Voyage to the Rock

This is a work of fiction.
Names, characters, places, and incidents either
are the product of the author's imagination or used fictitiously.
Any resemblance to actual persons, living or dead, or events is
entirely coincidental.

Copyright © 2014 by (Rev. Fr.) Matthew Penney

All rights reserved.
For more information address the author at
father.matthew.p@gmail.com.

Lumination Press

ISBN 978-0-9937470-0-7 (print)
ISBN 978-0-9937470-1-4 (ebook)

Printed in the United States of America

First Edition

Front cover: Western Brook Pond, Gros Morne
Back cover: Christ Enthroned, *Book of Kells*

Visit
http://voyagetotherock.webs.com
to separate "the facts from the fiction"

and **Lumination Press** at
http://luminationpress.webs.com

VOYAGE

To the

ROCK

Fr. Matthew Penney

☦ Lumination Press ☦
2014

Table of Contents

Chapter 1: Here Lies Martin Shea...
Chapter 2: A New Existence
Chapter 3: The Beginning of a Journey
Chapter 4: A Choice
Chapter 5: A Voyage and An Abbot
Chapter 6: Mysteries of the Sea
Chapter 7: And the One Becomes Two
Chapter 8: Searching for Answers
Chapter 9: The Unnamed Islands
Chapter 10: The Antique Store
Chapter 11: The Manuscript Page
Chapter 12: Poetic Puzzles
Chapter 13: An Insult
Chapter 14: Lark Harbour
Chapter 15: Getting Complicated
Chapter 16: The Plan
Chapter 17: Taking Back the Cross
Chapter 18: A Vacation Away
Chapter 19: It's in the Little Things
Chapter 20: Sharing Secrets
Chapter 21: Hard on the Trail
Chapter 22: Searching through Shadows
Chapter 23: A Narrow Miss
Chapter 24: The Rabbit and the Wolf
Chapter 25: A Light in the Darkness
Chapter 26: Land of the Promise of the Saints

Chapter 1:
Here Lies Martin Shea...

The sickening sound of cracking ice. A white-lined spider's web streaking from his feet. A moment's panic freezing him to the spot. A single, sharp, intake of breath. The silent certainty that there is no escape. The burst into the icy depths.

This is how Martin experienced his mother's words. And like being plunged into a river of ice, Martin came alive in his struggle for life.

"No! We can't!"

"I know it seems difficult," his mother said, "but it's not as bad as it sounds."

How could it *not* be as bad as it sounded?

"But why?" he sputtered. "*Why?*" There was panicked force behind his words, as though this simple question would be enough to bring his parents to their senses.

"You know why, Martin." Even while trying to soothe, his mother's matter-of-fact tone was not absent. A drowning man could not be soothed!

"To start a *mission*? In the middle of nowhere?" He looked from his mother to his father, whose expression was hidden behind his thick, brown beard. "An Orthodox mission in Newfoundland?"

"Listen–" Martin's mother said as she adjusted the thin scarf around her neck.

"We can't move from Boston to *Canada*. To *Corner Brook*." Martin threw his arms wide in exasperation.

"You've always loved Corner Brook," his mother said. "We've had great vacations there."

"*Vacations*. Not to live there," Martin said. *They mean it.* He felt panic rise and begin to turn into hot anger. "I only said I liked it 'cause it's Dad's hometown. You don't want to know what I really think of it."

"Martin..." his mother said, brows knitting into a frown; his father, dressed as ever in his long black cassock, sat oddly quiet.

"Well, my life is officially over." Martin was going to burst. He felt like his head was under water—that his lungs would explode from the pressure. "And what do you think of this, Brigid?" he said suddenly, turning to his sister sitting beside him. "Tell them. Your life's over too, you know!"

His younger sister tugged on her long blond pony-tail; she had tears in her eyes.

"Calm down, Martin," his mother's tone was beginning to show a hint of irritation. Martin didn't care. When your limbs were beginning to freeze to death, you did whatever you needed to survive.

Martin tuned out as his sister began her protests. He stared across the dining room at the sun streaming through the patio doors leaving checkered patterns on the floor. How many times had he flown through those doors, basketball in hand, to spend hours shooting free throws in the backyard? During how many sleep-overs had he and Nick Zisis set up at the computer in the corner of their adjoining living room, the large floor lamp casting everything else into shadow as they conquered alien worlds and won World Series? How many Christmases had he spent sitting on the plush rug before the blazing fireplace, directing the perfect placement of tree ornaments? Martin had never felt so attached to the shelves of blue china surrounding him and the smooth surface of the long dining room table as he did right now.

This was his home: with the sounds of cars and groups of laughing kids outside the front window, with joggers and their dogs passing, and the trees that neatly lined the sidewalks which ran the length of the brick houses on either side of the street. Home was *not* some northern isolation in the Canadian

Voyage to the Rock

wilderness. Martin clenched and unclenched his fists as they rested on the table.

They were actually going to rip him away from his life in Boston to go traipsing about in the woods of Newfoundland. What was he supposed to do? Become a... a *fisherman*? Or learn how to swing an axe and become a lumberjack? He shook his head, denying it. This was completely *crazy*! He had to reason with his parents before it was too late. But what?

And then a faint ray of hope in the darkness: *School.*

"I'm finally fitting in at high school!" he said. "We can't move."

Brigid huffed at being cut off. His mother's tight-lipped face grew stormy, and creases began to line his father's brow.

"That was one of the reasons why your father and I decided that this is the right time for us to move." Martin's mother held her intertwined hands before her just a bit more rigidly than before. "High school starts later there, so you won't be the only new student."

What had his mother just said? It was like Martin's brain was becoming too numb to register everything. "Start from scratch getting to know everyone? I already did that once, *remember?*"

Martin," his dad's voice was low and intense. "Remember who you're speaking to." Martin knew he meant business.

"But Mom," Brigid said, momentarily letting her pony-tail drop. "Don't they have to go to middle school until grade nine?"

His mother's voice softened as she spoke to his sister: "That's true, honey. But on the bright side it will give you a chance to meet lots of friends before going to high school."

"This is so unfair!" Brigid said, slumping in her chair.

Martin couldn't stop himself from adding, "A huge, freezing, island, and nothing but trees and wilderness. On the edge of the world!" He gripped the edge of the table in his hands. "What makes you think anyone there even *wants* to become Orthodox? There's not even a *church* there." There was a touch of spitefulness in the question.

"You know your father has always dreamed—"

"Dreamed about what?" Martin demanded. "Of becoming like St. Herman of Alaska? Of living in the wilderness and teaching the people? That was 200 years ago! And he was a hermit. He didn't drag his kids there with him."

"Just think about it for a minute, Martin."

Martin ignored the comment. "Mom, what about your job at the school? Dad, the cathedral and your job at the university?" he asked, gesturing to each in turn. "You're both just going to drop everything?"

"Actually, your father's already found work in the Classics department of the university in Corner Brook. And I'm going to start working full-time on my iconography."

"Well, I see you guys have this whole thing worked out. Just one problem—you forgot about me and Brigid. Our lives are ruined."

"Don't be so dramatic, Martin." There was his mother's matter-of-factness back. "You'll see, you'll both be able to keep in touch with your friends—"

"But my friends are all here. My real life is *here!*" Martin let the words burst free from his mouth as though letting out a final, fleeting lungful of air, in defiance of the icy darkness that was swallowing him.

But he had pushed too far this time.

His mother did not yell at him. But her eyes were flint striking stone and her words snapped like the crack of a whip: "Well, you'll just have to make *new* friends then, won't you."

Martin may have physically winced. He knew one thing, though: Discussion-Was-Over.

"And what about Facebook and all those messages you send back and forth?" his mother asked. "You don't think you can do that from there?" She was staring so intensely at Martin that he wavered under her gaze. "You'll have *plenty* of opportunity to stay in contact with your friends."

In a last effort of defiance—courageous or stupid, he wasn't sure—he obstinately crossed his arms on his chest, and looking

Voyage to the Rock

away, muttered one final statement under his breath: "This can't *really* be happening."

It wasn't meant to be heard, but it was.

"Yes, *Martin*," his mother's voice still crackled, "this really *is* happening."

* * *

Things had gone worse than Martin had hoped—a lot worse. And so instead of a glorious evening of triumphant two-on-two with the guys, he was left for the evening reeling in his room.

Despite everything that had happened, despite all his feelings, despite everything else he couldn't bear to even think about, one thing itched at him: his dad's silence.

Martin had never experienced that before. His dad always did all the talking. So why had he said nothing this time? Why just sit there? It didn't make any sense.

The question had loomed at the back of Martin's mind for the last couple of hours as he'd tried to distract himself from the problems of his new reality. He'd flipped through magazines, laid on his bed staring at the trophies on his bookcase, listened with eyes closed to the tick-tick-tick of his wall clock; nothing worked. He was so desperate he'd even tried *cleaning* out his desk. But it was there, avoid it as he might. It nagged at his thoughts.

There was a knock at the door.

Martin knew who it was before his dad poked his head in. "May I come in?" Martin had been expecting this from the moment he left the table.

"Okay," Martin said hesitantly.

His father entered and sat at the edge of Martin's bed. Then he did the last thing Martin could have expected.

"I'm sorry, Martin," he said.

Martin didn't know what to say. His father *apologized*... to *him*.

His father went on. "Martin, you always knew I hoped for this. Ever since I became a priest I wanted—if God ever gave me the opportunity—to return to my home, to offer to others the same gift that's been offered to us: the Orthodox faith, in all its amazing beauty." His dad adjusted the folds of his long cassock. He was now staring at the icon of St. Martin of Tours that hung on the wall across from them.

"There are so many people there who have never even heard of Orthodoxy, let alone had the opportunity to encounter it. We possess such a treasure." His eyes were bright, though his voice was quiet.

"I know this is difficult for you," his father said, tucking a long, dark strand of hair behind his ear and turning to Martin. "But the chance to start an Orthodox mission in Newfoundland, it's a prayer answered."

Martin just stared with a frown at the poster on the far wall. He wished *he* was a snowboarder right then, gliding away from his problems down some snow-covered slope. "Your prayer. Not mine," he said.

His dad, taking his long beard in one hand, sighed. "I knew this would be difficult for you. I had hoped that maybe you could at least understand a little why this is important to do." His father stood to leave. "I'm sorry, though. I'm probably asking too much of you."

Martin kept his gaze fixed unsympathetically forward.

Out of the corner of his eye, he could see his father silently leave the room. To his own annoyance, Martin had to fight fiercely against the tiniest hint of something bitter in his mouth—the taste of guilt.

* * *

"Well, enjoy the snow, Dude!"

It was a hot, muggy day, the kind that made Nick's joke an even starker contrast to Martin's life to come. Up and down the street were a few weekend early-birds packing trunks and loading

Voyage to the Rock

roof-racks in neighboring driveways, trying to escape the city before the bumper to bumper rush. The irony was that all of Boston would be anxious to escape the city, while Martin would give anything to stay right there in his little driveway, beside his small patch of green lawn.

"It's a shame you'll be up there ice-fishing while we're hanging at the pool all summer," Nick Zisis said.

Martin nailed him hard in the arm. "Alright, alright," Martin's friend said, holding up long thin hands to ward off the next blow. "I'm just kidding".

"Well, you deserve it anyway," Martin said, pointing at his bean-pole friend. Then he sighed and leaned against the family car, staring off into the sky.

"This really sucks," Nick said as he leaned on the car next to Martin. "I never would've imagined you'd be taking off to Canada."

"You wouldn't have? I live with them, and I didn't see it coming," Martin said, trying to keep from rubbing his temples.

"Can't you talk to the bishop or something? Go over your dad's head, I mean?" Nick said. "He's a priest after all. He's gotta listen to the bishop, right?"

"Don't I wish?" Martin pulled back his shaggy brown hair with his two hands and sighed. "It was a bishop that asked him to move to Corner Brook in the first place. Dad just happened to jump at the chance." Martin kicked at a rock and scuffed a sneaker across the driveway. "Cue the music for the end of the world, would ya? Here lies the dusty old bones of Martin Shea. Died of boredom in a town of 20,000 people. Didn't even finish high school."

"But learned how to talk with a perfect Newfie accent!" Nick said with a laugh, his long legs giving him a head-start as he sprang away from Martin. Martin gave chase around the car.

When they were both out of breath and sore from exchanging punches to the arms, they stood there together until the awkward moment was right in front of them. "Well anyway, man, it won't be the same around here without you," Nick said.

"Yeah," Martin said, putting his hands in his pockets and looking down. "It won't be the same without you either." The silence stretched out before them again.

"So anyway, I should go pack the rest of my stuff."

"Yeah, that's cool. I gotta get going anyway. So... take it easy, bro," Nick said, raising his hand.

"You, too," Martin said as he grabbed it and they pulled each other in for a quick hug.

"Don't go too wild this summer," Martin said as Nick turned to walk away.

"I won't," he said, looking back. "And that goes for you, too. Who knows, things might be better there than you think! Call me on Skype once you reach *The Rock*."

"*The Rock*... man," Martin said shaking his head. "I'll call...if I survive the five hour ferry ride. We'll be talkin'."

"For sure." Nick waved and then a few moments later disappeared around the corner to the next street.

Better than I think? I doubt it. Martin gave a little slap on the railing post as he headed inside.

Voyage to the Rock

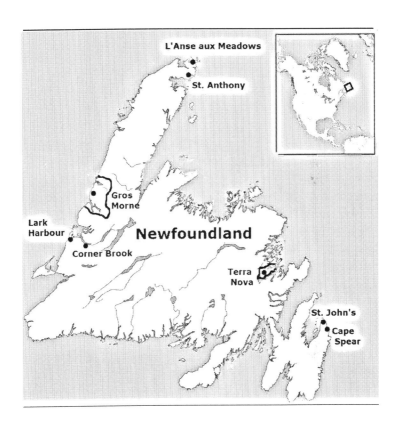

Chapter 2:
A New Existence

Martin's mouth watered at the smell of fried bacon, eggs, and home-fries. A week of packing, cleaning, moving, and travelling didn't make for too many home-cooked meals, so he was looking forward to this. That didn't even count the fact that they'd fasted from meat and cheese for the last month for the feast of Sts. Peter and Paul.

The family gathered around the table. His dad began to say grace, "Through the prayers of our holy fathers..." He blessed the food and then the whole family sat down and started to eat. A plate full of eggs and crispy bacon was just what Martin needed in the midst of his otherwise unsettled life.

Right now his life wasn't the only unsettled thing, though. The half-opened boxes, packing paper, and scattered dishes and pots gave the dining room and adjoining living room a cluttered feel. This was offset by the sheer size of the rooms which were large and open in the style of old farmhouses. There were hardwood floors and large trimmed doorways and windows. The shimmering blue bay was visible through the windows toward the back of the dining room, and thick green evergreens rose steeply from the rocky shore on the other side to be broken only occasionally by small clusters of houses.

Corner Brook itself was all piled together like a spilled container of Lego, starting from the coast and the sprawling Bay of Islands, and moving from a large paper mill to climb the surrounding hills with twisting streets, businesses, and homes. Everything seemed to be either down a slope or up one. His legs already ached at the idea of having to bike up those streets.

Voyage to the Rock

His father's voice interrupted his absent-minded chewing. "So today is the first day of our new summer schedule." Martin rolled his eyes and started spreading jam on his toast. No one else even seemed bothered by the suggestion of a *new summer schedule*. Brigid worked away at the breakfast sandwich she was putting together, while his mom added a spoonful of honey to her yogurt.

"Well, we all know that there'll be a lot to do if the church temple is going to be built for September 1st, the Church New Year. This isn't news to either of you," their father said addressing Martin and Brigid. "We talked about this before we left Boston. As your mother and I mentioned, we'll need you to pitch in a few hours each day."

Martin was still ticked about this. It wasn't bad enough that they'd packed him away like a runaway prisoner, but hard labor all summer as well? Weren't there laws against this kind of thing? He was no fool, though. He wasn't going to poke at that sleeping bear again: He may have escaped trouble when it came to their fight about the move, but his parents had been less "understanding" with his protests about the summer work schedule.

What bugged him most, though, was how irritatingly pleased Brigid seemed by the whole thing. She was all wide-eyed anticipation.

"So Martin and I will be working on the carpentry aspect," his dad continued, "while you ladies will be responsible for preparing the paints, boards, and canvases for the icons. There's plenty to be done." He took a gulp of hot coffee. "So... every morning we'll need to be up and dressed by 8 a.m."

Martin and Brigid both groaned.

"I know, I know. It's early," their father said, "but it's the only way to fit everything in. Up at eight, then morning prayers, breakfast, and clean-up. Then four hours or so of work at our respective jobs."

His mother smiled reassuringly before popping another spoonful of yogurt into her mouth.

"After that the afternoon is yours," their dad said. "Once your stuff is unpacked, that is."

Martin quickly shoved a piece of cheese into his mouth to choke back the protests that were dangerously close to spilling out. So this was "Day One" of his new existence.

And just like that everything went on as though nothing were said. His mother had her striped apron on and was starting to clear the table. Brigid began braiding her blond hair as she chatted with their dad about the possibility of Newfoundland hiking trips.

Martin stopped listening. He wanted to be 2,000 miles away right then, in Boston, with friends—playing basketball, hanging out at the skate park, swimming in Nick's pool, and having the great summer he was supposed to be having... before his life *ended*.

As his father stood up from the table to say the Thanksgiving prayers, Martin stuffed a few more pieces of bacon into his mouth; just because his *life* was finished didn't mean his appetite was! After the prayer, Martin drained his orange juice and carried his dishes to the sink.

"Just lay them here, Hon," Martin's mother said. "Brigid and I will be taking care of the clean-up."

"Mom!" Brigid said, freezing in the act of pushing in her chair.

"That's part of our job, Brig," their mother said, shrugging as if to ask: What can we do about it?

"Enjoy that," Martin whispered as he brushed past Brigid.

Brigid turned and shot daggers at him just as his dad called, "Martin! Time to go. Our work awaits us."

Brigid's frown turned to a mockingly sweet smile: "Yes, Martin, your work awaits you. *Enjoy that*."

It was Martin's turn to scowl.

He trudged toward his father as his mom called from behind: "Have a productive time, guys!"

"I'm *sure* we will," Martin mumbled as he left the house.

Voyage to the Rock

His dad gave him a friendly clap on the back as Martin reached him at the end of the walkway. "The first day of our new project. I have to tell you, Mart, I've really missed this kind of work. This'll be great. You'll see." His father gave him a tentative glance, which Martin couldn't help but find odd.

Heading around the side of the house, Martin's father led them to the tool shed at the end of the driveway near the back of the house. Grabbing two tool-belts and two pairs of work-gloves, his dad turned to him: "Here, these will be yours." Martin took the belt by the straps, looking at it uncertainly. "It has everything you'll need," his dad continued, "Hammer, nails, screws, tape-measure, utility knife, safety glasses—lots of stuff. Just remember, the first rule of any carpentry work: you're responsible for your own tools. Take care of them because they're the only ones you've got."

His father strapped his belt around his waist, the hammer dangling at his side. He hung his safety glasses around his neck and grabbed a screw gun. Then he gestured for Martin to do the same. Martin wasn't so sure about all this, but he grabbed the screw gun and followed his father to the site of the future church.

The church was being built next to their house. They moved across the side lawn and to the other side of a little thicket of trees. The site was on a sloping hill. Martin looked down the back yard which ended in tall evergreens. Through an opening, the large bay was visible. Again a cloudless sky stretched out above it all.

"Beautiful, isn't it?" his father asked, his voice quiet. "What a great location for a church."

"Yeah," Martin said disinterestedly.

It's not that Martin was unaware, exactly; he wasn't. But he was a teenager. He cared about the scores of basketball games and hockey play-offs, about cool sneakers and hoodies, about girls, too, truth be told; about scenic views, in small towns, for little churches, he did not care—and especially not in his present situation. Why should he spare a thought for it?

As they approached the site, Martin saw that the foundation began as a bit of gray near the front yard and grew to a full wall as it descended towards the backyard. The thing must have been about as long as half a basketball court. Standing above the cement foundation it looked more like an empty swimming pool than it did a future church.

Martin stood one foot on the edge of the foundation as he peered in. It wasn't empty inside. There was wood everywhere, tools and electric saws were piled in one corner, and across the top of the foundation were long beams of wood.

His dad had already started down a big wooden ladder set up for coming in and out. Martin sighed and followed. This was going to be a lot of work.

His father walked around and took stock of everything. He went from piles of wood to boxes of screws and nails to the work benches, humming a bit as he did. Martin started weaving his way around inside having climbed down.

"Well hello, me B'ys! How is ya?"

Martin turned to see a man standing at the top of the ladder with a cardboard tray of coffee cups and his tool belt slung over one shoulder.

"We're doing just great!" his father said. "Aren't we Martin?" His dad's face was split with a wide grin as he turned back to the visitor who was now coming down the ladder. His father went over to take the coffee tray from him.

The man clapped him with a hearty handshake: "Well, don't you look like the Ol' Moses himself! How've ya been, B'y? It's been ages, it has, Greg'ry. I guess that's *Father* Greg'ry now, eh?"

His dad stood beaming. "Things have been going really well, Shawn. And what about you, me Son? And Maggy?" He was slipping into speaking like a Newfoundlander.

"Ah, well, you know, it was a bit of a change this last year, what with moving back to Corner Brook, but Maggy's happy to finally be home again after all these years. And how's Lizzy? Where's she? Up to the house?" Shawn asked.

Voyage to the Rock

"Yeah, with my youngest, Brigid. Elizabeth'll be so excited to see you and Maggy again," Fr. Gregory said.

"And so this here is Martin, eh?"

By now Martin had come over and was standing somewhat awkwardly nearby. "Sure is," Martin's dad said. "Martin, this is Shawn. We grew up together. We were in the same class every year from grade one 'til twelve."

"Class? Think we spent more time in trouble than in class." Shawn winked at Martin.

Martin looked uncertainly at Shawn as the man shot out his hand. "Good to meet ya, me Son. I ain't seen you since you was about up to me knee. You're tall now, though, ain't ya?"

Martin didn't really know what to say. "I guess so," he said as he shook the man's hand.

"And your son, Jeremy?" Fr. Gregory asked as a young man of about nineteen popped down the ladder.

"Yes, B'y," Shawn said. "Jeremy, you remember Fr. Greg'ry, don't ya?"

Jeremy hesitated a bit.

"He was young, Shawn, and I had a lot less hair back then. Not to mention all the black I'm wearing, eh Jeremy?" Jeremy clearly did not remember Fr. Gregory, though he smiled at the joke about his striking appearance.

He wasn't the first person in Newfoundland to have noticed his dad. The long black cassock he normally wore, his cross that hung to his chest, his priest's hat and long beard, these attracted more than a few curious looks. But that, at least, was something Martin was used to—even from when they lived in Boston. He always found the startled or inquisitive looks funny—except when they turned into long conversations about Orthodoxy during which Martin got to *wait patiently* for his father.

Fr. Gregory and Jeremy shook hands.

"And this is Martin."

"Nice to meet ya," Jeremy said to Martin, in an accent much less thick than his father's.

"Yeah, you too," Martin said.

"Well, B'ys, the coffees are in the tray and there's cream and sugar on the side. Do you drink coffee, Martin?" Shawn asked looking at him.

"Ah... not really," he said putting his hands in his pockets again.

"Good!" said Shawn. "Filty stuff. Though it's great on the job. I brought ya a hot chocolate just in case."

"Thanks," Martin said, moving to take it.

"Well then we're all set. The rest of the B'ys is finishing up another job, but they'll be here by noon. Late start for us all today."

Late start? It was 9 a.m. They were early by half an hour!

"How many men do you have on your crew, Shawn? You sure got this foundation dug and poured quickly, and I see you're already onto the joists for the basement ceiling," Fr. Gregory said.

"We're six altogether, counting me and Jeremy—a good little crew. But you said you're hoping to have the basics done by September 1st, so we've tried to get a jump start on the work. Thankfully, the permits all worked out miraculously quick! But that's your business, I suppose, working miracles that is." He raised his eyebrows and smiled at Martin. "It'll be a hard working day for us for the next two months or so, but it'll be ready—unless it rains all summer." If Shawn hadn't been so confident, Martin wouldn't have believed it could be done so fast.

Here we go! Martin thought.

Martin and Fr. Gregory were given the task of building walls from the stacked 2x4's. Before long his dad had explained everything to him and they were hard at it. After a short while he knew how to mark the boards, how to line them up, and how to hold them for his dad to nail together. He also learned that the thing that looked like some kind of futuristic weapon was an air-nailer, and how the compressor worked that gave the "firepower."

Voyage to the Rock

Two and a half hours of practice later, Martin's arms and ears also knew a few things: soreness and ringing. He would *definitely* be wearing earplugs the next time he did this job.

When Shawn called over that they should break for fifteen, to say Martin was *pleased* would be an understatement.

"Here, Martin," Fr. Gregory said handing Martin five dollars. "Go and get an ice-cream down at the corner store. And take thirty minutes. You've earned it."

"Thanks, Dad," Martin said. Escape for awhile!

"Oh, and Martin..." his dad said as Martin was heading out the back doorway, "Go get Brigid, too."

Martin sighed without looking back. "Sure, Dad," he said as he left.

* * *

"Martin, you can't imagine how difficult it is to mix the right colors for the icons. I spent like an hour just trying to find the right shades for all the different parts Mom was painting." Brigid and he were descending the hill of their street toward the store.

The houses on either side were separated from each other by stretches of tall evergreen trees. From what Martin could make out, they were all two-story houses similar in style to theirs. As they moved further down the hill the houses turned into bungalows with small yards and fences; on one lawn were scattered toys and a bicycle.

They walked down the middle of the road as there was almost no traffic on the street. The whole town seemed strangely empty to Martin. There was a marked absence of cars honking, the steady din of voices, and the presence of crowded sidewalks of people moving about the city. Instead, he was in a "quaint" town, whose brightly painted, historic-looking shops and tiny mall made up the main attractions of its downtown. The place couldn't have felt *more* isolated to Martin—and it didn't help that his house was in the more heavily-wooded, outer neighborhoods.

Brigid was still talking but Martin was in no mood to listen. He was just then feeling acutely the injustice of everything, and now the ache in his back and arms as well.

"So what are you going to get, anyway?" Brigid asked.

Fed up, Martin finally turned on his sister. "Listen, I may have had to bring you, but I don't have to talk to you," he said.

Brigid rolled her eyes and played with her long braid, unfazed by her brother's remark.

After about two minutes without speaking, Brigid continued, "You know, Mom says we might be taking a trip on Wednesday... to the Viking settlement." She said it as though she hadn't even heard his last remark.

Martin responded with cold silence.

Heading up the steps of the store's front patio, Brigid made her way happily in. Martin waited a minute before he followed, annoyed by Brigid's good mood. How could she not be upset? That was Brigid for you, though, always doing whatever their parents wanted. No complaints. No arguments. And happy as a clam. It infuriated Martin!

The store was small inside, but looked pretty much like any other convenience store. It did have some strange touristy items though—like ball caps with moose antlers, t-shirts with "100% Newfie" printed on them, and pure maple syrup candies.

"Thanks," Brigid said, as the woman handed her an ice-cream. "My brother's paying." She gestured to Martin, and then headed outside.

Martin went over to choose his ice-cream, but waited at the glass as the woman went to answer the ringing phone. A few minutes later, he had his ice-cream cone and was heading out the door. As he stepped into the sunshine he noticed the parking lot was empty.

Where was Brigid?

Then he noticed a lawn with some picnic tables to the right of the store. Sitting at one of them was Brigid talking to some kid. As Martin walked over, he could see that the boy was around their age and had a mass of red hair and freckles.

Voyage to the Rock

"Yeah, we just moved here last weekend," Martin heard Brigid saying to the boy. "This," she said on seeing him approach, "is my brother Martin."

"Hello!" the kid said, turning to Martin.

"Hey," Martin said politely enough.

"Martin, this is Ashley. He lives on the same street as us."

"Yeah, I lives in the light blue house," Ashley said, gesturing up the road as though it would be possible for them to see it.

"I told him about how we've moved here from Boston, and about how you and Dad are building a church." Brigid was speaking a mile-a-minute.

You'd think she was never allowed to speak and so had to tell the world everything she could whenever she got the chance. Couldn't she ever keep things private? Martin was not interested in meeting some *Newfie kid*, and certainly didn't want Brigid blabbing their whole life story to a complete stranger.

"Is your dad the one with the black robe and the long beard? I saw you guys movin' in," Ashley said.

"That's our dad, alright," Brigid said. "He's hard to miss."

"So your dad's a minister or something? What religion are you B'ys anyhow?" Ashley asked. "I ain't never seen a minister dressed like that."

Martin was annoyed—with both of them. It was bad enough that he was stuck on this stupid island, but there was something cruelly ironic about his being exiled here because he was the son of an Orthodox priest, when no one even knew what Orthodoxy was. "We're Orthodox, actually, and my dad is a *priest*, not a minister." Martin's words were thick with a frustration that really had little to do with Ashley's questions. But it was there nonetheless.

"Orthodox? Sorry, but I ain't never heard of them. Is that like Catholic? I thought priests were Catholic?"

Martin gave the kid a flat stare, the kind that made a person want to start shuffling their feet and avoiding eye contact. Martin knew there was no chance that this Newfoundland boy was going to have heard of Orthodoxy when many adults in

Boston had never. But he was in a bad mood and didn't feel like being reasonable.

Brigid piped up in Martin's silence. "No, we're not Catholic. Orthodox Christians and Roman Catholics were one church until about a thousand years ago. And we call ours priests, too."

Ashley cocked his head slightly. "Well, I guess it's like my pops always says, 'a trout feeds like a salmon, swims like a salmon, and dies like a salmon, but it'll always taste like a trout.'" He was nodding his head as he finished. "So how come I ain't never heard of the Orthodox? Are there many of you?"

It was Martin who spoke up. His words mirrored his mood—like a wasp nest shaken up with two hands. "You've probably never heard of Orthodoxy because there aren't any Orthodox Churches around here. But it's the *original*, unchanged church. There are millions of Orthodox. Besides," Martin's tone became even more condescending—he didn't even *care*, "every Christian for the first 1,000 years *was* an Orthodox Christian. So yes, I'd say there *are* lots of us."

Brigid's icy stare could have frozen the bay itself. Martin ignored her.

Ashley, though, was staring wide-eyed, and looked like a boy caught by his teacher without his homework done. He didn't seem to have noticed Martin's tone. "Well, B'y, I thinks I'm following you. But there's one thing I'm still confused about."

"And what's that?" Martin asked with a flat tone.

"Well I always thought priests couldn't get married."

That was Martin's limit. "I don't have time to talk with you, *Ashley*, nor to wait for you, Brigid. I've got work to do!" And with that Martin spun around and headed back up the road.

The last thing he heard before he was out of earshot was Ashley asking, "Was it something I said?"

Chapter 3:
The Beginning of a Journey

It was still dark when Martin, along with the rest of the family, stumbled into the car. Martin pulled his hoodie up on his head and wrapped himself in his fleece blanket. *5:00 a.m.* That was definitely earlier than Martin liked! But at least it was a break from working at the church. On the seat next to him, Brigid was already snuggling into her pillow against the car window. His parents were in the front placing coffees in cupholders and getting everything ready.

"Everyone awake to pray before we set off on our journey?" His dad was as alert and as chipper as though he'd slept until mid-morning. "I found a really great one. Everyone still up?" Once Fr. Gregory heard two groans from the back, he began: "In the name of the Father, and of the Son, and of the Holy Spirit. Amen. Shall I abandon, O King of Mysteries, the soft comforts of home? Shall I turn my back on my native land and my face toward the sea?"

Martin found himself already drifting into the quiet jumble of images that lay just on the edge of sleep. A prayer, and Boston; he was on a boat, and he could see the ocean.

"... my final prayer in my native land?" he heard his father's voice. "Shall I then suffer every kind of wound that the sea can inflict?" A gray sky and rising waves; he was near the edge of his little boat; it was rocking in the wind. He suddenly jerked awake, just as he was tipping into the sea.

He heard his father finish: "O Christ, help me on the wild waves. Amen." There was a momentary silence.

Matthew Penney

"A great travelling prayer, eh?" Fr. Gregory asked. "I read it in the life of St. Brendan the Navigator last night!"

"Beautiful," Martin heard his mother quietly answer.

Martin was already drifting back to sleep. Before he slipped finally across the divide that separated waking from dream, one last phrase repeated itself in his mind: *Abandon home.*

* * *

When Martin next opened his eyes, to his right a golden sunrise greeted him from between green mountains that stood in the distance. A wide expanse of wild green and purplish grass rustled as the wind whistled along the open space that separated the mountains and the road. To the left their car followed the winding coastline. Martin yawned and stretched as he watched the blue water that spread out as far as he could see. There were small white caps as the waves rolled toward the shore. It looked cool despite being early July. Martin couldn't help but feel the relaxed calm of the beautiful scenery, the gentle rhythm of the car, and the warm contentedness of waking.

"Well, good morning, Martin!" Fr. Gregory said in a playful tone. "Slept well, I hope? You're waking up just in time. We'll be entering Gros Morne National Park in the next ten or so minutes. The mountains are beautiful at this part of the highway."

Brigid was now stirring, and his mom was looking out the window as the wild grass was gradually receding and the road came closer to the looming mountains. They vaguely reminded Martin of a picture of the Scottish Highlands he had once seen: towering rock walls that seemed to go straight up with soft green grass covering the tops—without any trees. They were sort of like giant soccer fields thousands of feet up.

"You know, Martin," Fr. Gregory said, his sunglasses giving him a matrix-like appearance when combined with the rest of his black apparel. "We may be lucky enough to see some moose. Keep your eyes peeled."

Voyage to the Rock

"Moose?" said Brigid, rubbing her eyes and giving a small stretch.

"Yeah," Fr. Gregory said, "they're all over this park—all over Newfoundland. And we might just be lucky enough to see one. You can't imagine how big they are. And you know what?" Fr. Gregory asked looking at Brigid in the rear-view mirror.

"What?" Brigid said.

He raised his finger into the air. "There were no moose in Newfoundland originally."

"What do you mean?"

He began stroking his long beard the way he always did when he was going to be "informative." "It wasn't until 1904 that the first moose were brought. But they're certainly here now—in the hundreds of thousands. When I was young", he took off his sunglasses so as to be able to look at them in the rearview mirror, "I once saw a giant bull moose while hiking in Gros Morne with your grandfather. It was massive. I'll never forget it."

"Wow. I hope we see one."

"As long as we don't see one up close," Elizabeth said matter-of-factly, peeking over her shoulder at Brigid. "I like my moose from a distance! How about you, Martin?"

Martin needed to keep up appearances, so despite the fact that he really *did* hope to see a moose, he only muttered an unenthusiastic, "Sure", while continuing to look out his window at the mountains that were now looming dark and tall near the right side of the car.

Martin ignored the rest of the conversation as the others chatted on about moose stories, the trees, the water, and similar things.

In the end, they didn't see a moose in Gros Morne, and to be honest, Martin was disappointed. It would have been the most interesting thing about his exile so far.

The long drive down the lonesome Viking Highway was uneventful, though beautiful. After following the coast and the mountains of Gros Morne, the road had again opened into long meadows as the mountains receded farther and farther into the distance. There were whole forest areas of strange, bent-over, pine and spruce trees—*tuckamores* his dad had called them—blown sideways by ocean winds until they stayed that way. They were like a painting of a massive wind-storm permanently captured for any passerby to see. They drove by the Broom Point Fishermen Museum, a red shack on the coast in the middle of nowhere—the only other building being a tiny outhouse propped up against the wind by two driftwood logs; they saw fishing villages and old cottages painted brightly in reds, blues, or yellows. Martin found the various places they passed morbidly humorous: Dead Man's Cove, Nameless Cove, Mistaken Cove, Savage Cove, etc. A *very comforting place, Newfoundland.*

After a time, his mother spoke up, re-adjusting the forest-green scarf around her neck: "Gregory, why don't you tell us more about the Viking settlement?"

"Yeah, Dad," Brigid said, sitting up straighter.

"Well, you know we're heading to almost the very *top* of Newfoundland," Fr. Gregory said, "to L'Anse aux Meadows, the famous landing site and camp of Leif Erikkson."

Martin stifled a groan as his father unconsciously grabbed for his beard. He just kept his gaze directed out the window at the blur of trees and brush.

"Do you remember when exactly Christopher Columbus discovered America?" Fr. Gregory asked.

"1492," Brigid said before anyone else could answer.

"Yup. But... do you know that he wasn't the first European to visit North America? So can you guess when the Vikings arrived?"

"1310?" Brigid said.

"Nope."

"1250?" she said, grabbing Fr. Gregory's seat with two hands and bouncing a little on her own seat.

"Wasn't it in 1030?" Elizabeth said, tilting her head slightly.

Voyage to the Rock

"Nope and nope," Fr. Gregory said, a large grin splitting his face.

"1003 A.D.," Martin said, not even turning to look at the rest of them.

He heard his sister huff.

"Exactly! 1003 A.D.," Fr. Gregory said, as though Martin was as enthusiastic as the rest of the family. "Almost 500 years before Christopher Columbus. The Vikings were the earliest European visitors—at least that we have evidence of—and there are two Norse sagas that tell the story of Leif's arrival. He called it Vinland."

"Why Vinland?" Brigid asked, wrinkling her nose.

"Well, because Leif and his men found lots of wild grapes growing in the forests. Vinland, 'Land of Wine,'" her father said.

"Really, there are wild grapes in Newfoundland?" Brigid said, again leaning on Fr. Gregory's seat.

"There *were* wild grapes in Newfoundland—at least until the late 18th century. But after some harsh winters, they disappeared. They still have wild grapes just over in New Brunswick, and they think Vinland was the name of this whole area of Eastern Canada, not just Newfoundland."

"Are there other Viking settlements, then?" Brigid said.

"Nope. Just this one that's ever been found. That's what makes it so special!"

"So what happened to the Vikings in the end?"

"Nobody really knows for certain," Fr. Gregory said as the trees opened out to an open stretch of green to the left of the car, blue ocean to the right. "But the sagas say it was a combination of fighting with Native Americans, and the lack of trade. Either way, after only a few short years here, they never returned."

Never returned. Who can blame them? Martin half wished he could sail off in a Viking ship. He grabbed a fist of shaggy hair in his hand and exhaled as he stared out onto empty landscape.

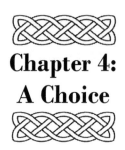

Chapter 4:
A Choice

Seven long hours later they were at L'Anse aux Meadows Viking site, surrounded by flat, grassy meadows and the rocky beaches further off. From what Martin could see as they pulled into the parking lot of the National Park, it didn't look very impressive. There was a dark brown building with a large sign: "Interpretation Center". A wooden set of stairs descended to a walkway that led through a meadow toward some large grassy mounds and the coast. *Great!* Martin thought. *Seven hours driving for a museum and grass.*

They all got out. Martin leaned despondently against the car, thumbs tucked under the straps of his backpack and head drooping. Brigid and his dad were already walking toward the building. They were all smiles and eagerness.

"How are you doing, Martin?" his mom said, putting her arm around his shoulder and leaning on the car with him.

"Not good," was Martin's answer; he just stared down.

"I know it's hard. It's a big change moving here."

"Yeah, no kidding."

"But you know what?" she said, leaning in to whisper in his ear. "I really appreciate what you're doing—working hard to build the church, and helping your father. I know it's not what you'd like, and I'm really proud of the effort you're making."

Martin didn't say anything.

She gave Martin a playful shake. "Let's go and have a look around. We might as well since there's not too much to see out here. We did come all this way." Martin and his mom walked to catch up with Brigid and Fr. Gregory.

Voyage to the Rock

Inside it was just what Martin had feared: a museum. It wasn't very big and had glass cases full of items found at the site, pictures, and write-ups. It did have some interesting life-sized Viking models, though.

Martin was glad when a guide finally started gathering everyone into a tour group. While he started explaining the history of the place and about Leif Erikkson, Martin took the time to stare at a brightly painted Viking shield with a large red dragon on it, hanging on the opposite wall.

He turned his attention back as the group started to move out the door toward the site of the reconstructed Viking buildings in the direction of the coast. They walked along a wooden plank path lined with chest high pine trees that opened onto rocky meadow. In a few minutes they arrived at the large grass mounds that Martin now saw had doors, and windows in the roof; it reminded Martin of a story he once read about a "hobbit-hole".

"This first building," the guide explained as they entered, "is the forgery—or blacksmith shop. The Vikings were the first inhabitants to smelt metal in all of North America." He gestured at a man with a thick beard dressed in Viking clothes and pounding a glowing-orange piece of metal with a hammer: "As you can see, our local Viking, Gorn the Black-hand, is using his anvil, hammer, and tongs, to make one of the 2,700 nails in a Viking ship." Gorn grunted at the group and kept working, while the tour guide got volunteers to "pump the bellows" to help get the fire hot. Both Brigid and Martin got to take a turn—Brigid enthusiastic as usual, and Martin less so. They each received a hand-made nail for their trouble.

The group moved from building to building, learning about Viking life and Martin had to admit the whole thing was kind of interesting. Still if all the other stuff wasn't so exciting, the Men's Workroom had some redeeming qualities—namely swords, axes, and Viking helmets which you could pick up and wear!

After some time, the guide led them back outside to finish the tour. It was his concluding words, though, that returned Martin even more deeply into his sullen mood: "These Viking adventurers left everything they knew—their cities, their settlements, and their societies—to travel all the way here to these desolate and rocky shores of Newfoundland. They had no friends, nothing familiar, only their own desire to explore and to survive. They abandoned the comforts of home for the wounds that the wild sea could inflict, and then disappeared forever like ghosts back into the foggy mists—never to be seen or heard from on these coasts again."

Abandon home. The thought floated into Martin's head. *Shall I turn my back on my native land?* Where had he heard that? He couldn't remember. But the whole thing put a sour taste in his mouth.

As the group broke up to start exploring the settlement and the surrounding area, Martin saw his mom and Brigid head back to the Long House. When his dad came over and tried to convince him to go back to visit the forge, Martin refused.

"I'm just going to walk by the water."

"Suit yourself," Fr. Gregory said. "But we'll all meet back here in 25 minutes, so don't go too far."

With that Martin headed off down a gravel path that led toward the dark blue Atlantic waters. He scuffed his feet and kicked small stones into the brush to either side of the path as he went. Occasionally, he broke pieces of branches off the short trees around him and chucked them into the brush as well.

What was his life supposed to be now? How could he ever adjust to this? And why didn't anyone, anywhere, care what *he* thought?

The gravel path crossed a little stream that—now at low tide—was really just a bed of large damp rocks. Seeing that it also led windingly to the shore, Martin hopped down from the path. As he made his way among the stones, he picked up and threw rocks at different targets as he went. He brooded about his friends back home in Boston. *I should be there with everyone else,*

Voyage to the Rock

not here at the end of the world where even Vikings wouldn't stay. This is insane!

"I certainly didn't *decide* to 'abandon the comforts of home,'" Martin said aloud. He bent over and hefted a huge rock to his shoulder. "Didn't anyone ever think about asking *me?*" he grunted out this last, as he pushed more than threw the rock. It landed with a loud crack of stone on stone. He slumped down heavily on a large dry rock in the middle of the stream bed, all his energy gone.

Here he was, half-way between the coast and the path back to the Viking settlement, sitting in the middle of a dry stream. Could things be more hopeless? Hidden by the banks of shrubs on either side of him, he let his face sink into his hands and felt the utter isolation of the whole place. What was he going to do?

He sat there for a few minutes holding his head in his hands—his eyes closed, not moving. When he did finally move it was to rub the strain from his temples.

As he opened his eyes, though, he saw something. It was almost completely buried in mud from the stream, but was sticking out from between two large rocks. It was a strange green color. Not more than an arm's length from where he was sitting, Martin leaned forward to grab it.

It seemed to be a piece of metal or something. It didn't come out when he first tugged at it. So he leaned forward and began to dig away the mud and small rocks. As he continued, he felt the bottom edge of it and realized that it was fairly large— definitely longer than his hand. Grasping tightly around the base, he gave a final yank, and with a popping-sloshing noise, it pulled out in a spray of water and mud.

He wiped his now dirty face with the back of his sleeve and moved to a clear puddle of water next to him. Martin thrust the heavy object in to try and get a better look at it. The water became a murky brown as he washed it off. But when Martin finally pulled it out, what he saw took his breath away.

It was a *cross*! A crucifix, to be precise.

Matthew Penney

On it was a carved figure of Christ, who—strangely—was wearing a robe and was surrounded by what looked like a sea of green intertwining vines. The patterns whirled in intricate designs all over the arms of the cross and there was a large ring around its center. Despite the fact that the metal was tarnished and green like the steeple of an old church, Martin could still make out the amazing detail. There was also a dark stone that protruded from the side of Christ, where he would have been pierced by the spear.

Martin was stunned!

He turned it over and rubbed a finger over its rough scratched back and roughly finished edges. It looked ancient! How could it have gotten there and how long had it been buried there? Where could it have come from? Martin's mind was racing with unanswered questions.

It definitely wasn't something someone had forgotten there recently—it was *way* too old. But at the bottom of a stream that spends half the day completely flooded with ocean water? It didn't make sense. *No one would have thrown away a treasure like this!* And who would have brought it out here to the Viking settlement?

A sudden thought actually caused goose-bumps to spring up all along Martin's arms. *Could it be from the Vikings? Leif Erikkson and the Vikings?* It *was* ancient-looking, but Viking?

Part of his mind wanted to say it was crazy, impossible, but the longer he stared at the Cross and its rough edges and out at the ocean in the distance, the more his doubts began to slip away. He quite possibly held in his hands a thousand-year-old Viking cross. What would it be worth? He would be *famous*! The possibilities were turning themselves over in his mind.

He sat staring at the amazing find, trying to decide what to do next. Should he tell his parents? Or the tour guide? He didn't really like either of those options. Well, he was certain that he wasn't just going to leave it there at the bottom of some stream.

Voyage to the Rock

Then Martin had a thought that made his heart sink precisely because he was pretty sure it was the *right* thing to do: give it to the people working at the museum.

But I found it. He thought challengingly. *It should be mine. If I hadn't come along it would have probably lain here for another thousand years!*

Unfortunately, it was already too late—just in those few short moments.

He knew you didn't just get to keep things you find at historical sites that belong to museums. But this more than anything made him so *mad*! Why did everything have to turn out so badly for him?

The little voice inside him persisted, though: "It belongs to the National Park, to the Viking exhibit."

If it even is Viking, he shot back spitefully. Even this was about to be taken away from him. No cross, no answers, no *nothing.*

He stared at the cross again for a long time. The figure of Christ hung there with a serene expression—almost as though sleeping. His hands were outstretched more as if holding something up than stretched out in pain.

Martin just sat there, wrestling with his own thoughts.

"Alright, alright," he sighed, speaking to the little Christ, and brushing hair out of his face with the back of his arm, "I'll give you to the museum." He couldn't help lightly rubbing his finger over the intricate-lacing pattern and the face of the Christ before he took off his backpack and carefully put it inside.

Standing up, he brushed the drying dirt off his legs and headed toward the path back to the Viking settlement. His mom and Brigid were already waiting, and his dad was coming out of the Long House when he finally arrived.

"Good timing everyone!" Fr. Gregory said. "If we hurry, we'll still have enough time to visit Norstead Viking settlement before hitting the road."

They started up the pathway. "You know, Norstead is a real re-created Viking village. It even has axe-throwing! How's that sound, Martin?"

"Sounds pretty good, Dad," Martin said, though only half-heartedly.

The further they went up the path, the more and more Martin felt the weight of the bronze cross on his back. *So... give it to the museum... There it is, a few feet up the hill... It's a shame, though, you won't ever find out who it belonged to... And more of a shame that you'll never get to see what it looks like all cleaned up... Bet those patterns would look amazing... I wonder what that stone at Christ's side is made of... It's too dirty to see it now, but cleaned up...*" The thoughts flowed from one to the other.

They reached the back of the building. Martin was walking behind the others. They were continuing along the side of the building toward the parking lot and the car. Martin followed. He reached the front of the building as the rest of the family continued toward the car. He stopped by the main doors.

Well, what are you waiting for? Take it in. He peered in the window and didn't see anyone at the desk. *Go on in.*

But Martin hesitated. *A shame the cross isn't cleaned up and polished. It would look great then! A shame to give it to the museum all dirty... and without any information about it at all.* Martin stared in the window. No one.

I could clean it up first... and maybe find out a bit about it ... You know, that's actually a really great idea! Then I could send it back here, with information and looking amazing...

He looked back at his family starting to load their stuff in the car. There was still no one at the desk. *I wouldn't keep it–just help out the museum and then return it. It's not like they'd notice it was gone. They haven't noticed it for over a thousand years!*

"Martin?" his mother called. "Are you coming?"

Since no one is at the desk...

"Yeah, Mom. Coming!"

Martin turned and headed for the car; the others were already getting in. He pulled off his backpack and reached for

Voyage to the Rock

the car door. "Excuse me, me Son," he heard a man's voice say from behind him.

Martin froze. He slowly turned around.

A man in a navy blue jacket with SECURITY written across his chest stood before him. Martin's eyes widened!

But before Martin could confess everything, the man was holding something out to him. Martin looked down to see his fleece vest in the security guard's hand.

"I thinks you dropped this back there," he said gesturing over his shoulder. When Martin didn't immediately answer, the man said, "It's yours, ain't it?"

"Yeah...," Martin said, "yeah, it is. Thanks."

"No problem, B'y. Have a safe drive." And the security guard was gone as quick as he had appeared.

Martin blinked in stunned silence, and then did the only thing he could think to do: he got in the car.

Chapter 5:
A Voyage and An Abbot

It was nearing 4:30 p.m. when Martin and the family were finally back in the car and heading for St. Anthony's where they had a motel room booked for the night. Norstead Viking village had been every bit as interesting and exciting as it was supposed to have been: "real" Vikings working and living, making boats, cooking Norse food, weaving and sewing Viking clothes, and of course, axe-throwing and sword-fighting. Martin and Brigid were both able to throw an axe and have it stick in the pile of logs, and they both laughed when Fr. Gregory and Elizabeth could not. There were Viking stories and songs and lots of things to see and do. And to top it all off, they even saw a massive iceberg floating in the bay. In the end, the trip to L'Anse aux Meadows had been a good, long, and tiring adventure.

"So what did everyone think?" Fr. Gregory asked as the car headed back south the way they'd come.

"It was awesome!" Brigid said, raising her hands for emphasis—a blond pony-tail in one of them.

"Yeah, a really great idea, Gregory," Elizabeth said.

"Martin?" his dad peeked in the rear-view mirror.

"It was great, Dad." His parents exchanged a small satisfied look that wasn't lost on Martin.

Martin had only half been thinking about the Viking village when he answered. His mind was now fixed on the object that rested between his feet in his backpack. While at first, he had been a bit freaked out about having taken the Cross, as the day wore-on, those feelings were replaced by pure excitement. He had continued to run over the possibilities all day, but there was

Voyage to the Rock

something he saw in Norstead Viking village that had *really* gotten his attention.

"Hey Dad," Martin said after the car had fallen silent for a few minutes. "Did you notice that chapel back in Norstead? Why was that there?" Martin secretly hoped to have confirmed the thought that had made his heart leap when he saw it.

"Well, Martin, despite the fact that most people believe that the Vikings were savage pirates and pagans, Leif Erikkson and his crew were actually converts to Christianity. Leif had brought the Christian faith, along with a priest, to Greenland from King Olaf I of Scandinavia. I was very pleased to see that Norstead has re-created an early Christian chapel there, especially since those Vikings shared the same Orthodox faith as even we do."

I knew it! Martin tried to keep the goofy grin that was threatening to burst onto his face under control.

"Wow! Orthodox Vikings!" Brigid said. "I wonder what their *Pascha parties* were like?" Elizabeth let out a laugh.

Martin, who was too excited to listen to Brigid, quickly said: "So you mean they brought things like crosses... and icons?" He tried not to be too obvious.

"Well, I don't know about icons exactly, but I'd be pretty surprised if some of them didn't have crosses," Fr. Gregory said.

Ha! A real Viking Cross!

"So we aren't the first Orthodox to come to Newfoundland!" Brigid said, curling her fingers in her hair.

"We certainly are not," Fr. Gregory said as he glanced left out at the ocean waters beginning to show the faint orange traces of sunset. "But likely, the Vikings weren't either."

"But I thought you just said the Vikings were Christians?" Brigid said, scrunching her brow. "Who could have been Christians here earlier than them? The Native Americans?"

"Well, I don't know whether or not there were ever Native American Christians before the Vikings, but I didn't mean them," Fr. Gregory said.

Now Martin was interested: "Well, who then?" he said leaning forward.

"Why, Saint Brendan the Navigator, of course!"

"Now Dear," Elizabeth said as she reached over and put a hand on Fr. Gregory's shoulder, "maybe they've never heard of St. Brendan." This was a classic prompt from their mother trying to entice their father to quit creating suspense and to fill them in. While his father may have needed prompting to cut to the chase, he needed no prompting to elaborate.

"Never heard of St. Brendan? But we read one of his travelling prayers this morning before we set out!" The beard was already in hand.

"Aww, Dad, come on," Brigid said. "Tell us what you mean about St. Brendan. Did he come to Newfoundland, too?"

"Some think that he may have." Fr. Gregory said this with eyebrows raised and the hint of a smile on his tight-lipped face, as if he hadn't decided yet on whether he would let everyone in on the secret.

"When, Dad?" Martin's tone was flat and to the point.

"Well...," Fr. Gregory said—pausing for effect, "It would have been some time in the sixth century, with a group of seventeen other monks." A wide grin spread across his face.

Sixth century!

"Well, why do people think he came here? Is there a camp of St. Brendan like Leif Erikkson's Viking camp?" Brigid asked.

"Not that anyone has ever found," Dad said. "But... we have the description of his voyage from all those centuries ago."

"And it says that he came to Newfoundland?" asked a wide-eyed Brigid, her blond hair twirled so tight that if it were attached to a propeller she'd be airborne on release.

Was he really related to Brigid?

"Of course not," Martin said. "This place wasn't even discovered back then, let alone called Newfoundland."

"You're right, Martin," Fr. Gregory said, "*and wrong.*" His tone had become a touch more sober. "They may not have called it Newfoundland, but if one reads the details of the voyage carefully, one finds many things that certainly *could be* Newfoundland."

"Oh man," Brigid said. "First Orthodox Vikings and now maybe Irish saints, right here!"

"Not such a boring place after all, eh guys?" Fr. Gregory said, smiling.

Martin didn't know what to think now. Viking, Irish? *Could the Cross really be IRISH, from St. Brendan? That would seem to make sense of all those intertwining designs on it. But could it really be 1,500 years old? Oh man!*

"Are you guys interested in hearing a bit about St. Brendan's voyage?" Fr. Gregory asked. "I've actually been reading it for the last few days."

"We're definitely interested!" Martin said, a little more enthusiastically than he intended.

Their father looked out at the flaming red sea for a moment. "Well then..."

The Voyage of Saint Brendan the Abbot

St. Brendan, son of Finnlug Ua Alta, of the race of Eoghan, was born in the marshy district of Munster, in the sea-side village of Ciarraige Luachra, in the year 485. Even before his birth and in his childhood, the future fame of this holy man was revealed in visions and signs, and by angels and miracles. And no one in Ireland was able to look upon his youthful face because of the abundance of the divine radiances and grace of the All-Holy Spirit within him. Growing in perfection and a prophetic spirit, he became a man famous for his great self-restraint and his many virtues, and was the Spiritual Father of nearly three thousand monks.

Matthew Penney

One evening to St. Brendan's monastery at Ardfert came the holy father Barinthus. When questioned by Brendan about where he had been and how he had arrived at the monastery, Father Barinthus could only weep tears of joy and fall at St. Brendan's feet, offering praise and prayer to God! But embracing the monk, St. Brendan cried out: "Father, why should we be sad while you are here? Have you not come to give us comfort, and to give us joy? In God's name tell us some divine mysteries and the amazing wonders that you saw while sailing the great ocean, and refresh our souls!"

And so Barinthus, as an obedient monk, began to tell his story while the brethren crowded round:

"To the island of my spiritual son, Mernoc the Solitary, I sailed, and was greeted by a multitude of monks who were awaiting my arrival, my coming having been revealed by God. When I had been shown all that the monks did and how they lived, and the whole island on which they dwelt, my child, Mernoc, led me to the western shore to a small boat, and said: 'Father, enter this boat and we will sail on to the West, towards the island called the *Land of Promise of the Saints*', which God will give to those who will live after us in the last times.'

As we set off, the fog was so thick that we were closed in on every side. We could hardly see the front of the boat before us. But after a while a great light shone around us, and there appeared a large and grassy land, full of all kinds of fruit. For fifteen days we traveled throughout—no plant

Voyage to the Rock

without its flower, no tree without its fruit, and precious stones all around—and still we could find no end to this land. We finally came to a flowing river and wanted to cross. But not sure what to do, we waited for the Lord to direct us.

Then suddenly, all-shining bright, a man appeared to us and said: 'Welcome, Father Barinthus! Welcome Father Mernoc! Worthy Brothers! The Lord has revealed to you this land which he will grant unto His saints—the Paradise of God. One half of this place you have seen; the other half you are not permitted, yet, to enter. Rather, it is time, Fathers, for your return.'

'But what is your name, O Holy Sir, and where are you from?' we questioned the radiant man.

'Oh, Fathers, shouldn't you ask instead about this land, and the wondrous things that you have seen? Just as you see everything now, exactly the same has it been since the beginning of the world. Have you not noticed that you have neither ate, nor drank, nor slept for these past fifteen days, nor has the darkness of night come? But I know for certain that here it is forever daytime, without a shadow of darkness. For the Lord Jesus Christ is the light of this place! And if mankind had not sinned and disobeyed the commandment of God, in this land of delights would people always have lived.'

And so Father Mernoc and I were moved to tears by what we heard, both for the joy of experiencing such a blessed place and the sadness that human beings had lost it. Returning with us to the shore, as we got into our boat the man was taken from our sight. So we continued back into the thick fog and to the Island of Mernoc and his monks.

The monks all raced to see us when we returned. 'Why have you left us so long, O Fathers!'

But I said to them: 'Do not be upset, Fathers, for we have been in the Paradise of God, without food and drink, but so completely refreshed in both body and spirit! Do you not know by the beautiful scent of our clothes that we have been in Paradise?'

'Yes, holy Father, we do, since we have often smelled this beautiful fragrance from our abbot Mernoc, which stayed with him for nearly forty days.'

And so after forty days with Abbot Mernoc and the monks I left for this your monastery, Father-Abbot, and will leave for my own tomorrow."

When St. Brendan and the monks heard the story of Father Barinthus, they fell to the ground and gave glory to God: "Righteous are Thou, O Lord, in all Thy ways, and holy in all Thy works! Thou, who have revealed to your children so many great wonders. Thank you for allowing us to have such spiritual comfort from this story!"

After a night of prayer, St. Brendan with the agreement of all his monks decided to fast and pray for forty days and then to try themselves to sail to the holy Island. Of all his monks, he selected fourteen to accompany him on the journey.

* * *

Voyage to the Rock

"Well, I guess we should stop there," their mother said as the lights of the town became visible. She wrapped her scarf more snuggly around her neck. "Does anyone else find it chilly tonight?"

"Ah, your mother is right, guys," Fr. Gregory said. "We're almost there and I don't want us to miss the hotel."

"Okay, but just one question," Brigid said holding up a hand. "So people think Newfoundland is the *Land of Promise to the Saints?*"

"No, no," Fr. Gregory said. "The *Land of Promise to the Saints* is Paradise, and isn't simply *any* earthly place—though it's not completely heavenly either. But Newfoundland may have been one of the many places St. Brendan and his monks encountered on their journey to it."

"You need to tell us more!" Martin said, and actually grabbed onto the back of his father's seat.

"Now that's the old Martin back again!" Fr. Gregory said. "I'd love to continue... but not tonight. Right now we need to check-in to our hotel room and then find somewhere to eat." Martin sank back into his seat. "It's going to be an early morning again tomorrow, and we still have our prayers to finish before bed," Fr. Gregory said as he turned the car off the highway. "Tomorrow, though, we can hear as much about St. Brendan and his voyage as you guys want."

The rumbling in Martin's stomach told him that food wasn't such a bad idea but his desire to discover more about the Cross still tugged at him. Martin sighed inwardly. Well, his answers would just have to wait until the morning.

Chapter 6:
Mysteries of the Sea

Martin was shielding his eyes from the morning sun as they sped along the highway back towards Corner Brook. It was a beautifully clear day and everyone was refreshed after their long trip the day before.

As planned, they had gotten to bed early the previous night, and so after a quick breakfast they had started off. They were driving now for about thirty minutes. Brigid was reading next to Martin, and his mom and dad were chatting about work in the front. Martin was trying to wait for the right moment to bring up St. Brendan.

To say Martin hadn't slept *at all* the night before would have been an exaggeration, but it was certainly to the soft, slow breathing of the others that he finally fell asleep. *The Cross.* It had captivated his mind before sleep, and filled his dreams afterward. So Martin was more than patient by the time he finally brought up the subject that had been consuming his thoughts non-stop.

"So Dad, do you think we might be able to hear some more about St. Brendan?"

Brigid looked up from her book.

"Well," said Fr. Gregory, "since your mother is driving, if everyone wants to hear more, I'm fine with that."

"Sure, Dad," Brigid said, as she stuck in her bookmarker and put the book in the back window.

"Liz?" Fr. Gregory looked over at their mother. She was her bright-eyed morning self. "That's fine with me. There's something fun about hearing a traveling story while traveling." She pulled her scarf up nearly to her chin—*naturally*, since it was before 10 a.m. Martin was hot just looking at her.

"Okay, then," Fr. Gregory said, laying his black hat on the dashboard. "Back to St. Brendan and his preparations to set out..."

* * *

It was at the mountain called St. Brendan's Seat that the monks built their boat. The frame inside was made entirely of thin wicker sticks—about two fingers thick—all twisted together and joined with leather cords. It looked like the ribs of some small whale. Over the sides they attached cow-hide leather soaked and hardened in an oak-bark liquid. After they sealed all the joints and seams with tar, they were ready to set sail to wherever God would lead them.

But just before the fourteen monks and their Father-Abbot Brendan got into the boat, three other monks approached and fell down before the saint and begged to be taken along. St. Brendan, being filled with the Holy Spirit, agreed, but not before he made this prophecy of warning to the three: "Have your will, my children. For God has shown me why you have come. One has acted well and from a yearning heart, and God has prepared an excellent place for him, while for the other two of impurity, they will find harm and judgment." And so the voyagers set forth with only forty days' worth of food and water in the name of the Father, and of the Son, and of the Holy Spirit.

Matthew Penney

The first island they reached was after nearly all their food was gone. It was a rocky and steep place and the monks circled the island but could find no place to land. And so with such weariness and fear, the monks wanted to take a drink from a flowing waterfall. But St. Brendan stopped them and said: "Brothers, don't do such a foolish thing. If God has not shown us a place to rest, do not take this water without his permission! But I know that in three more days the Lord Jesus Christ will show us a place to land." And so it was that on the third day, they found a small cove and place to enter. St. Brendan then blessed the landing-place and they all got off.

It was then that springing down the path there came a dog, who when he came to St. Brendan acted so lovingly that it was as if the saint were its master and not some other. "Come, Brothers! The Lord has sent to us a guide to lead us to our rest." It was to a great mansion that they were led, and they entered into a spacious hall filled with bread and fish. But before St. Brendan blessed the food and the starving monks began to eat, he warned them saying: "Beware that Satan doesn't lead you into temptation. For I can see him urging one of our Fathers to a wicked theft. Let us all pray fervently for his soul this night."

After their meal and their evening prayers the Fathers laid down to sleep. But St. Brendan saw sneaking in the night a black demon creeping up to steal a silver horse's bridle and gesturing to one of the three late-coming monks

Voyage to the Rock

who took it and placed it in his robe. The saint then silently arose to pray all night.

In the morning, though they saw no man, the table was again set with food. And when the monks had said their morning prayers and ate, they headed to the shore.

It was at the shore that St. Brendan said: "Dear Fathers, let us not show evil to our host and defile our journey with a theft. For I tell you, that the Father of whom I spoke last night has given himself over to the demon's will and taken a silver bridle."

At this the unfortunate monk fell down and cast the bridle onto the shore. "It is I, O Fathers, who have done this crime. I am guilty. Forgive me and pray that my soul not be lost!" And with a mighty prayer the Fathers fell upon the ground to pray to the Lord Jesus Christ. And then with a howl, a black demon jumped from out of the monk's chest, this repentant Father saved after seven years of temptation and sin. By the command of St. Brendan, in the Lord's name, the demon was cast out and the monk was told to receive Holy Communion, since the saint knew that he was shortly to die. And die the monk did, but was delivered from Hell, and angels of light were seen receiving his soul.

* * *

"Agh! That was terrible," Brigid said. She must have braided and unbraided her hair at least five times from the moment Fr. Gregory had mentioned the demon until the end of the story.

It had added more than a little to Martin's own growing anxiousness. He involuntarily shivered. Until that moment, Martin didn't know it was physically possible for someone to actually feel the blood drain out of his face. But he had as the story went on, and now that it was at an end, he felt as though *he* could fall over and die.

No, not die! He clenched and unclenched his fists in the pockets of his hoodie as though he were pumping his own heart. *Oh man, oh man!*

He could almost feel the ancient Cross with its little Christ looking up at him from within the bag between his feet. He felt sick. *I'm going to send it back, St. Brendan. Really, I am!*

"Terrible, yes," said Fr. Gregory, turning in his chair to look at Brigid, "but also something wonderful, too. Do you see how even after seven years of being conquered by this demon of theft, even after St. Brendan had prophesied the monk's death, that God was still able through the help of His saint to show mercy and save the monk?" There was something soothing in Fr. Gregory's tone, and Martin involuntarily felt his shoulders relax a hair. "*Angels* came to take his soul—even though he had been a thief for seven years! It's a great lesson for us."

"I never really thought of it like that," Brigid said.

The comfort was short-lived. Now added to the already very unpleasant feelings of fear, a new sensation was creeping in: shame. *Well, there's nothing I can do about it now,* he thought. *It's not my fault no one was there. I would have given them the Cross. That was my plan from the start!*

"Are you going to keep going, Dad?" Martin said a little more sharply than was wise. He wanted to hear evidence of Newfoundland—settlements, or grapes, or tuckamore trees—not about dying monks and demons!

"Patience, Martin." His father's voice had lost its comforting tone. "We'll have plenty of time to hear the story. But, yes, let's continue..."

* * *

Voyage to the Rock

The next island they reached was all filled with sheep, and there they also saw all kinds of fish. So they stopped to perform the Divine Liturgy on the Feast of the Lord's Supper—Holy Thursday—and they remained there until Holy and Great Saturday. Here they met the shepherd of this place who himself was a holy man enlightened by God. He gave them food and told them that they must again sail out, but that they would find another place that night to celebrate the Pascha feast, and then quickly on to the Paradise of Birds.

And so it was that they found the new island which was quite small, with no grass or trees, and no sand on the shore. And while the monks got off and spent the night in prayer, St. Brendan prayed aboard their boat, knowing all too well the secret of this island.

In the morning light as Pascha came, they offered to God the Divine Liturgy, with St. Brendan himself celebrating from within the boat. And having finished, the Fathers thought to cook some fish over a fire that they had lit. But as the fire burned hot the island shook, and the Fathers in terror jumped into the boat just in time to see the island sink into the ocean—though not completely because later they saw their fire still smoldering in the distance.

"Dear Fathers, fear not, for God has revealed to me last night in prayer this mystery. This island that we sat upon was, in fact, no island, but the largest of all God's fish of the sea—a whale, named Lasconius."

Soon afterwards they saw the next island: the Paradise of Birds. Having rowed up a river inland, they came upon a marvelous waterfall which flowed with water, crystal clear. And above the fall, on a short, wide tree, sat a multitude of snow-white birds. Their number was so great that the saint could not help but pray to God to know the reason of such a gathering. And in a moment the answer: one snow-white bird soared down to land upon their boat's own prow. Its flying was as the tinkling of bells and it spread out its wings as a sign of gladness. Then the marvel: it spoke.

"In answer to your prayer, O Father Brendan, we are sharers in the great ruin of the ancient enemy—the fallen angel, the Devil. He was our leader and when he fell, we with him also fell—though not by our own will or choice. The Almighty God, who is righteous and true, has not sentenced us to suffer as with them. But here we abide where we suffer no pain and where we can partially see the Divine Presence.

"And yet, we stand apart from those angels who stood faithful. And so it is on holy feast days we are permitted to take the form of snow-white birds and to sit here and sing our Creator's praise! I will tell you that, as you have journeyed now for one year, so you must journey again for another six before you reach your desired end. Each year you will be led in circle: first, to the Island of Sheep from Holy Thursday until Holy and Great Saturday, next, to the back of the Whale Lasconius for the Lord's Resurrection and Pascha feast, then here, from Pascha until Pentecost, and last to a place where you have yet to go—St. Ailbe's Island—from

Voyage to the Rock

Christmas until the Feast of Christ's Presentation in the Temple and the Purification of the All-Holy Virgin Mary. After those seven years, through many and diverse dangers, you will find the *'Land of the Promise of the Saints'* which you are seeking, and then you will again reach home."

And so with that the bird again joined the others, and all at once at the time of Vespers, the Psalms in human voices they began to chant. And this was their pattern for each and every day, at each of the Hours of Prayer, from the time of Pascha until Pentecost, when the Fathers and St. Brendan once again returned to their boat. It was to the chanting of the birds that the monks sailed off: "*Hear us, O God Our Savior, the hope of all the ends of the earth, and in the sea afar off.*"

*   *   *

"You mean they actually had church on the back of a giant whale?" Brigid finally cut in. "And talking birds?" Her smile seemed to say: "Let's be adults about this".

"That's what the story says," Fr. Gregory said. "No stranger, I think, than the Prophet Jonah being thrown into a stormy sea which suddenly becomes calm, followed by being swallowed by a whale. Imagine that was the sea right there," Fr. Gregory said gesturing towards the whitecaps rippling across the ocean like water-color paint spilled on blue canvas. "And even if that was likely to happen," he raised a finger in the air, and brought it down to point at his daughter, "do you know what happens in the stomach of whales?"

Brigid gave her father a flat look.

"Digestion," he said, snapping his fingers. "So how could poor Jonah survive for three days in a whale's belly and not become whale food? The same way a group of monks can stand and have liturgy on its back: through God's miraculous care. That's faith, I guess."

"Well, I guess that makes sense," Brigid said, "if you put it that way."

If Martin hadn't been having just the same thought, he might have been annoyed that the story kept getting interrupted. He pulled his hoodie over his head. As it was, he was just curious enough not to mind too much.

"Now the *Birds* are much harder to explain in one way but easier in another," Fr. Gregory said, stroking his beard.

Elizabeth drummed her fingers along the steering wheel: "Now that's the one I want to hear more about."

"The simple answer," said Fr. Gregory, "is that they're not really birds; they just *appear* as birds sometimes."

"Okay," Brigid said, blue eyes intent, "but what are they *really*, then?"

"Fallen angels, I guess. But not ones who acted against God directly. Just ones that were ruled over by the devil before he rebelled against God." Fr. Gregory shrugged.

"What do you mean 'ruled over?'" Brigid asked.

"Well, the angels are a bit like soldiers. They have a commander and ranks. If your commander and the other officers make bad decisions and give bad orders, you can get caught doing the wrong thing without knowing it. Is this the same thing? Well, it's hard to say," Fr. Gregory said.

"Does that make sense, honey?" Elizabeth said.

"Well, I guess," Brigid said. "But it's a little hard to picture."

"How about you, Martin? What do you think?" his mother asked, their eyes meeting in the rearview mirror.

"I like the story," Martin said nodding his head, "but how about we keep going?"

"Well, I always love an eager audience," Fr. Gregory said, "but it's break time for me. Always keep them wanting more!" He added this with a flourish of his hand. "Besides, I'm sure

Voyage to the Rock

your mother would like to switch up the driving for a little while."

"But when do we hear about them arriving in Newfoundland?" Martin asked frowning.

"Oh, we'll be getting to that soon enough," his father said. "Besides, if we don't have time to finish St. Brendan's story on the way home, you and Brigid can always take turns borrowing the book."

Martin just rubbed a hand through shaggy hair. "I guess so."

The rest of the morning was spent with Martin napping in the back punctuated occasionally by conversation from his parents. It wasn't until shortly before 1:00 p.m. that they reached Gros Morne National Park.

Martin was now fully awake, staring at the mountains to one side and the ocean to the other. Fr. Gregory turned the car off the Viking Highway and they stopped at a place called *Fisherman's Landing Restaurant* where they all ordered Fish n' Chips.

"So, you guys have liked your Viking adventure?" Fr. Gregory asked, as he dipped some fries into a paper cup of ketchup.

"You bet!" said Brigid with an expansive wave of her arms. Martin wasn't even too annoyed by having to duck to avoid a hand to the head.

"It has been pretty cool," Martin said with a nod and a half smile. He leaned back against the tall wooden booth they were sitting in and took a drink of soda.

"A great idea, Gregory," Elizabeth said, patting him on the arm.

"And St. Brendan's voyage is nice, too," Brigid said over a mouthful of battered fish.

"About that..." Fr. Gregory said hesitating. "I completely forgot that I need to get some work done on my homily for Sunday. So... I think St. Brendan's voyage will have to wait for another time."

"Come on, Dad!" both Brigid and Martin said.

"I know, I know. I'm sorry. But like I said, you can both borrow the book and read it for yourselves. It's much more interesting with all the details anyway."

"But I'm already in the middle of a book, Dad," Brigid said almost dropping the piece of fish from her mouth. Her mother gave her *the look*. "Sorry," she said quickly.

"That works out perfect then. Martin can read it first and you guys won't have to flip a coin for it," Fr. Gregory said, giving Martin a wink.

"But can't you at least tell us why you think it's Newfoundland?" Martin said.

"Well... I don't want to spoil the story for you," his father said looking from one to the other of his two children, "but... I'll mention a few reasons why I think it might be Newfoundland—if you're mother's not tired of hearing about this yet?"

"That's fine, as long as it won't take too long," Elizabeth said. "We do need to get back on the road soon."

"Well, let's say that there are at least a few things that hint to it being Newfoundland. If I had to sum them up I'd say: waves, fire, metal, fish, ice, and islands. There," Fr. Gregory said, looking at Elizabeth with a satisfied grin. "How's that for quick?"

"Dad!" Brigid and Martin moaned in unison.

Elizabeth gave her husband a playful frown. "Well, maybe you could elaborate a little more, Dear."

"If you all *insist*," Fr. Gregory said, holding up both hands as if to say *I surrender*. "Why Newfoundland? Waves: that's the seven years the monks sailed West. There's not much west of Ireland. Fire: that's for the fire-belching volcanoes they encountered; just what you'd find on Iceland. Metal: that represents hairy, metal-smelting, men. Sounds a lot like a certain group of Vikings we just heard about, and it just so happens there were Viking camps all over Greenland. Keep heading West. What do we find next? Fish: the monks found massive schools of fish just like the Europeans found when they came to Newfoundland. Ice is for the floating crystal iceberg the monks discovered; yesterday we saw one for ourselves, now didn't we? And Islands: three of them unnamed, one of them filled with grapes like our Vinland; and since the monks were going in circles each year, maybe really just one big one? I'm just guessing, of course, but it sounds a lot like a journey from Ireland to Newfoundland to me." Fr. Gregory took off his skoufa and made a little bow. "Thank you, thank you. No applause necessary."

"Kids," Elizabeth said in mock solemnity, "never let it be said that your father cannot be brief when he chooses."

Fr. Gregory pretended a look of shock. "Is someone suggesting that I like to talk?"

"No Dad," Brigid said, "You just get *cornered* by mobs of parishoners long after coffee hour is finished with us waiting in the car."

"Well, imagine that," Fr. Gregory kept up the joke. "Can you believe them, Mart? Accusing me, of all people, of being long-winded."

Martin just shook his head, but he was obviously fighting back a smile.

"Since it doesn't seem I'm going to find anyone to defend me," Fr. Gregory said, "what did you all think of my little description?"

"It's awesome," Brigid said.

"Yeah, Dad, really awesome." Martin couldn't believe the way things were unfolding. *The Cross must be from St. Brendan's voyage!*

"It really does sound amazing," Elizabeth said.

"Yup. I told you it was great," Fr. Gregory said, so pleased that it seemed as if he, and not St. Brendan, had accomplished the voyage. "I told you guys that Newfoundland had more to offer than you thought."

Whatever Martin's feelings about the place, it certainly was true that this rocky, isolated island on the edge of the world was turning out to be much more than he could ever have imagined.

Chapter 7:
And the One Becomes Two

The sky outside Martin's large window was dark except for the bright moon and its reflection over the bay. The darkness of his room was broken by the light of his desk lamp which shone on the object before him: the tarnished-green Cross.

Under the bright light it seemed even more beautiful and mysterious: the lines and curves and intertwining knots carved into it, the disc-like circle that lay interposed over the center of the Cross, the roughly carved crucified figure in his long robes, and the little unidentifiable stone at Christ's side. There was something so simple about the Christ-figure but so intricate about the whole Cross.

The rest of the trip home had been uneventful. His father had worked on his homily as his mother drove, and Brigid had tried to speed through her novel in the hopes of finishing quickly and borrowing the book on St. Brendan. Martin had taken the time to try to work out some sort of plan of action.

Next to him he had out a set of drawing pencils and a notepad of paper: the first step of his plan. After another moment of gazing, Martin picked up the Cross and laid it on a blank page of the large notepad. He took out a sharp pencil and carefully began to trace the Cross. It began wide at the bottom, gently narrowing as Martin's pencil moved up towards the arms, then following the curve of the circular section connecting the arms and the main body of the Cross. This was repeated with each arm of the Cross, starting wide and becoming gradually more narrow at the middle and following the curve of the ring at the Cross's center. Once he had an outline made he removed the Cross and laid it next to his notepad. He began with the Christ trying to copy his size and position on the Cross as exactly as possible.

After some drawing, then erasing, and then drawing again, Martin tried to sketch the details of the little Christ's hair, closed eyes, nose, and beard; he also added a dark little scribble where the dirty piece of stone was. This part was somewhat easier since the details of the face were not as complicated as the rest of the Cross. How he was going to copy all the intertwining curves was another matter. He began with some of the details on the large ring; there was basically just a slightly thick band that wound along the outside edge.

"Well, here we go, Mart. The real work." He brushed his hair out of his eyes and chewed at his bottom lip as he began.

It took a long time—until Martin's hand hurt from the pencil and his eyes were strained from trying to follow all the lines. As much as he would try to follow one he found it impossible to continue since they were continually overlapping and underlying other curved lines. He would start, then stop, then erase, then start again, and again stop and erase. This went on and on, but slowly some of the patterns were starting to emerge and resemble—at least loosely—what he was seeing on the Cross.

The moon out his window seemed to have glided across the bay when next Martin looked up. He clicked the pencil down on the desk and leaned back in his chair, stretching his arms high over his head. He sat upright again and looked at his work. "Not bad, if I do say so myself." He was grinning. He had a somewhat accurate copy of the Cross.

This'll work just fine, he thought.

There was one thing strange about the designs, though—and it was no mistake in his drawing. All the curved lines seemed to curve and connect and intertwine so that there were no beginning and no end to them. Even as they came near the edges of the Cross or the body of Christ they would suddenly curve back toward the middle or downwards or upwards, continuing in their inter-woven dance. But some of these intertwining lines *did* come to an end on the outer sides of the Cross. On the top, the bottom, the right arm and the left, there were two "dead-end" lines each; it was even stranger because there was no pattern to it that Martin could see.

"You'd think they could have managed to fix those," Martin furrowed his brow. "The rest is so *complicated*, so *perfect*..."

A ninth "sore-spot" ran from the edge of the Cross directly to the little stone at Christ's side. Could someone have put them there on purpose? *But why?*

"What is that?"

Martin almost jumped out of his chair!

It was Brigid.

"Where did you find it? At the Viking settlement?" Brigid said. She was nearly climbing over Martin's shoulder.

Voyage to the Rock

Martin quickly swept the Cross underneath the notepad, and turned to meet Brigid. "Don't you know how to knock? This is my room! What are you doing in here?"

Brigid's wide-eyed astonishment turned indignant. "Mom told me to come up here! I didn't want to. But you've been holed up in here without a peep for hours! She wanted me to bring you those cookies and milk," she said pointing to a plate and glass on his bedside table. "So don't start yelling at me!"

"Well, you could have at least knocked," he said as he got up from his chair to close the bedroom door. The last thing he needed was his mother to come upstairs too!

"I would have if I wasn't carrying snacks for *you*," Brigid said, pointing the end of her blond braid at him. "But now I see why you've been so quiet! A little secret you've been hiding, huh?" and she moved toward the notepad.

Martin wasn't quick enough, and Brigid was now holding the Cross. She hopped back from Martin's reach, but then stood mesmerized by it. "It's amazing! And heavy," she said, one hand tracing the rough edges of the arms. "So did you find it there?"

Okay. Martin knew he needed to handle this delicately or things were about to get bad for him. Stealing from a National Park, hiding it from his parents, and then caught by his little sister before he could return it himself was not how he wanted this whole thing to end!

"Alright, Brigid. Sit," Martin said pointing to the stool next to his desk. She hesitated. "Do you want to hear the story, or not?"

"Of course, I do." Brigid looked at Martin suspiciously while still clinging to the Cross.

"Well, then sit... and promise me that whatever I tell you, you won't repeat a word of it to *anyone!*"

"Why should I promise?" asked Brigid, jutting her chin slightly. "I could just mention this to Mom and Dad and you'll *have to* tell the whole story."

"Brigid!" Martin said. Brigid actually started. "Brigid, please," he repeated more quietly, forcing himself to unclench his fists. "Because if you tell them—or *anyone*—we'll never discover if this Cross really is from St. Brendan's voyage."

There it was. He knew he needed to let her in on the whole thing; that was the only way to make sure she didn't say anything.

This got Brigid's attention—exactly the effect Martin was counting on. "What do you mean?" Brigid's eyes were as round as the moon out the window. "Do you think this is really from St. Brendan's voyage?" She glanced at the Cross in her hands again.

Martin knew he had his sister hooked and that if he played this right, his secret would be as safe as if no one had discovered it. "It *could* be," Martin said as he moved to take a cookie from his bedside table and lay back on his bed with his feet crossed. "Unless, of course, it is just Viking," he said between a bite of cookie.

Brigid's eyes shot up. "Or Viking?" she said almost to herself.

"So," Martin said sitting up at the edge of his bed, "sit, and I'll tell you the whole story." He reached his hand out for the Cross and Brigid hesitated a moment before handing it back to him and plopping down on the stool.

Martin then began to tell how and where he'd found the Cross, his initial ideas about it being Viking, and he added a very *confident* and *convincing* account of how innocent his taking of the Cross really had been, how he had intended to return it but that the museum had appeared closed. He told how he was motivated only by a desire to benefit the museum and possibly history by his potential discoveries. He spoke so well he almost had himself convinced. Almost.

He went on to explain how his ideas had changed on hearing about St. Brendan's voyage, and how now he was firmly convinced—which he wanted to be at least—that the Cross must be a sixth century Irish cross from St. Brendan's voyage.

Voyage to the Rock

"All that's left, really, is for me to go to the library tomorrow and confirm that this is actually an Irish cross," Martin said as he finished his narrative.

Brigid was too caught up in the possibilities and the adventure of it all to realize just how over-confident Martin was actually being about the whole thing. She clearly *wanted* to believe it was true, and so was unwittingly willing to let Martin spin his tale.

"Wow. This is unbelievable," Brigid said, taking a deep breath and letting it out.

"So you won't tell anyone about our discovery?" Martin asked.

"*Our?*" Brigid asked. "You mean you're including *me* in all this?"

"Well, you are agreeing not to tell anyone, and to let me continue the research I need to do to confirm it all, aren't you? Well then that makes it *our* discovery." Martin added this last to make certain Brigid wouldn't be revealing his secret.

"Of course I won't tell anyone," Brigid said, clasping her hands tightly at her chest. "And if there's anything I can do to help just tell me!"

"For now, just make sure nobody finds out about the Cross. When I need your help I'll ask," Martin said. "But make sure you don't speak to me about this unless we are absolutely alone and can't be overheard. Got it?"

"Got it," Brigid responded with barely contained excitement. "This is so awesome!"

"I know," said Martin, "but it's time you left before anyone gets suspicious. We'll talk later."

"Yeah. You're right. Okay, I'll go." And with a final glance at the Cross in Martin's hand, Brigid slowly opened the door, peeked out, and then was gone.

Martin quickly locked his door and slumped down on his bed. *Whew. Disaster averted!* He lifted the Cross to look at it. Seeing the hanging Christ, Martin couldn't help but feel a tinge

Matthew Penney

of guilt about what he'd just done. *But I have to keep you secret for just a little while longer.*

With this last, Martin was actually, inadvertently, speaking to the little Christ before him. *I'm going to send you back soon. Really.*

Getting up he put the Cross safely back in his backpack, along with his sketch and the copy of *The Voyage of St. Brendan the Abbot*—which he knew he wouldn't have time to read that night.

He'd have to move on to stage two of his plan: visit the Corner Brook Public Library tomorrow. He needed the internet to research and they weren't going to have it at the house for another week at least. Besides, maybe he could talk to someone about books on St. Brendan, or on Irish and Viking crosses. This was really his only hope, except for any clues that he might still find in the *Voyage*. It was the library or another long day of unanswered questions.

Chapter 8:
Searching for Answers

Martin was already waiting and ready by the family icon-corner when Fr. Gregory entered the room for morning prayers. The lampadas in front of the icons were lit, and the coal for the incense was glowing hot.

Fr. Gregory looked surprised to see Martin standing before him dressed and with everything prepared. The prayer book was even open to the correct page on the reading stand. "Wow," his dad said. "What's gotten into you?"

"What? Nothing," Martin said with all the wide-eyed innocence of a little child. The truth was that Martin couldn't wait to eat and be out the door to work. He hoped if they started a bit early that he might get permission to leave sooner for the library.

Fr. Gregory raised an eyebrow. "Still excited from the trip maybe?"

"That must be it," Martin said, nodding his agreement. Excitement couldn't even begin to describe how Martin was feeling since the trip.

Soon—though not soon enough for Martin—the whole family was there. The prayers finished, they ate a quick breakfast before Martin and Fr. Gregory were saying their goodbyes and finally heading over to the site of the church.

They worked hard and quickly that morning, both of them refreshed from their trip, with Shawn and Jeremy working as diligently as ever. And so before Martin realized, it was time to finish up for the morning. He was tired, but at least the time had flown by and his mind had been too occupied to be staring at his watch all morning.

"Dad?"

"Yeah, Mart, what is it?" his father said as he slung his toolbelt over one shoulder.

"Do you think I can go to the public library this afternoon?" Martin undid his own belt.

"The public library?" Fr. Gregory asked with a half-smile.

"Well..." Martin began, "I was hoping to look a bit into the Vikings and into St. Brendan's voyage." He still couldn't help but feel somewhat like a fugitive with the large metal cross tucked away in his backpack.

"Sure you can," Fr. Gregory said clapping a hand on Martin's shoulder. "I know it's close but do you think you can manage to find it alright?"

"No problem. I've already looked at a city map and have the directions in my bag." He pointed to his bag beside a make-shift tool bench. "I'll just take my bike."

"Okay, then. After lunch you're free to go," Fr. Gregory said as he brushed dust off his black sleeves and chest.

"Actually, Dad, I already made some sandwiches this morning. I was kind of hoping to head out ASAP."

"Well then I don't see why not," Fr. Gregory said, clearly impressed by his son's new-found enthusiasm. "Just make sure you're back by supper-time."

"Perfect," Martin said, grabbing his bag. "I'll see you then."

And with that Martin was heading out the back door of the church's basement and running up and across the hill toward the house and his bike. Hopping on and fastening his helmet, he sped off down their street toward the center of Corner Brook.

It was a beautiful, sunny day and Martin coasted much of the way toward downtown. He sped down streets with little one-story houses and fenced-in yards. He zoomed past playgrounds with squealing kids and heard dogs barking after him as he

Voyage to the Rock

whizzed by. As he neared the city-center, he tried to stay close to the sidewalk as the cars passed.

At Main Street Martin stopped, took out his map, and found his bearings. He only needed to turn right onto Mount Bernard Avenue and then to follow it straight up until he reached the library. It would be easy to spot since it was apparently the tallest building around—a whopping 15 stories. *A small apartment building in Boston.*

He found Mount Bernard Avenue easy enough but underestimated how tiring it would be to bike up to the library. It wasn't a very steep street but it was long. By the time he actually arrived at the large white building with all its windows, his legs were burning from the exertion and he was sweating. He wiped his forehead with the back of his sleeve and couldn't quite help feeling that he was like King Arthur on his quest for the Holy Grail; so what if he was only riding his bike to the local library. He had a reason to be excited.

Locking up his bike and helmet, he headed inside. The information board on the wall clearly read: "Corner Brook Public Library—2nd and 3rd Floors". Heading into the elevator, he pressed the button for the second floor. The doors opened onto a large open room. There were people sitting at tables in the middle quietly reading, and around the outside of the room were various shelves of books. Across to one side he saw the main desk. Martin headed straight for it.

"Hello," the woman at the counter greeted him. "Is there anything I can help you with?"

"I was wondering if I could sign up to use the internet?" Martin said as he laid his backpack at his feet.

"Let me check the availability," she said glancing at the sign-up sheet. "Unfortunately, there aren't any free until 4:30 this afternoon. Would you like me to put you in at that time?" she asked.

"No, thank you. That's a bit late," Martin said, putting both hands in his hoodie pockets.

"Well, is there anything I can point you to?"

"Actually, I'm looking for books on early Irish and Viking voyages to Newfoundland—and especially Irish and Viking art."

"The person you needs is Mr. Evans upstairs in the non-fiction department. If anyone knows, he does. He's the old feller with the bow-tie, one floor up."

"Thanks," Martin said as he grabbed his bag and headed for the third floor.

In a few minutes he had found "Mr. Evans" standing amid the book shelves. He was looking from book-spine to shelf, book-spine and back to the shelf, and then quickly sliding the book in before repeating the process with another.

"Excuse me? Mr. Evans?" Martin asked.

"Yes?" the elderly man straightened his reedy form and looked at Martin over the tops of his wire-rim glasses.

"I was hoping you could help me find some books on Viking and Irish art, and anything to do with Viking or early Irish voyages to Newfoundland."

"Ah... a main-lander, eh? Just arrived on the 'Rock', have ye?" He had the distinctive Newfoundland accent. "Looking for books on Vikings, and maybe St. Brendan?"

Martin couldn't help a shiver. "How'd you know I was looking for something about St. Brendan?"

"You aren't the first person interested in the 'first visitors' to Newfoundland. Many people have been captivated by the Viking voyages, and a few who know better—about whether the Irish didn't in fact beat them here." Mr. Evans gave a knowing wink.

"So you have some books then?"

"Well, we do have a few that might be of interest to you. Follow me." Mr. Evans seemed almost to move on tip-toe as he hastened down the aisle, Martin close behind. He led Martin to a section of books near a large window and sitting area at the far wall. From the window Martin could see the main area of the town and the large bay behind it.

"Here you go." Mr. Evan's spread out a thin arm like some sort of scarecrow performing a magic trick. "You'll find just

Voyage to the Rock

about anything we have on Vikings and the early Irish here. I puts this section together just for people like you!"

"Thanks," Martin said.

"Well, if you needs any help, you just finds me!" Then he straightened his bowtie, adjusted his glasses, and was off back down the aisle they'd come from.

Martin smiled and shook his head in spite of himself. Then he turned his eager attention to the shelves. There were at least five of them full of books, divided roughly between books about the Irish on the right and those about the Vikings on the left. Further there were little tags on the shelves suggesting different types of books: General, History, Society, Voyages and Trade, and Art and Architecture.

Martin decided to start with Art and Architecture to see if he could eliminate one or the other right away. He grabbed a book entitled *Norse Art 800-1100 A.D.* He flipped through the book looking for similarities to the Cross. There were lots of full color pages so he was able to see tons of different examples of Viking art. There were some similarities between the Cross and what he was seeing; many of the pictures twisted and intertwined with lines going on forever. There were even ones with crosses and the circle behind them. But the pictures didn't quite look right; they were too "free" and not as symmetrical and consistent as the patterns on the Cross.

It wasn't impossible that the Cross was Viking, but when he looked at a whole book full of Norse art, he just didn't feel like it fit with those examples. There was both a sense of disappointment, since he was pretty sure he had discovered the Cross wasn't Viking, but also of excitement since that must mean it was Irish. He would not dwell on the alternative: that it was neither.

He put the book back and reached for one from the Irish Art and Architecture section. The first book was no good since it didn't have any pictures except for a few rough sketch-drawings. He quickly replaced it and took another. This one wasn't helpful either since it was mainly about architecture and only had pictures of old Irish churches. The third book, though, paid off.

On the cover of the book itself he saw a tall stone cross that looked quite similar in shape to his cross—it even had the large circle that surrounded the Cross' center. The book was called *Ireland's High Cross*. As Martin flipped through he saw page after page of different versions of *his* Cross; it was a temptation not to reach into his backpack and pull it out to compare.

Instead, he slipped his hand in and took out his drawing of it. It definitely looked like a high cross, though the arms of his cross were wider and more proportionate than the high crosses. He looked at the designs on his copy and then back to the book. There had to be something to confirm whether his Cross was the same.

Some of the high crosses did have interlacing patterns like his, but some didn't have any at all. Others had scenes of people or a seated Christ in the middle and different kinds of patterns. *How to be sure?*

It seemed that his Cross could be Irish—it was so similar, but the Viking ones had been similar too, to an extent. Without seeing more of the weaving patterns it was hard to tell.

He glanced at the spines of the books to see if there was another that might answer his questions. Nothing caught his eye.

Martin jumped as a hand was laid on his shoulder.

"Sorry to startle you, me Son. I just wanted to check in with you." It was Mr. Evans.

"Ah, thanks..." Martin brushed shaggy hair out of his eyes.

"Is there anything I can help with?" asked the thin old man.

"Actually...," Martin hesitated. "Have you ever seen anything like this before?" and he took his drawing of the Cross from behind the book he was holding.

"Well now," said Mr. Evans reaching out knobby knuckles and taking the drawing. "Now isn't this interesting?"

"What?" Martin asked leaning forward. "You recognize it?"

"Recognize it... well, no."

Voyage to the Rock

Martin's heart sunk.

"Not exactly, that is," Mr. Evans said. "But it looks to me to certainly be a form of Celtic Cross—in the same style as an Irish High Cross."

"Yeah?" Martin perked up. "But what about the designs on it?"

"Now *those* are what's interesting. High Crosses do have this sort of design, though usually not so intricately or so often; and they certainly have this here 'ring'," Mr. Evans said pointing to the disc with his folded glasses. "Some people says this 'ring' is a type of halo, you know," said Mr. Evans looking up at nothing in particular. "Some says it represents eternity; some says both. A beautiful thing, Celtic Art."

Martin was waiting anxiously at what he felt was the moment of victory or failure.

"You knows what some people say is the most beautiful piece of Celtic Art?"

Martin shook his head, barely able to handle the delays.

"The *Book of Kells*," Mr. Evans said leaning forward as though revealing a secret. "It's an illumined manuscript—an early Irish edition of the Four Gospels written in Latin, produced in the 800's or even earlier, filled with countless illustrations." He put the edge of his folded glasses to his cheek. "It represents a perfect example of Irish Celtic art and is one of the best examples of these Celtic knots you've drawn all over this here Cross," said Mr. Evans pointing to Martin's drawing.

"It is?" Martin asked.

"Certainly it is, and that's why I'm a bit surprised you've never heard of the book. How did you manage to draw these?" Mr. Evans said.

Martin suddenly felt panicked under his gaze; he had to consciously force himself not to clench and unclench his fists. "I just copied it from a picture I had at home. That's why I came here—to find out more about it."

"Well then, me Son," said Mr. Evans handing the paper back to Martin. "I suggest you looks at the *Book of Kells*, since what you drew seems to be a pretty good copy of some of the more intricate interlaces from it. Here," he said, grabbing a book from the shelf and handing it to Martin, "this is what you're looking for."

Martin took the book. "Thank you, Mr. Evans. You've been a great help!"

"Yes, B'y, that's my job. And I was just thinking earlier that there are two more books that might be of interest to you. This one by Tim Severin," he said picking a book from the shelf. "And this one." He handed both books to Martin. "The second one of these is actually by one of our own Newfoundlanders— Dr. Brendan Arthur. It contains just about everything there is on St. Brendan, his voyage, and Newfoundland. The stuff in here may be a bit controversial to the rest of the world, but I thinks Arthur presents a good case for why Brendan and his monks may have indeed landed in Newfoundland. Main-landers always think they knows better," Mr. Evans said with a furrowed brow, and then looking back at Martin added, "Ah... not all main-landers, of course. But especially those academic types! Anyhow, I knows Dr. Arthur personally—lives nearby in Lark Harbour, he does—and I thinks he may be on to something with this book." He paused and shook his head, "Poor old feller. Well, now, I ought to be back to work."

Before Martin could ask more, the frail—but spry—figure of Mr. Evans was gone.

Martin looked at the three books in his hand: the *Book of Kells: An Illustrated Introduction*, Tim Severin's *The Brendan Voyage*, and Brendan Arthur's *St. Brendan the Abbot: The Incredible Journey to Newfoundland Shores*. Martin smiled to himself; yesterday he had no information and now he was finding more than he'd have time to read!

He quickly opened the *Kells* book, sat in the chair near the window, and flipped through page after page of colorful pictures of old manuscripts. He studied the book for a long time. He was captivated by intricate illustration after intricate illustration. They were filled with birds and animals, with saints and angels,

Voyage to the Rock

with Christ, and all of the pages were covered in the "Celtic knots" that he himself had copied from the Cross last night. It was an Irish cross! It had to be.

The question remained though: Was it St. Brendan's Cross?

Finally starting to feel a bit tired, Martin glanced at his watch. It was almost 4:30 p.m.! He needed to be home by supper or he'd be dead. Plus, he still needed to get a card so that he could sign out the books.

As he gathered his things to go, there was a loud growl from his stomach that reminded him of something else—he had forgotten to eat his lunch!

Chapter 9:
The Unnamed Islands

After a satisfying supper—three helpings—followed by dishes and clean-up, Martin was back in his room and ready to continue his research. Unfortunately he wouldn't be poring over any of his new books since he wasn't able to get a library card. He had forgotten his birth certificate at home! So instead he was going to use the time wisely and try to finish the book that lay in front of him: *The Voyage of Saint Brendan the Abbot*.

On the cover of the book was a dark green and gold border that framed a picture of St. Brendan standing in long gray robes. He was resting one hand on the large mast of his boat and part of the sail was visible. His face was thin with a long white beard and he was bald except for thick tufts of hair on either side of his head. His eyes were a deep blue color, and it was like he was staring right into Martin's room. The picture was almost an icon, really.

"Well, here we go, St. Brendan."

Martin opened the book to find out where they had left off...

* * *

And so it was for nearly eight months more they sailed with the food given to them by the holy man from the Island of Sheep—dried bread and salt fish, and water that was carefully kept. When finally there appeared a new island, the Fathers sought and sought to land, but like before no place

Voyage to the Rock

was found and they were tempted to drink from fresh-flowing waterfalls. "My Children, take nothing here without the permission of the holy fathers from this place. For they will give you freely what you desire to take in secret!"

They shortly found a landing place, and a silent and ancient monk they met to lead them to his abbot and the other fathers there. But to all questioning words, he opened not his mouth, but only with signs and waves did he urge them on. St. Brendan told his brothers: "Keep silence so as not to offend our hosts by foolish speech, for I can see that they have a rule of holy stillness."

They were led to meet twenty-four monks and the abbot of this place who spoke to them in a holy song: "Arise, you holy ones and come forth to meet us; sanctify this place and bless this people in peace." Then the abbot embraced St. Brendan and all his companions and led them into the monastery and washed their feet. Next they went to eat in the strictest silence, but the abbot spoke clairvoyantly and said: "Fathers, now take and drink a loving cup in the gladness and fear of the Lord, that which you had wished in secret to drink today. Be of good cheer!"

After the meal, they went to the church and offered their praises to God. But all was done in the utmost silence and no one spoke except the monk whose turn it was to chant the verse of the Psalm. Even to the abbot the monks did not speak, but made gestures to which the abbot answered by writing on a slate. And later when questioned by St. Brendan the abbot confessed: "For eighty years we have kept this rule of silence and no brother has ever heard the voice of another except while chanting psalms and spiritual songs." Brendan was amazed that men of flesh and blood could carry out such a great form of struggle for God and wanted to stay, but the abbot reminded the saint of Brendan's own quest and service to God.

Voyage to the Rock

Suddenly, while they were still speaking, a fiery arrow shot through the window of the church, and as if it were a bolt of lightning, flashed from lamp to lamp that hung within the church and before the holy altar table lighting them with a glowing flame. The abbot said: "Come and see the secret of all this, that the wicks of the lamps do not burn down, nor ever need to be changed, nor does oil need to be poured in them. But they burn and are not consumed, nor do ashes remain in the morning, for the light is entirely spiritual." And when St. Brendan wondered about this the abbot reminded him of Moses and the Burning Bush, which bush burned with the spiritual light of God's energies, but was not consumed.

St. Brendan and his monks remained there for many days, following joyfully the rule of the holy Fathers that lived on St. Ailbe's Island, until it was finally time to leave again. So with the blessing of the abbot and his monks, St. Brendan's company set sail.

Under the protection of God alone, St. Brendan and his monks used neither oars nor sail, but drifted about every which way until the beginning of Great Lent. And then one day, with their food three days gone, they came upon another island. And so it was that here in this land the monks found many springs and herbs and vegetables, and fish of every kind. St. Brendan thanked God for the comfort He showed and the rest that the brothers were given. But from here they left after not many days for the monks had become careless and taken too much to drink, and were scarcely saved except for St. Brendan's prayers. And so they continued their circular journey towards the Island of Sheep and the Lord's Supper—the Holy Thursday feast.

* * *

Was this the first of the 'unnamed' islands Dad had mentioned? There didn't seem to be too much to show it was Newfoundland: 'springs and herbs and vegetables'. Still, it also said, 'fish of every kind', and Newfoundland is definitely known for having lots of fish. He pushed his hair off his forehead and turned back to the book.

* * *

Again they repeated their accustomed Feasts to the Isle of Sheep until Holy Saturday, then for Pascha on Lasconius, and Pascha-tide until Pentecost upon the Island of Birds, and back to St. Ailbe's Island for the Christmas feast.

And it came to pass that once during the time between Pentecost and Christmas that the Fathers were seized with a dreadful fear. For a giant whale was making its way towards their little boat. With cries they shouted: "Help, O Father Brendan, help us!" But the saint only replied: "Fear not, you of little faith! For God who is always our protector will protect us now!" And as he prayed aloud, Behold, the miracle! God sent another monster of the deep that attacked the whale, and left it dead, half-devoured and in three pieces. And the faith of the monks was strengthened.

Voyage to the Rock

Then it was that the travelers found another island. It was filled with herbs and fruit and vegetables, like the island on which they drank too much and almost lost their way. And as they approached they saw upon the shore a large part of the giant whale and were commanded by the saint to take and prepare to eat. But St. Brendan would not take from the meat, he being a priest and never eating flesh that once had held the 'breath of life'.

On this island, they remained some time, for the ocean was all storms and wind. And the holy fathers used this time to rest, and explore, and gather more of the giant whale to eat. But they found no living man.

* * *

This was obviously the second 'unnamed' island. *The 'storms and wind' are a lot like Newfoundland,* Martin thought. But he knew that lots of places near the ocean might be like that. He pulled up his chair and kept going.

* * *

At another time upon their watery quest, they came upon an island all-flat and filled with flowers of white and purple. Upon this island as the saint foretold lived three groups of monks: boys, young men, and aged elders. And when pressed by the monks to tell them more, St. Brendan said to them: "On this island to remain is one of the three who joined late at the shore."

And as he said so it came to pass, and standing on the shore were three groups in choir : the boys, clothed in snow-white robes; the young men, in robes of violet; and then the last, the elder monks, all-arrayed in purple vestments. And after their chanting had finished, a cloud of marvelous brightness overshadowed the entire island, and chanting as from a heavenly host of angels continued through the entire night.

In the morning when the Holy Sacrifice of Divine Liturgy was ended, two members of the young men's choir came with a basket filled with purple grapes, and placed them in St. Brendan's boat. "Eat of this fruit, O Man of God, this fruit from the Isle of the Strong Men, and give to us our chosen brother, and then depart in peace." And St. Brendan and the other monks having given their brother and fellow traveler the kiss of peace, said farewell to him, and departed while the chanting choirs sang: "Behold how good and pleasant it is for brethren to dwell together in unity!"

When those days had passed, after the Fathers had finished a three day fast, in the sky there flew a radiant bird which coming near the boat, dropped more of the Strong Men's grapes within. "Never have we seen or read of such grapes—so large and sweet and fragrant!" The size of apples, and yielding juice for all, the fruit was a precious miracle from God. And to the island which had given such fruit, the company had soon arrived.

Here it was that they found similar fruit—an isle all filled with grapes. "Set up your tents and be of good cheer for

Voyage to the Rock

God has given such excellent food in this land which He has shown us." And there they dwelt for some forty days, feasting on grapes, and herbs and vegetables, and glorifying God for such a marvelous place. This was the third such island, laden with food, and no one that was seen. And the name of the place—Isle of the Strong Men—remained to the Fathers a mystery.

*   *   *

Was this the third island? But it had a name? *Did Dad get it mixed up?* Martin drummed his fingers on his desk while he thought.

The island sure seemed like the other two. It even said 'this was the third such island, laden with food', and also, 'and no one that was seen'. It had grapes, too, and didn't the Vikings name Newfoundland *Vinland* because of that?

It has to be the third island, doesn't it?

*   *   *

At another time as they celebrated St. Peter's feast, the monks beheld an awesome sight. Beneath their boat and all around they saw a multitude of silver fish. They swam and swam and filled the sea, and joining them were numerous whales, so that the monks were filled with fright. But St. Brendan made bold by such an amazing sight grew louder as he said the prayers, and the creatures as though answering jumped in the water all around, and then swam far away.

One day, a towering silver mountain of crystal before them appeared. Its height pierced the sky with its surface like cold marble. The thing was so large that they could not see its top, but they could see its clear and icy bottom plunging into the ocean deep. "Let's take the boat in closer, that we may view the wonderful works of God." And into an opening the saint directed the monks, and beheld the sea that looked like transparent glass within a crystal cave. Inside it shone with the light of the sun, as bright within as from without.

After some time in the crystal cave, upon a ledge they found a gift. It was a chalice all of hard cold crystal, and next to it a diskos. St. Brendan at once took them up and to the Fathers said: "The Lord Jesus Christ has displayed to us this wonderful marvel of His love, and given to us these gifts therefrom. So let us honor Him as is fitting and celebrate the holy Liturgy with them!" And so from there they sailed again, but to more fearsome islands and more dreadful trials.

* * *

Martin stopped to consider these last two events. The reference to 'multitudes of silver fish' was exactly what the Europeans found when sailing to Newfoundland—just like his dad had said. *That's a good clue to it being Newfoundland!* And the 'silver mountain of crystal' was definitely an iceberg; he saw one shimmering in the sunlight just two days ago, and so knew only too well that it looked like a mountain of crystal! These last two clues were impressive.

Martin considered it all: the three islands, the schools of fish, and the iceberg. It wasn't a lot to go on. But it at least made it *possible* that the three islands were really one very *large* island.

Voyage to the Rock

And by the descriptions, it *was* possible that it was Newfoundland.

"But is it?" Martin sighed heavily and leaned back grabbing two fistfuls of hair. *Did the Cross belong to Irish monks?* This was still the question that made or broke the whole thing. He could read books all day long and guess at story clues or pictures, but how could he be *certain* about anything?

Martin stood up and began pacing his room. "Think, Martin," he chided himself. "If it were a perfect world, a perfect situation, what would you need so that you could figure this out?"

A signature on the back? Not likely! He was staring at his reflection in the window. "Well, then what?"

An expert. Exactly, but how can I find one of those? And where? His dad would start working at the university in September, but that was too long from now and there was no way Martin could find a professor who might know something without his dad finding out. Even Mr. Evans who seemed to know a lot wouldn't be able to say for certain how old the Cross was or if it was real.

Then who else? "Who can tell if something is old and valuable?" He stared intensely into his own face trying to will the answers out of his brain. "Who knows old things...?"

And then it clicked: an antique dealer! If there was anyone in this city who might know, an antique dealer must—or at least he'd know who to ask to find out.

Martin sprang up and headed downstairs to find the phonebook. He passed the living room where, curled up on the couch, his mother was showing Brigid some photos of icons from a large book and his father sat reading the newspaper in the armchair in the corner. Martin didn't pause as he headed for the kitchen.

"Martin, are you *still* hungry?" his mother asked from the other room.

Hungry? What would he tell his mother? Why did he need the phonebook? "Yeah, Mom," he lied. "Is there anything?"

"There's some fruit in the bowl on the island," his mother said.

"Okay," he said, grabbing an apple in one hand, but his true object—the phonebook—he put under the opposite arm so as not to be noticed when he passed the living room again.

Brigid cast an inquiring glance his way as he scooted by, but Martin didn't stop to make eye contact. In a moment he was back upstairs in his bedroom with the door shut, and flipping through the phonebook for "Antiques".

He found an advertisement for the only dealer in the city: *Sullivan O'Connell's Fine Heritage Antiques*. The write-up specified that Mr. O'Connell had over 45 years of experience. He received objects of all kinds and all time periods, and best of all "Specializing in Irish pieces." *Jackpot!* Not only that, it read "Certified Appraisals, or Free Uncertified Appraisals on all pieces. " This was too good to be true.

But can I really trust showing the Cross to someone?

He wrestled with this question for awhile. Sighing, he pushed himself out from his desk and spun himself in a quick circle. He knew that if he didn't take the risk he may as well just send the Cross back to the museum now. How else would he discover for certain anything about it?

By the time his spinning came to a stop it was decided. He would take the Cross to Mr. Sullivan O'Connell tomorrow on his way back from getting a library card and his books.

"Martin!" Dad called from downstairs, "Time for bedtime prayers."

Martin closed the phonebook and tucked it away. He glanced at the open copy of St. Brendan's *Voyage*. He wasn't going to finish that tonight like he'd hoped. But he would make sure to add one extra prayer that night: to St. Brendan for some answers tomorrow.

Chapter 10:
The Antique Store

A sharp wind blew against Martin's face and his hands were getting red and cold as he coasted down the street toward the downtown. The dark clouds overhead didn't look promising. Martin needed to get to the library and antique store, and get back home before it started to pour.

It being Saturday and his day off, he needed to make the most of it. The antique dealer was the top priority, but he still felt uneasy about revealing his secret. He had decided on the library and his books first... to get his courage up somewhat.

And so it wasn't long before he was back in the library at the main desk. They had held the books for him and he filled out the form to get his own library card.

"Here you go, B'y," the girl working at the desk said. She was young and it occurred to him that she probably went to the high school he would be attending in the fall. Unconsciously he felt his shoulders tense. The last three days had worked wonders for jamming his problems into a tight little ball in a back corner of his mind.

"Thanks," he said as he took the card and his books. He knew he couldn't keep everything back there forever, but for right now the promise of answers and fame was going to have to be a good enough distraction.

That was just the kind of resolve Martin needed because he was now on his way out and heading for the antique store. A few minutes later he was pedaling down Broadway Street looking left and right for the shop.

He stopped his bike. He was in front of a beautiful old two-storey building that had obviously been well-maintained. The top half was covered by long wooden shingles painted a dark green that ran the width of the building. There were two small wrought-iron balconies with a fine chair and table on each in front of large French doors. The lower half of the building was made of large rough stonework, broken by two picture windows and the door to the main entrance. Carved on an ornate wooden sign with flowing gold script, it read: *Sullivan O'Connell's Fine Heritage Antiques*.

From the window were visible antique tables and book cases filled with treasures of bronze, gold, or silver. There were fancy lamps and ornate dishes. Martin thought he even made out a suit of armor further in.

This was it. This was Martin's last chance to forget the whole thing, to give up his search, and to just send the Cross back to L'Anse aux Meadows without a return address—never to be discovered and never to be in trouble. He hesitated and weighed things in his mind; he took even longer to make his decision than he thought he would. But there was something in the air, something about the antique store that made him uneasy. Was it simply the fear of his secrets being uncovered? Or was it the gloomy and chill weather?

Whatever the reason, in the end Martin knew he couldn't abandon this small bit of adventure in an otherwise all too boring life. He swallowed his fear and entered the store.

A bell above the door rang and the smell of old wood and varnish greeted him. The store was fairly large but was so filled with items everywhere that it gave Martin a claustrophobic feeling. Everything was neatly arranged and displayed; Martin had stepped into a museum—or into a castle. As he had seen from the window there were lots of antique tables and chairs, bookcases and wall-hangings, and the room seemed to shimmer from all of the expensive metallic objects that sat arranged on every bit of table space and which reflected the dim light.

Voyage to the Rock

There was indeed a suit of immaculately polished armor, and he now saw upon one wall, rows of mounted swords of different lengths, thicknesses, and styles. Every other wall was covered with elaborately framed old paintings, wall-hangings, and large pieces of intricately carved wood. Behind glass doors, in the dark, shining, wooden bookcases were row upon row of old books. The entire room made Martin afraid to move in case he accidently broke anything.

He slowly and carefully weaved his way further in, trying to find someone who might work there. He walked into an adjoining room through the large double-door opening, but all he saw were more antiques—though interestingly, there were some large stone crosses and other similar objects against one wall.

"T'is ain't no place fer kids to be foolin' round in!"

Martin could have won the Olympic high jump with the amount of air he got in that moment. He spun and towering over him was a bulky, rough-looking man scowling down at him.

"I... I'm not... not fooling around, sir," Martin said, unconsciously taking a step backward. "I'm looking for Mr. O'Connell, about an antique." He spoke this last with a little more confidence.

"Hmmph," the thick man grunted. "Wait 'ere, then. And don't touch anytin'." Martin moved to one side as the man walked past him and out around a corner toward the back of the store.

Martin was more nervous than ever. He slid his prayer rope off his wrist in an attempt to calm down. "Lord Jesus Christ, have mercy on me; Lord Jesus Christ, have mercy on me; Lord Jesus Christ, have mercy on me," he whispered as he pulled the knots between thumb and forefinger. He tried to get himself to breathe more evenly.

What am I doing here? He couldn't stop the thought. *I've got to get out of here.* He squeezed his rope tighter and tried to concentrate on the words of his prayer, "Lord Jesus Christ, have mercy on me," to keep himself from running out of the store.

Just when Martin couldn't take it any longer, a tall, thin man, dressed in a suit and tie, emerged from around the back corner. He approached with a long stride, and had silvery-gray hair combed back. As he got closer Martin saw that he had a stern, sharp, face.

"Mr. Duffy says that you were requesting to speak with me?" The man spoke with a different accent—Irish, maybe, but very educated sounding. He also spoke with more than a touch of aloofness, as though he were speaking more to a servant than a potential customer.

"Yes sir, I did. You see, I have something..." Martin couldn't help shifting his weight from foot to foot as he spoke. "Well, I was hoping you might be able to take a look at it... to see maybe if you could tell me anything about it and when it may have been made." Martin was babbling but he couldn't help himself. The man was so intimidating.

"I don't appraise baseball cards or comic books or any of those sorts of things, young man," Mr. O'Connell said peering down at Martin. "I specialize in fine antiques and artifacts." He raised a nonchalant hand to indicate the pieces all around them.

"Yes, I know... Well, I read that in your ad, I mean..." Martin said, stumbling over his words. "But that's why I came to you, sir. Actually, I have this cross." Martin reached into his backpack. "I think it's Irish," he said as he pulled the Cross from his bag and held it out to display it.

Mr. O'Connell's flat expression disappeared, and just briefly his eyes widened. Immediately, though, his eyes narrowed as he looked from the Cross to Martin. "Where did you get this?" Mr. O'Connell's voice was low and intense; his gaze was now firmly locked on the Cross.

"Well... actually..." Martin said. He had totally forgotten to think of what he was going to say if asked just such a question! He mentally punched his own arm. Hard.

Mr. O'Connell looked up, his piercing green eyes searching Martin's face.

Voyage to the Rock

"It's been in my family," Martin said, brushing brown hair quickly out of his eyes. "I was just trying to figure out where exactly my grandfather had gotten it." Gazing up at those shining green eyes, Martin suddenly had the uncomfortable feeling of being a helpless rabbit before a hungry wolf. He looked away.

"In your family, you say?" Mr. O'Connell took a step closer. "Your grandfather's?" He leaned forward slightly, hands clasped together before him. "And you don't remember where he got it?"

"No, sir, I don't." Martin's own hands were so slick he felt like the Cross could slip right from his fingers. "Neither do my parents," he added.

Did Mr. O'Connell believe him? He couldn't tell.

"So you're parents sent you here with it?" Mr. O'Connell said while staring intently into Martin's face.

"Well, no... Actually, I didn't tell them I was bringing it," he said, trying his best not to step back under O'Connell's penetrating gaze. "I mean, they don't know, that is."

Strangely, the tight lines on Mr. O'Connell's brow and around his eyes and mouth seemed to soften and he straightened somewhat. "And so you want an appraisal from me, do you?" An inviting smile suddenly appeared on his face. "To tell you where it's from and when it was made?"

"Yes sir, very much," Martin nodded, his own shoulders relaxing slightly. "The ad said that if it was uncertified, the appraisal was free. Is that true?"

"Ah yes, it is indeed! I must say, I'd be happy to take a closer look at that," he said pointing a long finger at the Cross. Mr. O'Connell held out his hand for the Cross.

There was something in his voice that Martin didn't quite feel comfortable about, though he didn't know why exactly. He hesitated only a heartbeat before handing the Cross to the old gentleman.

"You'll need to leave it with me for a few days, though," Mr. O'Connell said as he held the Cross in two hands, staring down at it, "so that I can examine it more closely and do some research on it." His voice had become almost a whisper.

"Okay... I guess that would be fine," Martin said. His mouth was dry and he swallowed. "When would I pick it up again, though?"

"How about sometime early next week—Monday or Tuesday? How does that sound?" Mr. O'Connell said looking up suddenly, and then paused. "That is, if your parents won't notice it's gone."

There was something in his eyes and tone. Was it a hint of mockery?

Don't be stupid. You're turning paranoid now! Martin tucked his hands into his pockets. "Yes, that will be fine, sir; and no they won't notice it's gone."

"Well okay, then. Good day!" Mr. O'Connell turned with cross in hand to walk away.

"Excuse me, Mr. O'Connell," Martin said, unconsciously raising a hand to stop him. "Don't you need my name or something? Shouldn't I take a ticket or receipt or whatever?"

Mr. O'Connell turned back to him. "Do you think I won't remember who you are? Do I look that *old* to you?" he said, a blank expression on his face.

"No sir, I didn't mean that! I just thought..." Martin was mortified.

"Well, then, don't you worry about thinking," Mr. O'Connell interrupted him, "Just leave that to me. You can see yourself out, I trust?" Without waiting for an answer, Mr. O'Connell, in his pinstripe gray suit and gold cuff-links, strode quickly back the way he had come.

Martin didn't know what to think or feel about what had just happened. He knew one thing, though: he didn't have the Cross anymore. And that made his stomach turn.

Chapter 11:
The Manuscript Page

"So you didn't outrun the rain, eh?" Fr. Gregory asked as Martin came in the door.

Martin was utterly soaked in fact. The moment he had stepped outside the antique store it had started to pour, and despite the fact that he had raced home, he was still drenched. So now he stood dripping in the hall with his father grinning at him.

" Hopefully you were at least able to get your books?" Fr. Gregory asked.

"Yeah," Martin said.

"It's okay," his dad said, reaching out a hand and giving Martin's shoulder a squeeze. "Now you'll be able to better *get into* your reading about St. Brendan and his voyage. Imagine being in the middle of the Atlantic ocean on a little boat made of leather with a storm like this going on. Amazing!"

"Amazing for Irish monks in the sixth century," Elizabeth said as she entered and saw her son, a hand on one hip, "but not so amazing for a soaked young man."

Fr. Gregory looked from Elizabeth back to Martin. He held a hand to the side of his mouth in a pretend whisper and said, "I think that's you're cue to get upstairs and out of those soaking clothes."

Martin took off his sopping jacket. He shivered; even his mother's ever-present scarf looked enticing right then. "I'll take that," his mother said. "Up to the bathroom; I'll bring you some dry clothes." Martin took the stairs two at a time as he headed toward a warm shower.

Matthew Penney

It wasn't until he was in dry clothes with a towel around his neck that Martin finally sat down at his desk to take out his library books. Thankfully they hadn't gotten wet inside his backpack. He moved the steaming lemon and honey drink that his mother left and laid the books in front of him on the desk.

The first book he picked up was Tim Severin's *The Brendan Voyage*. Martin was excited about it because it told the journey of one adventurer in the 1970s who had wanted to prove that St. Brendan's journey was actually possible. He had used the same kind of boat and materials that St. Brendan would have used, with the *Voyage of St. Brendan* as a guide, and he actually sailed from Ireland to Newfoundland. This was important because it was modern-day proof that the Cross really could have been St. Brendan's.

Other than the success of the voyage itself, and the mention of the volcanoes, icebergs, and whales Tim Severin had seen along the way, there wasn't too much else that Martin needed from the book. Martin noted that whereas he had found the Cross at L'Anse aux Meadows—the northernmost point of Newfoundland, Tim Severin's crew had arrived further south.

He slid the book to one side and grabbed another: the *Book of Kells*. He had already looked through this book quite a bit at the library and so wasn't expecting to find too much more to help him. *After all that's why I took the Cross to Mr. O'Connell, wasn't it?* He sighed at the thought of that encounter.

Still, he flipped through more pages and read a little about the *Book of Kells*. It was called an Insular Manuscript, which apparently just meant that it was made in England, Scotland, or Ireland. The *Kells* book, though, was one of the most famous examples of this art form. Martin also discovered that it was mainly practiced by Celtic monks. These books were known for their intricate designs of spirals and curves, sometimes having animals interwoven into them like the Viking ones, but also with many religious figures. The colors, the 'Celtic knots,' and the pictures of Christ and the saints were incredible. To Martin they looked like an early form of Byzantine icon.

Voyage to the Rock

He pulled out the sketch he had done of the Cross and laid it next to the photographs of the *Book of Kells*. Many of the delicate Celtic knots looked identical—though there were no animal figures on his.

Martin suddenly paused and his jaw dropped. On the page before him was the face and clothes of a Christ that looked *identical* to that on his sketch: the Christ Enthroned. Almost the only difference was that on his sketch, Christ was upright with eyes shut, his head tilted slightly to one side and his arms outstretched, while in the other Christ was seated on a throne. Martin wondered what connection there could possibly be between his Cross and the *Kells* book—since his Cross would have been made about 200 years earlier than the *Book of Kells* to have been St. Brendan's.

A knock at Martin's door interrupted his discovery. Quickly tucking his sketch under one of the books, he turned and said: "Come in." It was Brigid's face that peaked into the room. Martin leaned back in his chair and drummed fingers on the desk. "Yeah?"

"I wanted to talk to you about... *the Cross*," she said whispering and casting a look back into the hallway to make sure her parents weren't within earshot.

"Ssshhh!" Martin said gesturing her in. He didn't have time for diversions; he had work to do.

Brigid entered the room—but not just Brigid. With her was the red-haired kid from the ice-cream store. "What is *he* doing here? You told me you wouldn't tell anyone!" Martin hissed.

"It's just Ashley. I didn't tell any *adults*. Besides, he says he's willing to help if he can." Ashley was standing behind Brigid, clearly awkward at hearing their exchange.

"Well, what does he know?" Martin crossed his arms on his chest.

"Nothing much. Just that you found a Cross at L'Anse aux Meadows, that it is very old and might have belonged to St. Brendan, and that we're trying to find out information about it to know for sure," Brigid said.

"So everything, then," Martin said, his face as expressionless as a stone.

"Well... I guess so," Brigid said, two hands wrapped around her pony-tail.

"And how do I know I can trust him not to tell anyone, since I can't even trust *you*?" Martin said jabbing an accusing finger in Brigid's direction; she avoided eye contact.

"I knows how to keep a secret," Ashley suddenly said, stepping from behind Brigid. "You ain't got nothing to worry about with me."

"Well I guess I don't have much choice, do I?" Martin said looking from one of them to the other. "So what do you two want?"

"What else? For you to fill us in on what you've discovered!" Brigid almost bounced as she said this. "And Ashley was hoping he could..."–Brigid lowered her voice–"see the Cross." She tossed her blond hair over one shoulder. "So is it St. Brendan's or the Vikings'?"

Martin ran a hand through shaggy hair. What choice did he have? "Well, it seems pretty certain based on what I've found that it's Irish and not Viking."

"So it belonged to St. Brendan and his monks!" Brigid was trying to stay so quiet that her squeal came out more like a munchkin voice.

"Not so fast, Dorothy," Martin said with a smirk. Even Ashley was grinning. Brigid glanced at the tall red-head and flushed. Martin continued, "I said it *seems* to be Irish—at least based on some of these books, but it all depends on how old the Cross actually is. If it was only made ten years ago, it won't really matter too much if it is Irish, now will it?"

"Well how are you supposed to figure that out?" Brigid said while Ashley stared intently at him.

"I have some clues from these books for one thing. But more importantly," Martin said turning somewhat in his chair to avoid their inquisitive eyes, "I've enlisted the help of a professional."

Voyage to the Rock

"A professional?" Brigid said, scrunching up her face. "What kind of professional?"

"An antique dealer."

"I hopes you don't mean that old Sullivan O'Connell," Ashley said shaking his head.

"Yeah, I do," Martin said, spinning back to look at Ashley. "Why?"

"He ain't no good. As my pops says: 'smells worse than a four-day dead flounder,'" Ashley said. "People round here don't trust him much. The *Old Wolf*, they calls him—at least us young fellars do."

"The *Old Wolf*?" Martin asked, remembering those prowling green eyes.

"Yes B'y. If you ever saw him, you'd know why," Ashley said. "He got a buddy of mine in real trouble, saying me buddy stole something from his antique store, which Danny swears he never did. He was up to him dropping off a package is all."

"Well as a matter of fact," Martin said, sitting up straighter, "I have met him. He seemed polite enough to me," Martin knew he was just trying to justify his actions to Ashley—*and to himself*. "He was quite helpful, and says he'll be able to tell me in a few days exactly how old the Cross is and where it was made."

"You showed him the Cross!" Brigid said putting both hands on her head. It was clear from her expression that she hadn't liked a word of what she was hearing about Sullivan O'Connell.

"Well... sort of..." Now it was Martin's turn to squirm. "Actually, I gave it to him—but only until Monday or Tuesday."

"You did what?" Brigid said, eyes wide and mouth dropping open. "And you gave *me* a hard time about telling *Ashley*!"

"What was I supposed to do?" Martin was angry because he felt foolish. "What other choice did we have? You want to know if the Cross belonged to St. Brendan, don't you? Besides, he seemed like a nice Irish gentleman to me, not some thief."

Ashley let out a whistle. "Well, I hopes you're right about the Old Wolf and not me buddy, or else you may have more troubles getting it back than you think."

"Anyway, do you want to see what the Cross looks like or not, Ashley?" Martin wanted to be talking about anything else right then. *I'm such an idiot! Ashley has to be wrong about 'the Old Wolf'.*

"I thought you said the Cross was gone?" Ashley cocked his head.

"It is. But this isn't," Martin said and pulled the sketch from under the book. "Here you go...but be careful with it."

After a few moments of Ashley looking at the drawing, he said, "This is real fine drawing—as pretty as a perfect cast, B'y. This Cross must be some impressive! I hopes to see the real one soon."

"What else did you find out, Mart?" Brigid asked.

Martin was more than happy to be changing the subject so he proceeded to tell them about the library and the books on High Crosses, *The Book of Kells*, and Tim Severin's journey across the Atlantic. They were both impressed by the pictures in the *Kells* book and the similarities of Martin's drawing of the Cross. Martin also showed them the picture of "Christ Enthroned" which they agreed was almost the exact face and clothes. Martin actually enjoyed being able to share all the excitement and anxiousness that he'd been carrying around for the last few days.

"What's this book?" Brigid asked as she reached for the third library book on Martin's desk, *St. Brendan the Abbot: An Incredible Journey to Newfoundland Shores*. As she reached past Martin to his annoyance, instead of grabbing the book, she accidentally knocked it off the desk. She gave a squeak and the book thumped open onto the floor in a flurry pages.

"Brigid!" Martin said raising his voice.

"I'm sorry! I was just curious." They both moved quickly to scoop the book off the floor. Brigid got to it first and tried to

Voyage to the Rock

smooth out a few creased pages. "See, it's fine," she said, showing him that the book wasn't damaged.

"Would you just give it to me?" Martin said, thrusting out his hand.

"Jeepers! I'm just making sure there aren't any bent pages." She leaned to hand over the book. But then something caught her eye, and she pulled the book back just as Martin was about to take it.

"Brigid!"

"What is that?" she asked, and opened the book to the page that had caught her attention. She turned it for Martin to see; even Ashley leaned forward trying to look. It was a page near the end of the book—a photograph or photocopy—of an old manuscript. What was so striking about it was that it was completely covered in Celtic knots. In the middle of the page was a large blank space in the shape of a Cross, and inside the blank space something was written in a language they couldn't read.

"Do you see that?" Brigid said pointing, her eyes wide. "Those knots are almost identical to the ones you sketched from the Cross!"

Martin stared hard as he unconsciously reached out to take the book; he didn't want to get ahead of himself. He looked more closely for a few seconds. The curves and the thickness, the style of knots, everything... *was the same.* They were identical. Hours of staring at the Cross trying to copy it had imprinted those Celtic knots on his mind.

"Martin? Well, what do you think?" Brigid said, starting to doubt herself a little.

"Identical."

"I knew it!" she said throwing up her arms, her long blond pony-tail again clutched in one hand. "And look at the shape—where the words are written—it's exactly the same as the Cross. Look!" She took the sketch of the Cross and placed it on the opposite page from the manuscript. "A perfect fit!"

"That's as much a match as I've ever seen, B'ys," Ashley said peering between their shoulders. "But what *is* this here thing?"

Martin read from the subscript: "sixth century manuscript found in a wall in the altar area at Clonfert Cathedral." He then moved the drawing of the Cross off the facing page and began to skim it. "It says here that Clonfert is the name of the place where St. Brendan had founded a monastery and where he is buried. The monastery was completely destroyed in the sixteenth century, and the only thing that remains now is Clonfert Cathedral and the church graveyard."

"So this is the proof that the Cross belonged to St. Brendan and his Irish monks, right?" Brigid said, clasping her hands together.

"Not exactly. It says here that the connection of the manuscript to St. Brendan is doubted, and that most scholars think it was just the work of a pious monk of the monastery a generation or two later, despite the fact that the manuscript appears to be quite old."

"Well, why do they think that?" Brigid said, putting hands on hips.

"It says here that it's because this is the only known copy of the manuscript, and that it doesn't accompany any of the other known manuscripts of the *Voyage of St. Brendan*, nor does it exist in any other known copy or language than this Latin one."

"Latin, eh? I was wondering what that there language was," Ashley said.

Martin went on. "But the author of this book claims that it's genuine. He says there is no reason to doubt the age of the manuscript. Also, he points out that it was obviously something important and treasured—otherwise the monks would not have gone to so much trouble in order to make sure it was preserved amid the various raids over the centuries and the eventual destruction of the monastery."

"So it must be real," Brigid said. "Just look at it, Martin. Isn't it obvious?" Despite her excitement there was hesitation in her question.

Voyage to the Rock

Pulling the book closer, Martin examined the manuscript page more closely. The shape and size were undoubtedly the same as his sketch, and the inter-twining knots seemed to be the exact style as on the Cross...but how could he be certain he wasn't just seeing what he wanted to see?

Finally he sighed and brushed his hair out of his face. "I don't know. Maybe... it could be... but who can say for sure?"

Brigid's own enthusiasm began to melt away along with Martin's, and two sets of shoulders visibly sank.

"Well, ain't you two a sight!" Ashley said. The siblings turned to look at the red-haired boy standing back between them. "You've found an amazing Cross; you've found an ancient manuscript to match it; and now, with a little uncertainty, you've lost all faith in what you're holding in your own two hands." He even tapped the book and the sketch for emphasis. "I may not be too smart about history, but I sure knows what that there Cross is a symbol of—and it ain't of *quitting*. Besides, as my pops always says: 'a dead fish can always float downstream, but it takes a live one to swim up it!'"

Brigid's cheeks grew red and even Martin had the good sense to feel a bit embarrassed. "You're right, Ashley," Brigid said laying a hand on his arm. "Look at us giving up before we've even begun." She gave her blond tail a tug for emphasis.

Martin looked at the book opened to the manuscript page in the one hand, and the sketch of the Cross in his other. Ashley was right. Why was he getting down about his search already? Where *was* his faith?

It was then that something seemed to leap off both the manuscript page *and* his sketch: nine Celtic knots that ended abruptly; nine inter-twining lines that stopped without continuing the unbroken winding of the knots! He remembered the nine "mistakes" as they had seemed when he was tracing the Cross—two on the top and two on the bottom, and two on each arm, with the last one leading from the stone at Christ's side. But now he saw these same nine "mistakes" on the manuscript page in the exact places where they would meet those on the Cross!

"The answer *is* in our hands!" he suddenly said, holding the book and sketch up. "I just didn't see it. Look!" Martin said as he pointed to the nine points on the Cross sketch and then on the manuscript page.

"Then it is a match, B'ys!" Ashley said as Brigid simultaneously gave a delighted squeal and a spin.

"Ssshh!" Martin quickly put a finger to his lips, frowning at Brigid.

"Sorry," she said in a whisper. "But what do we do now?"

What would they do now? Martin wasn't certain himself. He was stunned. It really was St. Brendan's Cross! He had really found it.

"Well," he said slowly as he looked down at the manuscript page, "I guess we should find out what this writing says. There must be a translation here."

They had all but forgotten about the Latin writing in those few moments of excitement, and it was with new enthusiasm that Brigid and Ashley leaned over Martin's shoulders as he laid the book open on the desk and began searching the page for a translation. It only took a moment before Martin started to read:

There's more to verse than simply words/
The words reveal a shining gift.
A fruitful land unnamed by Birds/
A Three but One to where boats drift.

A company of God—three lost/
Were first of Christ's own sons to land.
But another comes to find the Cross/
When unchanged faith arrives again.

Voyage to the Rock

A fiery portal shows the way/
To those before the Cross, they hail.
Not resting on or near the bay/
Between high water, rock, and whale.

To see the Cross as saving key/
To guide one to the heavenly room.
Recall: the first, the last shall be/
And know the same when Crosses bloom.

To God's new children from afar/
Ol' Brendan awaits his gifts to give.
With the blessing of the *Stella Maris*/
Faith to revive and to forgive.

"Well now, what do you suppose that means?" Ashley said scratching his head.

Martin's mind was racing. What was this poem? And what connection did it have to his Cross? He didn't know for certain, but he was sure of something: "This is about *The Voyage of St. Brendan*. At least the first part definitely is!"

"You're right, Mart," Brigid nodded.

Martin continued: "The 'unnamed' land—that's Newfoundland. That's what it means by 'a three but one to where boats drift'. I had already worked that out from my reading of the *Voyage*."

" This line, too, 'A company of God—three lost.' That must be St. Brendan's party, right?" Brigid asked. "And the 'three lost' are the three monks who he prophesied wouldn't return." She put a hand to her mouth, eyes wide.

"Just what I was thinking, Brigid," Martin said, and he actually couldn't help giving her a light punch on the arm. She smiled, but he just continued: "And the line, 'Were first of Christ's own sons to land' is about the monks landing here in Newfoundland!"

"This proves it, Martin!" Brigid said grabbing Martin by both shoulders and shaking him. "This proves it all!" A goofy grin spread across Martin's face; what had they discovered?

"Voyage of what?" Ashley said from behind Brigid. "And what's all this talk about *monks?*"

"It's from a book our dad owns, Ashley," Brigid said turning to explain. "It's about St. Brendan's voyage across the Atlantic ocean and the adventures and things he saw before arriving in Newfoundland. Or at least some people think it may have been Newfoundland."

"And this proves it all," Martin said, as if to himself. "But what does the rest of the poem mean?" He turned to lay the book and sketch onto the desk directly under the lamp.

Brigid didn't hear this last part and was already going on about how they would be famous and be on the news and maybe even get to do television interviews. "We'll tell Mom and Dad, and then they can call the museum at L'Anse aux Meadows and the reporters. We'll go down in history for proving that St. Brendan and his monks really were the first Europeans to arrive in North America! I'm going to get Mom and Dad, and they can..."

"No!" Martin said spinning and grabbing Brigid's sleeve. "We're not telling anyone yet!"

"Well, what do you mean we're not telling anyone?" Brigid said, yanking her arm free. "We're just going to hide that we have the only proof that sixth century Irish monks landed in Newfoundland? Are you *crazy?*" She said already gripping her pony-tail in two hands; again Martin had the distinct impression that his sister was wishing it was his neck right then.

"Sit down for a minute, Brigid," Martin said gesturing to his bed. "Both of you." He rolled his own chair over and sat on it backwards. "Listen, we can't very well turn this over to the museum and news yet; we'll never learn what this all means.

Voyage to the Rock

What about the manuscript and the poem? Don't you even want to find out why this manuscript was so important that monks tried to keep it safe for hundreds of years when even their monastery was destroyed? Don't you think it's strange to have the Cross here in Newfoundland and the matching manuscript in Ireland?" He grasped the back of his chair and leaned further and further forward with each question. "I don't know about you two, but I'm not ready to let someone steal this mystery from us. I found the Cross and I plan to finish this."

Having dropped her pony-tail, Brigid didn't look anymore as though she was ready to strangle him, but she still looked skeptical with her arms now crossed.

"Yes, we've found some answers: we know the Cross is Irish, and we know it belonged to St. Brendan and his monks. But now there are new questions to be answered, and I plan on answering them. Or at least trying. It's just like Ashley said: we're holding this in our hands." Martin instinctively reached out his own hands. "Are we ready to just give it away? I for one am not."

Brigid looked thoughtful; Ashley was impossible to read. Martin hoped his expression was *pleading* enough.

"Okay," she said after a few moments hesitation. "But only until we can't find any more answers. Then we tell people."

Martin knew that was the best he was going to get out of her and that if he pushed it things could turn out a lot worse. "Okay, then. What about you, Ashley?" Martin turned to face him. "Are you in? Are you going to let what we're *holding in our hands* slip away?"

"I'm in, I'm in. I'm as curious as you to figure out this poem, or mystery—whatever it is." Ashley put his hands on his knees and leaned forward. "Besides, the only thing lost in catching trout is a fly, and I likes a good challenge!"

Martin's brows wrinkled slightly at this strange Newfie kid, but he said, "Alright, then, we're agreed. No one takes this from us until we've hit a dead end."

"Now, there's just one problem left," Ashley said sitting back again.

"What's that?" Martin asked frowning.

"We ain't got no Cross in our hands just now."

Martin swallowed hard at the same time as he heard Brigid groan the name: *"The Old Wolf!"*

Chapter 12:
Poetic Puzzles

Reaching a hand to his mouth, Martin tried to stifle a yawn. He straightened his back while balancing himself momentarily on the balls of his feet to let his legs relax a bit.

The morning sun was shining brightly through the patio doors into the dining room. Thin tendrils of smoke appeared and disappeared in the light before continuing to spiral their way upwards. The sun momentarily caught the form of Fr. Gregory whose vestments glittered a brilliant gold as he bowed; the tinkle of bells and new puffs of smoke filled the air as he continued his censing. He made his way methodically around the small table which was set up as the "holy table" this morning; the dining room table had been moved to the kitchen.

Martin could hardly believe how quickly his living room and adjoining dining room had been transformed into a little chapel. They had set up two long pieces of wrought-iron lattice that went from floor to ceiling, with a large icon of Christ hung on the right side and one of the Mother of God on the left. These separated the "church"–their living room, from the "altar area"– their dining room. There were icons set up around the living room and on the shelves and walls so that it felt more like a real church.

This was to be their Sunday routine until the church was ready to start holding services. Martin was used to long services—his dad was the priest after all—but having to get up thirty minutes early to set-up on top of it all was pushing it.

There were only a few people standing in the living room, but to be honest, Martin was surprised there was anyone at all.

He had more or less expected his family to be the only ones there this morning. But surprisingly there were about ten people.

Martin quickly moved to take the censer from his father who had rounded the "holy table" and put more incense on the coal before handing it back. He had to catch himself from wiping fingers on his own golden robes. If he got dirt on his server vestments, his mom would kill him.

For the hundredth time that morning, Martin had to struggle not to let his thoughts stray too much to the Cross. Every time they did they progressed from excitement to inquisitiveness to anxiety and then to what always left him with a shiver: to the *Old Wolf*. It wasn't all bad, though, since this usually led him to *beg* for help—*to whoever would listen*. To Christ, to St. Brendan, to the Mother of God, to every Irish saint he could ever recall! But inevitably, if he wasn't careful, this led *back* to thinking about the Cross. It was no easy morning.

He had even missed taking the candle out at one point. It wasn't until his father had peered back around the metal lattice with an arched eyebrow that Martin had even realized he'd forgotten.

His mother's soft chanting caught his attention as she began, "*Today is salvation come unto the world...*", which signaled that Divine Liturgy was about to begin. He took the censor from his father and hung it back on the brass stand. As his mother finished the hymn there was a momentary silence as his father stood before the altar table. Making the sign of the cross on himself he touched his forehead, stomach, right shoulder, then left, and made a bow touching the floor.

Martin crossed himself and leaned forward in a bow as his father intoned the words to begin the Liturgy: "*Blessed is the Kingdom of the Father, and of the Son, and of the Holy Spirit, now and ever and unto the ages of ages.*" An hour and a half later, Martin was pulling his robe over his head and laying it over the back of the chair in the corner of the dining room.

Voyage to the Rock

The living room was now filled with the conversation of those who had come. He saw his father introducing himself to an old couple who seemed to be Russian and a woman holding the hand of a small boy: "...Well it's wonderful to meet you all! And if you ever need anything you know where to find me..." his father was saying.

His mom was engaged in conversation with a middle-aged couple, all of whom were laughing about something. He overheard her say, "Oh, Fr. Gregory and I know all about that..." and then more laughter. Towards the back, there was another younger couple who were holding a baby girl while talking to a young man who had stood in the doorway during most of the service. Brigid, he noticed, had cornered an older lady and her son and was telling them both about why she thought the cooler summer of Corner Brook was even better than the hot summers in Boston; the woman wore a delighted smile.

Martin took the opportunity to slip out through the kitchen. He even escaped for a while. But Brigid found and dragged him back downstairs on his mom's orders so that he could meet and have lunch with everyone. Needless to say, it made for a long morning. Still, by the end of the lunch, when everyone had left and the living room and dining room had been set up again as normal, Martin had had plenty of time to ponder just what the poem might mean. He had narrowed it down to two conclusions: either it was just a poem immortalizing St. Brendan's amazing journey, or... it was something else. But what that something else might be, Martin had no idea.

And so it was with great eagerness that they all sat down together to try to puzzle out just what the poem might mean—Ashley had just *happened* to stop by again. The three of them sat with chairs pulled up around Martin's desk, the book open in front of them. Martin started by reading the poem aloud again as the others listened.

When he finished he asked, "Have you guys had any ideas since last night?"

"Not me," Ashley said shaking his head.

"No. Did you?" Brigid asked.

"Not exactly. But I'm sure I'll come up with something," Martin said while shrugging nonchalantly.

Brigid rolled her eyes.

"So what do you make of this treasure it's talking about?" Ashley asked.

"Treasure?" Martin and Brigid said at the same time, and then frowned at one another when they realized it.

"Yeah," Ashley said. "The *'shining gift'* that the *'words conceal'*. What do you think it is?"

Martin looked down at the page. He hadn't even noticed that line before now. Was this a clue to the meaning of the poem?

"That's it," Brigid said, drumming her hands on the desk as they all sat around it. "The poem must be a riddle to find some hidden treasure! Do you see the first line: *'There's more to verse than simply words,/ The words reveal a shining gift'*. 'Verse' definitely means the poem, and the *'shining gift'* is a treasure!"

Could Brigid be right? Martin wasn't sure. Could this be some sort of 'map' to a treasure? "Wait a minute," Martin said. "Look at the next line: *'A fruitful land unnamed by Birds'*. That's all it means—the *'fruitful land'* not some treasure. This is from the *Voyage*, remember Brigid? It's the Birds from the Paradise of Birds, and it must refer to Newfoundland—though why anyone would consider this place a *treasure* is beyond me." Martin's old mood was creeping back.

Brigid looked as though she wanted to argue with Martin about it, but she clearly had no answer for him.

"I ain't sure that's all it means," Ashley said. "Look at this stuff down here about *'the Cross as saving key,/ To guide one to the heavenly room.'*" He tapped the line on the page. "What else does someone need a 'key' to a ' heavenly room' for, if it ain't to find 'treasure' hidden away?"

"I think that that might be the 'heavenly mansions' that Jesus speaks about in the New Testament," Brigid said. "And the Cross is a key because after Jesus died and was resurrected,

Voyage to the Rock

heaven was opened for people to enter." She spoke hesitatingly as if trying not to embarrass Ashley.

"Oh," Ashley said, "Well that makes sense then."

Brigid quickly put her hand on his arm. "But maybe it means both! I mean, it's not like the riddle is going to be easy to solve if it does lead to a treasure." There was a moment of silence as all three of them scanned the poem.

"Hey," Brigid said. "Look down here at the end: '*Ol' Brendan awaits his gifts to give.*' More talk about treasure."

Brigid peeked over to look at Martin, but Martin didn't respond. He was thinking about something else that struck him as strange. Furrowing his brow he said, "Shouldn't this say '*But another comes to* bring *the Cross?*'"

"What do you mean, Martin?"

"It should read 'bring,' not 'find,'" Martin said shaking his head. "The 'another' would have to 'bring' the Cross—the Cross I found." Martin suddenly turned pale.

"What is it, Martin?" Brigid asked. She was looking intently at him.

"Brigid, how could the author of the poem know that 'another' would come and '*find*' the Cross? I mean, I found it at the bottom of some river bed in the middle of nowhere."

"Well, maybe it wasn't always there. Maybe it was left for someone to come and get," Brigid said. "Maybe *he* lost it afterwards... or never arrived to get it."

"Could someone really have left such a small cross out in the open and expect that some other group of monks, or whoever, was going to sail back across the Atlantic Ocean and be able to find it?" Martin said glancing at both Brigid and Ashley in turn. "Well?" He asked eyebrows upraised.

"Well, what are you saying, Martin? That you were *meant* to find it? That St. Brendan somehow knew and left it for us?" Brigid said giving Martin a skeptical look.

"I know it sounds crazy, Brigid, but you heard in St. Brendan's *Voyage*, how he knew things about the future. It's no different than any other Orthodox saint. Besides," Martin said, staring down at the Cross sketch and manuscript—his voice growing quiet, "when I read this line I get a strange feeling inside. Something just says *yes*."

Silence. The others didn't say anything.

"Well, anyway," Martin said as he pushed his chair out from the desk and got up, walking to his bookcase and straightening his trophies on one shelf. There was something about his words that obviously made them all a little awkward.

"*'But another comes to find the Cross, When unchanged faith arrives again,'*" Ashley said, breaking the silence. "Didn't you guys mention something about your Church being *unchanged*?"

Martin turned to look at Ashley, and then at Brigid. He walked back over and actually read the line out loud again. Could the line *actually* mean them? If not, Martin had no idea what it could mean. Both *finding* the Cross and it being when 'unchanged faith arrived again,' that seemed a strange coincidence—if it was only a coincidence. Besides, there was his *feeling*.

"Yeah, that's what I said the first day we met," Martin said slowly. "Though I've got to say, I didn't mean it in any nice way when I said it to you, Ashley. I was a bit... *upset* that day," Martin said as he rubbed the back of his neck while giving Ashley a sidelong glance.

Ashley just shrugged.

"Could it really be a *prophecy* written by St. Brendan for *us*?" Brigid asked, her blue eyes wide.

"I don't know, Brigid. But whatever it is, it seems 'Ol' Brendan' may have some sort of gifts to give to '*God's new children from afar*,' if they really are us," Martin said, plopping back down. "The only thing now is getting the Cross back and solving this mystery."

* * *

Martin opened the *Voyage of St. Brendan* to the point where he had left off. It had been a long day, but he was still excited—

Voyage to the Rock

and perplexed—about what they had discovered. He was eager to spend some more time reading before bed.

Please help me solve this mystery, St. Brendan, and please let me get the Cross back soon! This last was the other reason why he wanted to read: to help ease his nerves about Mr. O'Connell and everything that Ashley had said about him. He needed a little encouragement.

Pulling his blankets up to his chest, he took the book and began to read.

* * *

And so from there they sailed again on to more fearsome islands and more dreadful trials. The first such place was a rugged and rocky island without trees or vegetation. Here they saw hot fires burning and instruments of blacksmith forges. And St. Brendan turned to all the Fathers: "I am very uneasy about this place and feel a great anxiety. I do not wish for us to land there, but the wind seems certain to drive us on."

When they had come within a stone's throw of the island's rocky shores, they heard a wild noise of bellows blowing and the clanging sound of hammers ringing. With the sign of the cross the saint guarded himself and begged the Lord to deliver them. And from one hut came a hideous man, all hairy and grimy from fire and smoke, who saw the monks and began his shouting, crying aloud for the others.

"Put on more sail, and get to the oars, that we may escape this dreadful place!" And everyone alike signed himself with the cross and sprang to their work. But the savage men appeared at the shore with their tongs in hand and pieces of flaming metal, and threw them at the servants of Christ. But by the sign of the cross the monks were saved and not a single missile hit their boat. And the island became a blur of fire as the filthy inhabitants stood with their red-hot tongs, but St. Brendan encouraged his brothers and gave them a warning: "Soldiers of Christ, be strong in faith and courageous in the armor of the Spirit. For we are now nearing the boundaries of Hell; so watch and pray, and act with courage."

* * *

Martin shivered as he put the book down. This was not the *comfort* he had been hoping for. In fact, it had had the exact opposite effect on him. *Lord, please help me get the Cross back! Please don't tell me I was wrong to bring it to the Old Wolf. St. Brendan help!*

That was as much as he could stand to read that night. Putting the book on his bedside table, he turned off the lamp. But as he drifted to sleep the last line he had read floated through his head as though St. Brendan himself were whispering it into Martin's ear: *"...we are now nearing the boundaries of Hell... watch and pray, and act with courage."*

Chapter 13: An Insult

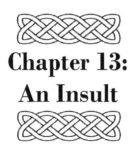

It was mid-afternoon Monday when Martin pulled his bike up to *Sullivan O'Connell's Fine Heritage Antiques*. The sun shining on the front of the building gave a completely different feel to the place than the one Martin had had while standing there under dark storm clouds. He almost sighed from relief.

Setting his bike along the building near a side-driveway, he adjusted his backpack and headed for the front door. He knew the Cross might not be ready yet, but his anxiety from the previous night had been too much for him. Mr. O'Connell did *say Monday or Tuesday*.

Gathering his courage and saying a silent prayer, he went in. The bell above the door announced his entrance, and though he saw Mr. O'Connell standing behind a narrow counter at the far end of the room, the man did not look up. He was bent over with some kind of eye-piece, examining something. Martin quietly made his way through the maze of antiques to approach.

When he reached the counter, Martin saw that Mr. O'Connell—again in his fine suit—was inspecting some kind of old pocket watch. He did not look up at Martin. Martin stood, his heart pounding in his chest, and just studied patiently the little lantern-like design on one of O'Connell's cuff-links while he waited.

After a few minutes of standing there, Martin gently cleared his throat in an attempt to get the tall man's attention. To this Mr. O'Connell furrowed his brows while still examining the watch. He did speak, though: "Can I help you with something?"

"Uh...Yes, sir," Martin said. "I was wondering if my Cross was ready?" Mr. O'Connell still did not look up. "You said it would be ready on Monday or Tuesday, so I thought I'd stop by to see..."

"I'm afraid I have no idea what you're talking about," the silver-haired man said, interrupting Martin.

Martin reached out a hand to stable himself as his knees suddenly went weak. "My Cross, the one I brought in Saturday afternoon—the Irish one," Martin said.

"A cross, you say? Hhhmm," the antique dealer said while looking up and tapping the side of his face, "no I don't think so."

"What do you mean you don't think so? I brought it to you on Saturday evening! A bronze cross!" Martin had to control himself so as not to yell from his sudden panic.

The antique dealer looked directly at him for the first time, his eye-piece still in his eye. It gave a chilling, futuristic look to his face. "Do not raise your voice to me, boy." His words were not loud, but were icy cold. "I told you that I don't have any cross of yours."

Now that he was looking at him, Martin couldn't help but begin to plead with the man. "But don't you remember me? We talked over there in that other room. I was wearing this same jacket," he said gesturing at himself.

"I've never seen you before in my life," the man said in a flat voice. Then he began to bow his head back to his work.

"Wait!" Martin was frantic now. What was going on? How could this man not remember him? Not remember the Cross?

The antique dealer looked up again and his one green eye that was visible stared at Martin. Martin shrank under the man's predatory gaze. But then his face softened somewhat, and there was a hint—just a hint—of a smile. "Well, can you show me your receipt then?"

Martin's jaw dropped.

Voyage to the Rock

And before Martin could gather himself, the man spoke: "I thought not." Then with a dismissive wave of a long, thin arm he said, "Now get out of my store."

"But you told me I didn't need to take one! That you would remember me!" Martin *was* shouting now.

Then he felt a strong hand grab the back of his neck and start twisting him around toward the door. "You don't mind that Mr. Duffy helps see you out, do you?" he heard O'Connell's amused voice behind him. "Oh yes... You can always go and tell your *parents*. I'm sure they'll notice your cross is missing."

He *did* remember, Martin realized with sudden horror!

The last thing Martin heard as he was thrust out of the store onto the sidewalk was mocking laughter. The *Old Wolf* had lived up to his name.

*   *   *

By the next morning—even before letting Brigid and Ashley in on the terrible news—Martin had come up with a plan. Truth be told, embarrassment was half the reason for why he'd spent the night puzzling out what to do. He'd even had to lie to Brigid when she asked him if he had gone to get the Cross; there was no way he was going to let her spoil anything by running and telling their parents.

So when he was packing up his tools and putting them into one corner of the church's basement, he knew just what he was going to say to Brigid and Ashley. They were set to meet at the picnic table at the little store down the road. Martin smiled inwardly thinking about his plan as he and his father headed over for lunch.

Despite Brigid's questioning looks over dinner, Martin wasn't willing to even glance in her direction. It was better if she was completely in the dark until he sprung his plan.

"I'll meet you at the picnic table in thirty minutes," he told her as he jumped on his bike and made as though he were biking into town to get the Cross. Instead, he drove a few circles around the streets just above theirs before pedaling off for the store.

When he arrived the two of them were sitting at the table waiting. He had to do this just right if his plan was going to work. Otherwise... no Cross, no adventure, no mystery solved—no nothing. Not to mention, if they did go to the police, it might not be just the *Old Wolf* who would be getting arrested for stealing.

Making his best attempt to look as he'd *felt* yesterday, he hopped off his bike and headed for them. He dropped himself heavily onto the bench, his elbows thumping on the table and his hands together. He let his head hang—just a touch.

"Martin! What happened?" Brigid said, sitting on the bench across from him. "Is everything okay? Did you get it?"

Martin hesitated a moment for effect.

"Martin? What ..." Brigid was cut-off by the sudden crack of Martin's open palm as it hit the table. Both Brigid and Ashley jumped.

"He took it," Martin said in a low, intense voice.

"He kept it?" Brigid said, nearly yanking her blond braid out of her head, just as Ashley muttered, "I knew it, I did!"

Martin looked straight ahead: "He stole it." Martin then went on to tell the whole story of the previous day.

"Ohhh Martin! What an evil man!" Brigid almost wailed. "How could he do this to us?"

Martin slowly looked over at them both, trying to look firm but not harsh. "*Us?*" Martin said. He had to play this just right. "What do you mean, 'How could he do this to *us?*'" Before she had time to answer, he went on: "How could he do this to *St. Brendan?*" His voice was full of indignation. "It's not *our* Cross the *Old Wolf* stole, it's St. Brendan's! It wasn't *our* plan for us to find the Cross. It was St. Brendan's!" He paused slightly to let the effect of these words sink in. "And it wasn't *us* who chose to solve the mystery of the poem. It was the *Saint*."

Brigid's eyes showed the wheels of her mind turning, but Martin pushed on.

Voyage to the Rock

"An insult," he said as though to himself, just quiet enough for them not to fully hear.

"What's that now, B'y?" Ashley said.

"An insult!" Martin said more loudly. "This is an insult to St. Brendan himself!" He felt himself walking a fine line now. He *did* think the theft was an insult to the Saint—he was just playing it up a little.

It worked, though. He could see by the fiery look in Brigid's eyes that it had. The effect of having just learned of the theft, combined with Martin's impassioned and "selfless" words in defense of the Saint had inflamed her heart.

"And we're going to go straight to the police and get the Cross back!" Brigid said raising herself up.

"No!" Martin said extending a hand toward her. *Control yourself, Mart.* "No, Brigid," he said with less urgency; Brigid looked at him in confusion. "That's exactly the wrong thing to do. It would just be *his* word against *ours*. He's an antique dealer," Martin said while staring intently at them both. Then he gestured toward them and himself, "And us? We're just a bunch of teenagers who claim to have found a 1,500 year old Cross in the *mud* at L'Anse aux Meadows. Who do you think they're going to believe?"

"But what about your sketch? That proves it!" Brigid looked as though she was about to start pacing back and forth. Ashley just sat there shaking his head and tracing a finger over some scratches in the picnic table.

Martin gave an ironic half-smile. "Oh yeah, the sketch from the guy who has just taken out a bunch of books on Celtic crosses and Celtic knots. There are lots of witnesses. But if the police never find any Cross—because the *Old Wolf* has hidden it—how are we going to prove that we're not just some bored kids telling lies about a respected antique dealer?"

"'Respected'? Ha!" Martin heard Ashley mutter under his breath. But it was clear that both Ashley and Brigid saw the logic of what he was saying. It *was* all true, after all, though worse for him if the police did get involved. Then they'd start asking him questions like: "Where'd you get this?" and those were questions Martin did not want to have to answer. So he prepared the next part of his plan.

"Well, what do we do then? Nothing? Just let that *Old Wolf* get away with this?" Brigid said throwing up her hands as she plunked back down on the bench.

Perfect. He couldn't have planned it better. "I have a plan," Martin said. "You remember the book with the manuscript page in it? Well, it was written by a man who lives here in Newfoundland. I found this out when I was at the library, and not only that, but he lives close." The looks Martin got were those of two fourth graders in university calculus—they had no clue what he was getting at. "We're going to find him and get his help."

"How can he help?" Brigid asked, brow furrowed.

"By telling us everything he knows about the Cross," Martin said. He turned to look at a group of kids who were shouting and laughing as they walked to a table further away. Martin lowered his voice and leaned in. "Maybe he'll be able to give us some clue that the police will be able to use to confirm our story *beyond any doubt*. Maybe he can give us some clue as to what the poem and this mystery is. If we solved it, I'm sure we'd find the proof we need to lead the police to the *Old Wolf*." Martin knew this wasn't going to get the Cross back exactly, but if he could at least learn something he could use—maybe even about Sullivan O'Connell—then he had to try. He certainly wasn't going to let the *Old Wolf* get away with stealing his Cross!

"Well, what do you say guys?" Martin asked looking from one to the other.

"I don't know, Martin," Brigid said shaking her head. "Getting someone else involved in all this—someone we don't even know? I'm just not sure."

"It's our duty, Brigid," Martin said in a firm tone. "We accepted this when we took the Cross. St. Brendan would want this." Martin *thought* he would.

"Well... okay," Brigid said.

Voyage to the Rock

"Ashley?"

"As my pops always says: you'll never catch if you don't cast. Count me in," Ashley tapped his chest with a thumb.

"Good," Martin said. "So there's only one thing I need from you two..."

"What's that?" Brigid said, eyes narrowing.

"I need an excuse for getting off work to go to Lark Harbour."

"Lark Harbour? What do you needs to go there for, B'y?" Ashley said.

"That's where Brendan Arthur lives—the author. I've looked it up on the map; it's not so far." In fact, it would take them all day just to bike there and back, but it was the only answer Martin could see if he was going to speak with Brendan Arthur.

"What, you plans on flying there?" Ashley said

"Close," Martin said, his voice unimpressed. "We're going to bike there."

Ashley raised his eyebrows: "That'll take us *all* day."

"Mom and Dad will never let us go, Martin," Brigid said shaking her braid at him.

"Mom and Dad," Martin said, clenching and unclenching two balled fists under the table, "will never know." He was getting tired of playing this game. "Listen up for once. Ashley, you're going to call our house tonight and ask for Brigid. Brigid," he said turning to her, "you are going to talk with Ashley and then go and ask Mom if you and I would be allowed to go on a biking trip with Ashley and his parents. You got that?" He pushed his hair out of his face. "That'll get us off work and give us the excuse we need to be gone for the day."

Martin had worked this all out while lying in his bed last night. "And she won't say *no*, Brigid," Martin said anticipating her objection. "She'll just be glad that I'm *making new friends*." Martin had to keep from curling his lip in distaste. NEW friends!

Brigid closed her mouth; it was obvious she had been about to make that very objection.

"So are you guys going to help get St. Brendan's Cross back, or not?" He knew their answer before they gave it. So despite a small protest by Brigid about being the only one who needed to "outright lie", they were onboard.

Martin couldn't help feeling a bit bad about the need to "guide" them to the right decision, but what other choice did he have? It was done now regardless. His plan had worked.

Chapter 14:
Lark Harbour

Martin stopped at the top of one of the slowly winding hills that the highway followed. To his left lay the Bay of Islands and a long stretch of river that led all the way back to Corner Brook. It was a beautiful day and the sun set the water sparkling like diamonds. There was a cool breeze in the air and the faint smell of sea salt. Newfoundland really was a beautiful place. It just wasn't Boston.

They had been biking now for about three hours and Ashley and Brigid were starting to slow down—to be honest, so was he. According to his map, though, just down this hill was *Blow Me Down* National Park with Lark Harbour on the other side.

"Are we almost there?" Brigid said, her chest heaving.

"Just down this hill and past the National Park," Martin said pointing.

"That there's Tortoise Mountain," Ashley said, waving toward the mountain that made up most of the park.

"Great," Brigid said, wiping her forehead with an arm. "I don't think I could have gone much farther."

Martin let his bike begin to coast down the hill. The wind whistled in his ears and whipped his hair, and he imagined he was on St. Brendan's voyage with wind, water, and sea-salt air. He began to pedal as he was coming around a bend in the road and in no time he was coasting past *Blow Me Down* National Park on his right. He didn't slow, but sped past the park's entrance. He needed to find a store or shop where someone might know where Dr. Arthur actually lived.

Martin glanced over his shoulder and saw that Ashley and Brigid were not far behind. He kept pedaling as the trees along the road opened up again. To his right now were the crisp blue waters of Lark Harbour, while to his left the road continued to wind among sloping hills of low pine trees and sections of grassy meadow.

Just ahead the road curved toward an area with some restaurants and shops. If he was to find anyone who knew Brendan Arthur, it would be there. Turning his bike off the main road, he drove toward the first sign he saw: *The Lark's Song Café and Restaurant.*

Parking his bike and leaving his helmet, Martin started for the front door.

"Wait, Martin!" Brigid called as she and Ashley pulled up. "Would you wait a second?"

"What, Brigid?" Martin said, halting on the first step and turning back. "I need to ask if anyone here knows where Brendan Arthur lives."

"Yeah, well Ashley and I are tired and want to take a break! We've been biking for over three hours now." Brigid's bright red face was proof of what she said. "And you hardly even let us rest along the way." She and Ashley both dismounted and were unfastening helmets.

Martin tried not to raise his voice. "Look Brigid, we don't have much time and I for one don't want to have to make this trip again. So we need to find this guy quickly."

"Alright, Martin. But we're *going* to take a break soon," Brigid said as she trudged toward him.

"Soon," Martin said as he hopped up the front stairs and entered the café.

The place wasn't very large. Inside were tables and a spectacular view of the harbor from a large picture window. There weren't many people inside; just a few older men were sitting at a table near the large window.

Martin walked up to the counter and heard Ashley and Brigid enter the café behind him. Sitting on a stool at a counter

Voyage to the Rock

was a lady reading a magazine. When Martin approached her, she laid it down and asked: "Can I help you?"

"Actually, I have a question I was wondering if you could answer," Martin asked, somewhat shyly.

"I'll do me best, Luv," the woman said, getting up from her stool.

"Well, I'm looking for a Dr. Brendan Arthur," Martin said, glancing over at the men as he did. "Do you know him?"

"Ol' Brendan, Go on B'y, yes," the woman said as she pushed her thick-framed glasses up on her nose. "I knows him; we all knows him around here."

"Really? Could you tell me where I might find him?" Martin said, some of his shyness melting away.

"Well, I knows generally where he is, but I'm not after seeing him for a few days at least," she said. Martin didn't quite catch her meaning, but she turned to ask the men by the window: "Hey B'ys, you knows where this kind young fellar can find Ol' Brendan?"

"Yes, me Son," the older man with the pipe said. "It's 11:30. He's up the hill, he is. Up there every day at this time, B'y."

"The hill?" Martin asked the lady.

"The hill you're after passing to get here. Back at the Park."

"She means 'Tortoise Mountain,' Martin," Ashley said over Martin's shoulder.

"That's it, B'ys," she said nodding. "Now I knows this here fellar is from the Rock,"—she gestured at Ashley—"but where are you from?" she said to Martin.

"I'm from Boston. Well... was..." Martin stumbled over his words.

"These two live in Corner Brook now, just likes I do," Ashley said, taking over. "Their pops is from there and their dad grew up there."

"What's your dad's name, Luv?" she said.

"Gregory Shea."

"Gregory, eh? Don't know any *Gregory* Shea," she said looking them over. "And how's she goin', me Ducky?" she said to Brigid.

Brigid looked confused, but said: "Well, thanks. I'm Brigid, Martin's sister. And this is Ashley."

"And I'm Katie," she said with a toothy smile, "and I'm glad I'm after meeting you all."

Martin and Brigid shared a confused glance but Ashley said, "We are, too," and all three of them thanked her.

"Well, Martin, as much as I'd like to join you on your long trek up the 'hill,'" Brigid said wrapping an arm around her brother's shoulders, "I think Ashley and I can wait here and have our 'break' while you find Dr. Arthur. It would *save time* after all." Brigid was wearing her most innocent face.

"Alright, alright," Martin said, shrugging his sister off. "I'll leave you two here to eat, but you meet me in an hour and a half at the park. Sound good?"

"Perfect!" Brigid said as she clasped her hands together and raised herself up and down on her tiptoes. "Katie, a table for the two, please," Brigid said.

"An hour and a half, guys," Martin said as he headed out.

With that Martin was pedaling back around the harbor, heading for the park. In moments he was driving past the large *Blow Me Down* National Park sign and only slowed long enough to ask the guard about Dr. Arthur before riding through the gates. Martin followed the road to the right until he came to an area where he could lock up his bike before heading to the long staircase that apparently wound its way to the top of the "hill". The guard had said he would be sure to find "Ol' Brendan" up there.

As Martin stood near a rocky overhang, he looked up at the *Governor's Stairs* that led to the mountain's top. The whole thing was impressive—but steep. Martin sighed as he began to make his way up. After only a few sets of stairs he was already huffing. He only paused for a brief glance behind him at the massive bay.

Voyage to the Rock

The higher he climbed, the more the wind blew Martin's hair in small gusts. He knew he must be nearing the top, but the trail seemed to climb straight-up and all he could see above were pine trees and rock.

Then the treetops overhead broke and he saw the clear blue sky above. With a last laboring effort he forced his legs, hands pushing on thighs as he climbed the steps to the summit. He stood there panting as he looked around him. The top was a rocky bald descending back into dark green pine trees atop the summit. There was a bench, and further away a wooden lookout platform that gave a spectacular view in all directions revealing the bay on both sides which sparkled in the noon-day sun. The wind blew more fiercely at the top, and now that he had stopped climbing he felt the chill of sweat down his back.

Zipping up his jacket, he looked for Brendan Arthur. The top was actually a little crowded with a few groups of people. For a moment Martin thought that he would have to start asking individual hikers if they were Brendan Arthur, but the groups filtered off the lookout and the rocky bald and headed off down another trail. One man remained leaning on the platform and staring out toward Lark Harbour. Could it be Brendan Arthur?

Martin made his way to the platform and climbed the handful of steps. The man didn't turn to look. He was wearing a dark green wind-breaker and a tweed hat with a brim on the front—like a fisherman or something. He stood with the end of a pipe in his mouth and there were small plumes of smoke whisked away in the wind as soon as they appeared. With his full red and gray beard, he looked like a mix between a fisherman and a monk.

Martin approached the man who had turned to face him. "Excuse me, sir?" Martin said while holding his wildly blowing hair out of his face with one hand. The man took the pipe from his mouth and eyed Martin up and down.

"Yes, me Son?"

"Are you Brendan Arthur, by chance?" Martin had to raise his voice to be heard over the wind.

"I sure am," the man said. "And who might you be? We haven't met before, have we?"

"No, sir," Martin said stepping closer. "My name is Martin Shea and I live in... Corner Brook. I was wondering: Are you the Dr. Arthur who wrote a book about St. Brendan and Newfoundland?"

The man's brow wrinkled slightly as he looked not at Martin, but the water beyond. "I sure am," Brendan Arthur said, turning his eyes back to Martin. "And how would you be knowing that?"

"I found out from the library in Corner Brook. I borrowed your book," Martin said.

"Ah... research for a school project?" Dr. Arthur said, nodding. Then he paused and narrowed his eyes. "But now why would you have come all the way up here to find me? And from Corner Brook, you say? What, did you drive here?"

There was a keen intelligence behind Dr. Arthur's gray eyes. "Actually, I took my bike," Martin said looking away.

"All the way here? So what is this all about?" Dr. Arthur asked. He had the intent look of a scientist about to dissect a frog.

Martin began to squirm somewhat. He had to be careful not to give too much away; it wouldn't be as easy as he had thought. "Well, I was wondering if you could tell me more about the manuscript page in your book, about the poem, I mean?"

Dr. Arthur took a long puff of his pipe and turned to lean back on the railing of the lookout facing the harbor. He let the smoke fly from his mouth into the wind before answering. "Now why would you be wanting to know about that thing," he almost seemed to spit the *that thing*, as though it tasted bad in his mouth.

"Please, Dr. Arthur," Martin said. "Anything you could tell me about it would be very helpful. What does the poem mean?" Brendan Arthur's reluctance to speak was obvious.

"Ah, who knows, B'y," he said looking at the pile of ash he was tipping from his pipe over the side of the lookout.

Voyage to the Rock

"Well, I know it's a riddle of some sort. And that it may or may not lead to some kind of *gift*, or treasure maybe?" So much for being careful! He was jumping in with both feet now.

"Now what makes you think that, me Son?" the old man said slowly as he looked up at Martin again.

"Well, there seems to be two parts to the poem: one that speaks about St. Brendan and his original voyage here, and a second part that seems to speak about another trip here... and a cross." Martin let his hair blow free for a moment and zipped his jacket to his chin. He hoped he wasn't being as obvious as he *felt*.

Dr. Arthur stared at Martin, and for a moment there seemed to be some sort of battle going on within him. But then he sighed—a long sigh. "Aye, Martin, some say there may be a puzzle to it. Not many, mind you; most think it's just religious poetry—but some think it's more."

"And what about you, Dr. Arthur? Do you think it's something more?" He looked closely at the old man's sad gray eyes.

"I suppose I used to," Dr. Arthur said, scratching at his thick beard. "But that was a long time ago now." He looked away and began to stuff his pipe again. There was something in his manner that set warning bells ringing in Martin's head. What if this man wouldn't tell him anything? He couldn't just let that happen!

"Look sir, I think it might be a clue left by St. Brendan himself—I know that may seem crazy," he held up his hands to keep Dr. Arthur from cutting him off, "but I'm sure he's speaking about *someone else* finding a cross which would help solve the mystery."

"So you really have paid attention to that poem, eh?" A light seemed to suddenly have flickered to life behind Brendan Arthur's eyes. "You're also familiar with the *Voyage of St. Brendan*, I see. I'm impressed, me Son." He had paused midway to lighting his pipe. It was as if some wall came down. "There should be a cross, I'd say, if anyone could ever have found it, and as the poem says this cross is the key."

"But 'key' to *what?*" Martin said, leaning on the lookout railing to speak more directly to Dr. Arthur.

"Well, my best guess is some sort of hidden encampment site, maybe even a chapel, B'y—with the whole 'heavenly room' bit," Dr. Arthur said while readjusting his hat.

"So Ashley was right," Martin said, nodding appreciatively and giving his knuckle a quick tap on the railing.

"Ashley?"

"Oh, no one—just a friend." Martin said quickly. "Please go on."

"Not much more to go on about, B'y. Without the Cross—who can say if there really is a hidden room?"

"And if someone had the Cross, what would it help?"

"Not sure. But without the cross, it's just guessing at the poem. Trust me, I know," Dr. Arthur said.

"What do you mean by that?" Martin said.

"Ah, what can I say?" Dr. Arthur took another long haul on his pipe. "You know how I said that only a few thinks the poem means anything? Well, I was one of them... and me wife. We studied everything we could on St. Brendan—even wrote that book from everything we collected. But in the end, we spent endless expeditions searching, and nothing." He looked distant—the face of a man searching for a photo within a box of old memories. "We knew it must be in Eastern Newfoundland somewhere from the line: 'A *fiery portal shows the way, / To those before the Cross, they hail.*' But we could never figure out what the 'fiery portal' was."

"What do you mean: you knew it must be in Eastern Newfoundland? What does 'To those before the Cross, they hail' mean?" Martin asked. He knew he must look like a wide-eyed kid right then, but he didn't care.

"Well, how else does one *salute* the Cross accept by making its sign—I mean to 'hail' it by making the sign of the Cross?" Brendan said, pointing with the end of his pipe as he spoke.

Voyage to the Rock

"And in this case, to do it standing 'before the Cross'—the Cross placed on the manuscript. Didn't you notice how detailed the 'blank space' was where the poem is written. I'd bet my last dollar that there was some cross that fit that pattern," Dr. Arthur said, shaking his head. "Touch head, stomach, left, then right—assuming we're talking co-ordinates on a map—and one ends up on the eastern coast of Newfoundland. At least that's what we guessed it must mean, me Son. We never did find anything, though. Likely we were wrong."

He was gaining *so many* clues from Dr. Arthur. Not answers maybe, but at least *something* to go on. "So you searched the whole eastern coastline?" Martin said. "And you didn't find anything?"

"No one said anything about the eastern *coastline*," Dr. Arthur said, again pointing at Martin with the pipe.

"Well, what do you mean?"

"Maybe you haven't looked at the poem as closely as I thought," Dr. Arthur said, though with a half-smile. "Don't you remember the line that says: 'Not resting on or near the bay?'"

"Right," Martin said feeling a bit stupid.

"But yes, we did look everywhere else inland and on the lakes beyond," Dr. Arthur said. "But like I said, without the cross we didn't have much to go on." Dr. Arthur became thoughtful again, and his light mood darkened somewhat.

"And here I go, getting all caught up in this mess again!" He gave a few furious puffs. "And now encouraging a young fellar into it, too." He turned to Martin: "You listen to me, me Son. You forget about Brendan's poem! It won't bring nothing but trouble, and without enough clues to find anything anyhow—real or imagined."

"Why not, Dr. Arthur? You've given me lots to think on!" Martin said.

"You see! You old fool Brendan, you see." He spoke out at the harbor. He turned back: "Remember, Martin, how I told you most people think this here poem is nothing? Well, not everyone does. There's someone here in Newfoundland that sure believed it, and didn't want anyone else out looking for it."

"What do you mean?" Martin said, his skin prickling at something in the old man's tone.

"I mean: things started getting dangerous when we were searching—supplies and food going missing, sabotaged boats, rock slides. Someone didn't want us searching," he said, his voice quiet. "Someone else was interested, too."

"So you just stopped? But how could you?" Martin said, wrestling with his own mixed feelings about everything that had happened since the day that he'd found the Cross at L'Anse aux Meadows. "How did you get yourself to, I mean?"

"It was easier than you think, me Son, easier than you think." Dr. Arthur's face became as hard as a Newfoundland cliff. He just stared far off at the bay.

"And your wife, she just quit, too?"

"You never-mind worrying about my wife!" Dr. Arthur turned so quickly, Martin involuntarily took a half-step back. "We stopped and you'd better stop, too!" Dr. Arthur said, punctuating his words with the end of his pipe. "Fool Brendan, opening your mouth to a kid," he muttered to himself.

"Dr. Arthur, was Sullivan O'Connell the one interested?" Martin *needed* to know.

The old man turned to face him with a wild light in his eyes. Martin inwardly shrank back from such fire. "What do you know about him?" Brendan's voice was quivering with intensity. "Never you mind. You just listen to me: Stay far away from that *creature!*" He actually turned and spat. "He's more wolf than man, he is. And a wolf often has its maw full of blood."

Martin shivered as chills ran down his back. He understood. He had felt Sullivan O'Connell's cold eyes on him: a wolf staring at a rabbit.

"Now enough of this foolishness. It's time to be heading down this hill, B'y. You coming?" Dr. Arthur said as he rose and headed back the way Martin had come.

Voyage to the Rock

Martin followed him, and the two made their way down the mountain stairs—much easier compared with coming up. They didn't say too much for a while and then Dr. Arthur spoke: "You says you're from Corner Brook, but you don't speak like someone from the Rock. So how do you come to be living in Newfoundland?"

"Actually, it's my dad who's from Corner Brook. He grew up there," Martin said. "My parents decided we needed to move here from Boston. My dad's an Orthodox priest and has this dream about being a missionary in his home province, so we're here starting a new church." All of Martin's frustrations that he had forgotten over the course of the last few days came washing back.

"Is that such a bad thing to want?" the old man asked. "You don't sound too happy about it."

"It's not such a *bad* thing except when you move your family and your teenage son from his life, his friends, and his high school to come live in the middle of nowhere." Martin realized he was clenching his fists and forced them to relax.

"That's the funny thing about life, eh, it sweeps you along whether you want it to or not. And as much as you might not want things to change, they always do—whatever we say." The old man had a sad look. "But it can be okay sometimes—and sometimes even great things come of it," Dr. Arthur said as he clapped Martin on the shoulder. "Take a lesson from St. Brendan and his crew—seven years of round and round before they could arrive where they were aiming to get. Maybe there's hope for us yet, me Son."

And then they were at the bottom and making their farewells.

"Thanks a lot, Dr. Arthur," Martin said as he unlocked his bike and helmet.

"You're welcome, Martin. It was nice to have some young lungs trying to keep up with me! So you say your dad's a priest, eh? Well, I haven't been to church in a long time. Maybe I'll stop by some time," and anticipating the worried look on

Martin's face, he said, "But don't worry; I won't mention your little trip out here to meet me." He gave Martin a knowing wink. "Just you be remembering what I told you," he said wagging a finger at Martin, "Forget Brendan's voyage. And stay clear of that *Sullivan O'Connell!*"

"Sure, Dr. Arthur," Martin said, and with that he got on his bike and headed back to meet the others.

Chapter 15:
Getting Complicated

"Can you hand me those drywall screws?" Fr. Gregory asked Martin, as he held a screw-gun in one hand and used the other to stabilize the sheet of drywall that was about to become a basement wall.

Martin reached into his tool belt and pulled out a handful of them. "Here, Dad," he said as he leaned to hold the wall. In a few short minutes the two of them had the wall fastened in place.

The church was really coming along. To see the place take shape right before Martin's eyes—it was pretty cool actually. But it all paled compared to his *real* work.

Solving his mystery was the important thing. He had gone over and over in his head his meeting with Brendan Arthur. He had a few new hints to chew on, but he kept coming up with dead ends. Brigid and Ashley hadn't been much help either, though they were excited by what he told them. He certainly hadn't told them everything that was for sure, otherwise Brigid would have run to his mom and dad no matter what Martin said. No, he had not mentioned anything about the *accidents* that had started to happen nor about what Dr. Arthur had said about Sullivan O'Connell. *Best not to get them worked up over nothing.*

It had been difficult evading Brigid's questions about everything he and Dr. Arthur had talked about. He had filled them in on as much as he dared. In the end he was able to convince her that he had done his best to learn what he could.

He had, after all, but more with the purpose of solving the mystery rather than simply finding a way to bring the *Old Wolf* to justice and returning the Cross to L'Anse aux Meadows.

What he *needed*—and he knew it well—was to get the Cross back to really make sense of it all. But if that was going to happen he needed to keep working on a plan. The reality was Martin was pretty sure what he had to do, he just didn't know how he was going to accomplish it yet.

The loud rumbling of his stomach interrupted Martin's thoughts and reminded him of the time. It was almost lunch. That brought his mind back to what his more immediate plans were: head back to the library to see if he could learn any more about the searches of Dr. Arthur and his wife. Martin was sure there must be some newspaper article or two that interviewed him. If he could narrow down a location, there was a better chance of both discovering where the true site might be and also of figuring out how he was going to get to Eastern Newfoundland to find it. This second problem was the biggest, but not so immediate, and so he left it for the time being.

"Quitting time, Martin," Fr. Gregory said. "You can head to the library as long as your mother doesn't need you for anything." It hadn't taken much to convince his dad to let him go again; he was actually pleased that Martin seemed to be warming up to Corner Brook. He had even gone on about how happy he was that Martin had taken the day off for the biking trip.

That had turned awkward for a bit as Martin had to tell a few small lies to avoid giving away the whole trip. He hoped Brigid had done as well in not letting anything slip. He knew she wouldn't be pleased with him for the next few days because of all the lying she'd had to do, but she'd get over it.

Martin unloaded his tools by the back wall. *It's not like there was any other way; I certainly didn't hear any ideas from them on what else to do.*

It turned out that it would be only Martin and his father for lunch. When they arrived at the house there were sandwiches

Voyage to the Rock

laid out and a note saying that his mom and Brigid had gone into town to pick up supplies for their icon-painting. Martin was glad since it meant that he was free to take off as soon as he was finished.

As he and his father ate things were oddly silent. Martin had the sinking feeling that his dad wanted to talk to him. Had Brigid said something? Martin could feel his heart beating faster and took a gulp of water to help his dry throat.

Fr. Gregory opened his mouth to speak and then stopped. Martin couldn't take it any longer—if he was caught he was caught. "What, Dad?" he asked more forcefully than he meant, putting down his sandwich.

"You know, Martin, there are more appropriate ways to speak to people," Fr. Gregory said, a hint of irritation in his voice. He went on: "But yes, I did want to ask you about how things are going? With the move and all."

Martin had to keep from sighing in relief and from rolling his eyes at the same time. So his dad didn't know anything. That was great news. But why did he need to drag Martin back to *reality*? "What do you expect me to say, Dad? That I'm happy we moved?" Martin slumped back in his chair. "No, I'm not."

"Of course not, Martin," Fr. Gregory said, leaning elbows on the table and running his hands through his beard. "We just haven't had much of a chance to talk, and I wanted to check in."

The mood Martin had almost completely forgotten over the past few weeks descended like a dark cloud over him. "That's a nice change," Martin said under his breath as he crossed his arms on his chest. "Look, Dad, I'm just trying to make the best of things right now,"—he wouldn't look at his father. "No I don't understand how you and Mom could make us leave our whole life behind to come here, and no I don't care about starting some *mission*. I just..." Martin paused. "Look, just forget about it. Can I please go to the library now?"

His father had a sad look on his face but nodded and said, "Of course, Martin. Have a good time." Fr. Gregory took his dishes to the sink and began to wash them.

Martin got up and left.

As he biked toward the library, Martin felt sick. He hated talking or thinking about Boston right now! And his dad, what was up with him? Martin just wished he'd start acting normal again. He squeezed his handle-bar grips as he pedaled up the hill.

Get your head together, Martin. He gritted his teeth. *You've got work to do.*

It wasn't long before he was heading up the stairs to the 3rd floor of the library. When Martin entered, he looked around for Mr. Evans. He guessed that if anyone could help, it was him. Martin didn't see him so he began to peek through the stacks. Sure enough, bent over with a stack of books beside him on a cart was the thin old man.

Martin went up to Mr. Evans who turned to look at him as he approached. "Ah, it's you again, is it? Looking for more books on Vikings and St. Brendan?"

"Well, not exactly," Martin said. "Do you remember that book you gave me by Brendan Arthur—on St. Brendan's voyage to Newfoundland? I was wondering if you had any newspaper articles on any of the excursions Dr. Arthur made while looking for a landing site. Did he ever do an interview about it?"

"Yes, B'y," Mr. Evans sighed and stood, "Brendan's 'excursions'. Now that you mention it, I recalls him having done an interview or two about it all. He'd never let on where he was searching, but he'd announced he believed he and Susan were close to finding proof of St. Brendan's journey." Mr. Evans paused to breathe on his lenses which he then started cleaning with a little cloth he produced from his pocket. "I don't know how serious anyone took him, but it captured people's interest for a while."

"Do you think the library might have a copy of these articles?" Martin asked with a smile.

"Certainly we do. It's on microfiche," Mr. Evans said as he put his glasses back on.

"Microfiche?" Martin said, his forehead wrinkling.

Voyage to the Rock

"Microfiche on a Microfiche Reader. It's nothing to worry about, me Son. You'll see. Follow me." He led Martin down to the second floor along the far wall that had tables with a large machine on each one. It looked like some old arcade machine; it had a large screen which sat back from the sides and top and was square-shaped. Mr. Evans flipped a switch and a buzzing sound began as the machine "warmed-up".

"Wait here," he said. "I'll be right back."

Martin sat in a chair in front of the machine and waited until Mr. Evans came bustling up with a handful of small cards. When Mr. Evans laid them on the table in front of him, Martin saw that they each looked like a rectangular card of photograph negatives—like the ones that used to come from film cameras.

Mr. Evans opened a tray on the front of the machine and put one of the cards in. "This is a microfiche, and as you can see..." he closed the tray again and began to turn some of the knobs, "these are photographs of old newspapers." The old librarian kept turning the knobs and on the big screen Martin could see rows of tiny newspaper pages. Mr. Evans kept turning and the machine zoomed in on one in particular which then filled the whole screen. It was a newspaper dated June 17, 1998.

"So basically you use this knob here to focus," Mr. Evans said as he turned the knob bringing the page in and out of focus, "and this lever allows you to switch from one slide on the card to another, so that you can find the newspaper page you're looking for. These other cards are other newspapers around the same time. What you're looking for should be in one of these slides, I'd say. If you need any more help, you can ask me or the other librarian down here."

"Thanks, Mr. Evans," Martin said as the old man left. *What a memory!* Mr. Evans had even remembered which year and approximate month that Dr. Arthur was in the paper.

Now Martin sat back to start the slow process of flipping through slides to see if he could find any articles on Brendan Arthur. *The Western Star* was the title of the paper he was looking through. Apparently, it was the newspaper for Corner Brook and Western Newfoundland. Page after page on the first card turned up nothing. So copying what Mr. Evans had done, he popped out the first card and replaced it with another.

He followed the same process again and again over the course of about an hour, until he finally found what he was looking for. It was a good thing, too, because he only had a few cards left. "Memorial University Professors of History Brendan and Susan Arthur Go in Search of the Ancient Irish in Newfoundland", the title read. The article was a full page spread and there was a large picture of a younger, more trimmed Dr. Arthur and his wife, a dark-haired Dr. Susan Arthur.

But as Martin read on his initial excitement at finally finding an article fizzled away. The article was just a general description of the history of St. Brendan and his voyage, the repeat journey by Tim Severin to Newfoundland, and some other facts that weren't going to help Martin find any campsite. He ran a hand through shaggy hair. *Oh well, back to puzzling it out on my own.*

Just to be certain, though, Martin decided to look through the last few microfiche cards to see if there were any other articles; he was already at the library after all. So he flipped through the cards—nothing.

Just as he was about to pop out one of the last slides, something caught Martin's attention: "Rockslide near Middle Arm Leaves Woman Missing". Something in the title pulled at his memory. The blood froze in his veins as he read, "Memorial University professor, Susan Arthur, missing after a rockslide capsized her small boat. Rescue and diving teams have been out all evening seeking for any trace of her..." Martin's stomach twisted. *It can't be...*

Martin read on to discover that Dr. Arthur and his wife had been on one of their expeditions to find St. Brendan's site. Dr. Arthur, who had been on land examining a rock face a little distance away, was barely able to avoid the slide by diving into the water. "To this point there has been no trace of Susan Arthur, though search teams will continue throughout the night."

Voyage to the Rock

"*Mysterious things started happening: sabotage, and* rockslides," Martin could hear Brendan Arthur's words in his mind as though they were being shouted.

Martin quickly loaded the next microfiche to see if there was more. On the front page it read: "Memorial Professor Found." Martin sat stunned for a moment, eyes staring blankly at the article before him.

Susan Arthur had *died*. They had found her body further down the bay early the next morning. It appeared that she had died instantly from the rockslide. "Tragedy!" it read.

"God have mercy." Martin said a silent prayer for her before quickly flipping to the next day's newspaper. Again, on the front page was another article: "Man Claims Foul Play in the Death of Wife." There was a picture of a grief-stricken Dr. Arthur, eyes sunken and face pale. In the article he claimed that just before the rockslide he had seen a man above them on the cliff. The article went on to say that while the police were looking into every possibility, there were no apparent signs of foul play.

Martin's jaw dropped. "They didn't believe him," he said aloud.

"They certainly didn't."

Martin jumped!

"Sorry, B'y!" It was Mr. Evans. "Didn't mean to startle you. Just thought I'd have a look to see how you was making out."

"His wife died!" Martin was shaking—literally, *shaking*.

Mr. Evans didn't seem to notice. "So you've found that bit of information, have you? I thought you might. A sad thing that was. I remembers it well," Mr. Evans said taking off his glasses and rubbing his eyes. "Ol' Brendan was never really the same after he lost Susan. We was friends, if you can believe it. But I haven't seen or heard from him in some years now." Mr. Evans looked even older—if that was possible.

"So did they catch whoever caused the rockslide?" Martin asked trying to control his creeping terror.

"Whoever caused the rockslide? No, me Son," Mr. Evans said, shaking his head. "In the end they said it was just in

Brendan's head—well they didn't say that exactly, but implied it—on account of the shock that Brendan had suffered from the event." Mr. Evans let out a deep sigh.

"Well, did you think it was just in his head?" Martin asked with wide eyes.

Mr. Evans looked as though he were remembering something. There was a pause before he said. "You know, I never did know what to think in the end. I mean, at first I was inclined to believe him, but Brendan reacted so strange to the tragedy that I started to wonder if it wasn't just his grief playing tricks on him." Mr. Evans crossed his arms on his chest. "Truth be told, I don't know what I thinks about it all. Haven't thought of it in a long while—not since your visit here last week anyhow."

"Did Dr. Arthur ever say who he thought it was? Did he even have a guess?" Martin asked, one hand gripping tightly the side of the table.

"He had a guess alright," Mr. Evans said with an ironic smile. "Almost landed him in court, it did. Certainly didn't help him to keep his job, I'd say. Said it was linked to that antique dealer... what's his name?" Mr. Evans said, tapping the side of his face.

"Sullivan O'Connell?" Martin said in a whisper.

"Yes, that's it," Mr. Evans said pointing to Martin. "Sullivan O'Connell. Said O'Connell had been asking some hard questions about the search for St. Brendan's site; said he had gotten quite 'irate' when Brendan and Susan weren't willing to share what they knew with him. Unfortunately, there was never any proof of the so-called meeting between them, and Mr. O'Connell had a clear alibi as he was back home in Ireland at the time of Susan's death."

"So why did Dr. Arthur almost end up in court?" Martin asked.

"Well, poor Ol' Brendan couldn't let it go. He was sure that O'Connell and the mysterious man at the rockslide must be connected. He started telling people that other 'mishaps' had been happening to him and Susan on their expeditions. Said it

Voyage to the Rock

was all tied to St. Brendan. If it had of stopped there," Mr. Evans laid a hand on the top of the microfiche machine as he spoke, "all would have been fine. But he started following O'Connell, even threatened him in the street one time. That's what almost landed him in court with a restraining order placed on him. It was a good thing—and a bit strange, too, I'll say," Mr. Evans said, putting a finger to his lips, "but O'Connell seemed to have such a peculiar aversion for dealing with the police that the charges never went anywhere. Otherwise, Brendan would have gotten himself in a heap of trouble. In the end, he was so grief-stricken and obsessed—and what with all the talk about St. Brendan and his voyage—everyone started to think Brendan had had a nervous breakdown."

Martin couldn't believe what he was hearing. Sullivan O'Connell was *definitely* bad news, but would he really have *killed* someone over all this? But Dr. Arthur had seemed a very normal and kind man—not some crazy making up wild stories. And O'Connell's *aversion* for the police? Didn't it prove he had something to hide? Unfortunately, neither alternative was particularly appealing to Martin: either a killer with his Cross, or a madman with the only clues.

"In the end, Brendan left his teaching position and retreated to his family home in Lark Harbour. Haven't heard much of him since." Mr. Evans just shook his head. "It's not that I didn't believe him exactly, but there just wasn't no proof. I always felt bad for Brendan, poor fellar. He was a good man... and Susan was a good woman."

"Well thanks, Mr. Evans," Martin said, brushing hair out of his face. "I should be heading home, though."

Mr. Evans stood up straight. "Yes, me Son, sure... Anything I can do to help again, you let me know. And I'll take care of these here cards. You run along."

Thanking Mr. Evans, Martin headed for the elevator.

Was the *Old Wolf* really a killer? Could Dr. Arthur have been mistaken? Martin didn't know what to think as he rode home. He could only think to do one thing at this point: he prayed to St. Brendan. *This is your Cross, your mystery, and your mission. What should I think about all this, St. Brendan?*

He pedaled up the hill toward home. Martin stopped his bike and got off. It was then that he experienced something that he couldn't have doubted even if he'd wanted to. Like a bell ringing inside his chest, he had one thought over and over again: *Trust Brendan.* Martin hesitated, but he was entirely convinced of what he felt.

Knowing what that meant about O'Connell, Martin understood something that made the hair on the back of his neck stand-up: things had just gotten a lot more *complicated.*

Chapter 16:
The Plan

It was difficult for Martin not to tell anyone what he'd learned about Dr. Arthur and his wife, Susan. All evening he had been trying to avoid Brigid's questioning looks and had done just about everything he could not to be alone with her—even volunteering for *dish-duty*. He needed to think, to plan. What was he going to do? He silently worked beside his mother, trying to run over in his head all the possible options.

"Penny for your thoughts, Mart?" his mother asked him as she handed him another dish.

"Oh... it's nothing," Martin said, a little caught off guard.

"Nothing?" Elizabeth said. "You've been pretty quiet this evening. And you even *volunteered* to do the dishes. Are you feeling alright?" She playfully put a hand to his forehead.

"Yeah, I'm fine," he said with a half-hearted smile in return.

"Well... how are you adjusting to things? A little better?" she asked as she washed another dish and peeked sideways at him.

"A little," Martin said, meeting her eyes before leaning back against the counter and continuing with his dry towel.

"I'm glad to hear it," his mother said. "Have you and your father talked about things yet?"

"No," Martin said, cocking his head at his mom. *What did she mean by that?* "Well, yes. But there's not much to talk about." Martin turned and put a dish in the cupboard.

"Oh, okay," Elizabeth said. "I was just wondering. Why don't you run upstairs, Mart? I can finish the rest."

"Okay," Martin said as he put the dry towel back on the oven handle.

Before he had left the kitchen, though, his mother said, "By the way, has your father mentioned you and Brigid visiting St. John's for a week or two?"

Martin turned back. "No. Why would we go there?"

"Well, your dad has a cousin there who's been after him to let you guys visit. I probably shouldn't have mentioned anything yet," Elizabeth said. "It's only if you would prefer seeing St. John's to working around here." She continued to wipe down the counters. "It's up to you—but I think you'd like St. John's. It's a much bigger city than Corner Brook, and beautiful too."

"Uh, I don't know, Mom," Martin said turning to leave. "I'll think about it."

"It would give you free time to keep reading your library books. What have you been reading about, anyway?" Elizabeth said.

"Just some stuff about the Vikings and the Irish, and voyages to Newfoundland," Martin tried to appear nonchalant.

"That's interesting," his mother said, pausing and looking up. "Do you have any leads? Was it the Vikings or St. Brendan who made it here first?"

"I'm not really sure," Martin lied. "But I'll keep working at it until I find my answers."

"Great," his mother said, while drying off her hands. "Have you finished the *Voyage of St. Brendan* yet? Were there any more clues in it?"

"I haven't finished it yet, but I did find some of the things Dad mentioned—about the three islands being one." Something pulled at Martin's memory as he said that, but he couldn't remember what.

"Well, St. John's would be a great opportunity to finish reading it—and to puzzle over the mystery. Maybe you'll find an answer," Elizabeth said with a playful smile, trying to entice him.

Then an idea hit Martin. He knew what his next move was going to be!

"Did Dad mention when we'd go?" Martin asked, interested now.

Voyage to the Rock

"Well, whenever you guys would like. The end of this week or next would probably work best for my and Brigid's work, but I don't know what would work for you and your father. Are you saying you want to go?"

"Definitely," Martin said more enthusiastically than he meant to. He hoped it would just give the impression that he was beginning to enjoy Newfoundland. Little did she know, what he liked about Newfoundland had nothing to do with him *adjusting* to some new life; he had a mission he was on. "I'd love to have some time to finish up my books and work on my mystery." Only he understood what that really meant.

"Well, alright then. I'll speak with your father about it tonight."

"Great! Thanks Mom," Martin said, and then headed upstairs.

Standing in front of Brigid's door, he knocked. He heard a scramble and the door quickly flung open. "Well it's about time!" Brigid whispered, tugging her braid for emphasis.

Martin entered the room, closing the door behind him. He sat on the chair by the window and Brigid sat on her bed. She was obviously anxious to hear what Martin had to say. But Martin wasn't worrying anymore; he had a new plan—and she would be a part of it again.

"So what did you find out? Anything?" Brigid demanded. "I don't know why you'd make me wait. Even doing the dishes... I mean, come on!"

"I'm sorry," Martin said, stretching out in the chair. "I just wanted to work out a few bugs before we spoke."

"What do you mean by that, Martin?" Brigid's eyes narrowed as she watched him.

"What?" Martin said wide-eyed and with a half-smile. "I've figured out our next step,"

"And...?" Brigid said, crossing her arms on her chest.

"And..." Martin said sitting up. "We're taking the Cross back."

"How are we going to do that?" she said, shaking her head. "We're going to suddenly *call the police?* After everything you said about them not believing us?"

"*We're* going to take it back," Martin said, gesturing at them.

"You have truly lost it, Martin!" Brigid shot up from the bed and began to pace back and forth in front of him. "We're not going to call the police, we're not going to tell Mom and Dad, but *we're* going to get it back?" She turned to stare at Martin, brows in a knot. "And how do you expect we're going to do that? Just walk up and ask him for it?" she batted her eyelashes as she said this last bit.

"*No*, we're *taking* it back!" Martin said.

"*Stealing* it, you mean!" Brigid's blue eyes turned fiery.

Martin shot up from his chair. "It's not stealing, Brigid, and you know it!" Their noses were just inches from each other, and the sparks from their eyes could have *smelted metal*. "It's ours and *he* stole it! If we can't go to the police, then we need to do something about it ourselves."

"Tell that to the police when they catch you," Brigid said, not backing down an inch, though her brother was half a head taller than her. "'It's not stealing, Officer,'" she said, making her voice foolish, "'I'm just *taking back* my valuable, historical antique that Mr. O'Connell *stole!*' I *will* visit you in prison, though, Martin. I promise." Brigid shook her head and moved to sit back on the bed. "Besides, if the police weren't going to find the Cross by searching his store how are you going to?"

"I'm not some idiot, Brigid," Martin said clenching his fists. "I've already thought this through. The problem with the police is that the *Old Wolf* will be *expecting* police. He'll have a plan for what to say and where to hide the Cross. Even *if* they believed us—which they are pretty much guaranteed not to—they will go and speak with O'Connell before any search. There will be no element of surprise; no catching him unprepared. It will be everything Sullivan O'Connell is already *expecting*. Very easy to avoid."

Brigid looked unconvinced. Martin pushed on.

Voyage to the Rock

"*Surprise* is the key, Brigid! By this point, I'm sure he knows the police haven't been called, and *won't* be called. Likely he thinks *I* stole it in the first place, and so can't go to the police about it." *Isn't that true?* The thought floated into Martin's head. "He's probably feeling quite comfortable with himself right now—very safe. We'll be the last people he expects," he said slamming his fist down onto his palm.

"Even if you're right, you already said it would be impossible to find it. He could have hidden it *anywhere*. If the police aren't going to find it, how are you?" Brigid said, her braid twisting and untwisting around her hand—a very good sign. That meant she was considering his words.

"Remember, Brigid, he's not expecting anyone to come after it; he's not expecting anyone *suddenly*, even if someone did come. He just got his hands on it," Martin paused here to let his words sink in. "He's studying it, Brigid. What else would he be doing but trying to puzzle out the same mystery as us?" Martin leaned forward in the chair, and willed with all his might to be convincing. "It's at his shop; I'm sure of it—maybe not out front in the open—but at his shop. That's where we'll find it."

Brigid's silence was proof enough that Martin's words were having an effect. She clearly saw the logic of what he was saying, Martin was sure of it. But was she willing to go along with the plan?

"No," she said finally, shaking her head. "It's too dangerous, Martin. Even if you're right—and I'm only saying *even if*—there's no way for you to get in and out unseen. What would you do? Break in at night? I'm sure the place has an alarm."

Good, he thought, she was engaging with his plan. All he had to do was to work out the bugs in her own mind, and then she'd agree.

"I told you that *surprise* is the key, and so we'll do what the *Old Wolf* expects the least," Martin said, a huge grin splitting his face as he leaned back in his chair, hands behind his head and feet crossed. "We'll walk in in the middle of the day and take the Cross from under his nose. But that, of course, is where you and Ashley come in."

"Alright, get out!" Brigid said getting off the bed and heading for the door. "You *are* crazy. I don't care anymore," she said as she reached for the knob. "Just go."

Martin slowly lifted himself. "Hey, that's fine with me then," he said as he brushed his shaggy hair back from his face and tucked his hands in his pockets.

As she swung open the door, he shrugged without looking at her. The hallway stood empty. Martin was about to step out when he leaned in and whispered, "I'm surprised you don't even want to hear the plan." He kept his eyes forward as he said this.

Brigid tensed all over and was obviously a few seconds away from yanking her braid right out of her head. Martin stepped past her with a foot into the hall.

"Oh shut-up and get back in here!" Brigid hissed barely louder than a whisper as she hauled him by the arm. She shut the door with a quick click behind him.

Leaning her back against the door, she said, "I don't know, Martin, the last time I listened to one of your *plans* I was lying to Mom and Dad left, right, and center."

"Calm down, Brigid," Martin said, gesturing with his hands. "It won't involve you lying to anyone." It would involve *Ashley* lying to someone, but Martin wasn't about to mention that right now. "Do you think Ashley will be interested in helping?" Martin asked.

If Brigid's eyes could have rolled any further, they'd be bouncing down the stairs. "Oh, he's more excited than anyone else; I'm sure he'll help," her tone was disapproving, but there was a flush in her cheeks. "I just hope you don't get him into *trouble!*" She sounded more like a protective mother than Martin's little sister.

"Good," Martin said, as though that was that. "Let's all meet tomorrow afternoon and I'll fill you in on the details of the plan."

Voyage to the Rock

"What?" Brigid said wide-eyed, chin dropping to her chest. "You're going to make me wait until *tomorrow*? I didn't even agree to your stupid plan yet?"

"Nor should you have," Martin said, his lack of opposition catching Brigid off guard. "It wouldn't be fair to Ashley, now would it? You just told me he'd want to help, and so it's only right to wait for him. I thought we were all in this together?" Martin said shrugging.

Brigid scowled at him, but agreed.

The truth was that Martin knew he could never convince Brigid alone; he needed Ashley, in more ways than one. If Ashley was really as willing as she said —Martin was counting on it, in fact—then tomorrow was the safest time to pitch his plan. *Can't have her vetoing it before the plan begins!*

"Now get out for real this time," she said and pushed him into the hall. "By the way, what did you learn at the library today?" She was still scowling, but had the good sense to lower her voice.

"Nothing." It was Martin's turn to hiss as he glanced left and right. "It's not important right now."

Brigid huffed as she snapped the door shut.

Well, that went as well as could be expected. Martin knew he'd almost lost her there. His jaw clenched as he thought about the need to play these foolish games. Why couldn't things just work smoothly? It was like his whole life—being pushed and pulled by the decisions of others!

As to his discovery about Sullivan O'Connell, it *wasn't* important right then. Besides, his plan involved being in broad daylight. There would be nothing dangerous to worry about.

Except getting caught.

He would just have to make sure he didn't get caught.

Chapter 17:
Taking Back the Cross

It hadn't taken much to convince them of the plan in the end. Ashley was enthusiastic, and seemed to think that he would be paying the *Old Wolf* back for the trouble he'd caused Ashley's friend. Brigid on the other hand was *furious* when she learned that Ashley would be expected to go in and meet Sullivan O'Connell *face-to-face* and *lie* to him about needing an antique gift for his grandmother. She had calmed down—a little—when Martin explained that Ashley just needed to distract O'Connell with questions about antiques, and that he wasn't really doing anything wrong.

Their main worry had been about the *Old Wolf* calling the police. If O'Connell decided to involve the police, they had objected to Martin, his claims would be *much* more convincing. "We'd be picked up in no time," they'd said.

Martin understood how serious a problem for his plan this would have been had he not heard from Mr. Evans about O'Connell's "strange" avoidance of police. Martin had explained this to both of them, and while it was still a bit risky, he had convinced them that it was *certain* that the *Old Wolf* wouldn't call the police.

Their getting permission for Ashley to come to St. John's had sealed it. They would all leave together the day after they got the Cross back and have a few weeks for the whole thing to blow over. While not having had a receipt worked to Sullivan

Voyage to the Rock

O'Connell's advantage in stealing the Cross, it now worked in *their* favor in avoiding being caught afterwards.

In the end, they had agreed, and that was why a week after he had found out about Susan Arthur, the three of them were camped up the road from the *Old Wolf*'s antique store in a small clearing behind a large unkempt hedge on the corner, surrounded by spruce trees on the back side. They were watching the side driveway and waiting. One or another of the three of them had repeated this ritual of peering through the shaggy hedge—a shift each day—for a week now. They knew that Mr. O'Connell's assistant, Mr. Duffy—the large Irishman—would be leaving from the back of the store in his white van, and in an hour would be back to unload the new antiques. This had been the part of Martin's plan that was the most uncertain, and he had been ecstatic to learn just how regular the delivery schedule was. Martin had *one hour*, though he planned on only using 5-10 minutes. Ashley could hardly be expected to keep Mr. O'Connell busy for an hour.

They waited from their lookout. Two o'clock. Time passed, but no van.

"Where is he?" Brigid said from behind Martin. Five after two—no sign of him. "Martin, what if he doesn't go today? The plan will be ruined if..." Brigid stopped as they all saw the van pull to the end of the driveway and stop before turning onto the road. They waited until the van was out of sight.

"Are you both sure you know what to do?"

"Been over it a hundred times, B'y. I thinks I could remember it in me sleep," Ashley said. The hint of a quiver in his voice spoke otherwise, but it was now or never.

"Okay," Martin said, clapping him on the back. "Remember I need at least ten minutes. Brigid, if you see Duffy returning, you blow the bird-whistle and I'll be out the back and around the next building—then you leave *very casually*." Martin's palms were sweaty, but otherwise he looked as though he'd done this kind of thing a hundred times. *Seems you're becoming an old pro at sneaking around.* He didn't respond to the thought. He had no time for his conscience right then. "Casual *especially* for you, Ashley," Martin said tapping him on the chest. "Don't get too nervous if you hear the whistle. Just finish up as naturally as you can and get out of there."

Martin nodded and the three of them made their way out from around the hedge. He and Brigid crossed the street first.

Brigid took up her place on a bench near the sidewalk one building over from the antique store. Martin sat down beside her, while Ashley paused a few buildings down waiting for them to have everything in place.

Brigid pulled out her book—she would pretend to be reading if anyone noticed her while still being able to watch for a long distance in either direction of the street. She laid the little bird-shaped whistle on the bench between Martin and herself. It was the perfect whistle and actually sounded like a flock of little birds if you blew on it. The high-pitched sound would be an easy—but thankfully, discreet—signal for both Martin and Ashley.

Martin and Brigid tried not to stare as Ashley headed past the remaining two buildings and came to the front door. Ashley didn't even glance over at them before entering; Martin had to admit, he was actually impressed with him for that.

Martin checked his watch. In two minutes he'd slip around the back of the building—just enough time for Ashley and Mr. O'Connell to start talking. Each tick of the second hand seemed an hour. *Help me, St. Brendan!*

"Be careful, Mart," Brigid said with a touch of worry in her voice.

"I'll be in and out before you know it," Martin flashed his best smile; inside his belly fluttered so fiercely he felt like he would start floating.

When he was convinced no one was watching, Martin got up, gave Brigid a wink, and slipped around the building next to the antique shop.

He quickly peered around the back corner and finding it empty, entered the backyard. Staying close to the back of the building he made his way across until he reached the driveway to

Voyage to the Rock

the antique shop. There was an open garage door that he quickly passed in front of as he slipped to the back corner of the *Old Wolf's* building.

He waited.

There was a solid backdoor to the shop and a large window next to it. Martin prayed the door was open!

As slowly as possible he tried to glance in the window that looked into the back of the store. He wasn't about to just open the door and find himself face to face with someone. The afternoon sun shone in the window illuminating the room slightly. There was no movement inside.

Martin's heart was pounding right out of his chest!

He slowly moved to the door.

Reaching for the handle, Martin hesitated. This was the point of no return; if he was caught now, it would be the police and likely jail!

He slowly turned the knob, half-expecting the lock. Instead the knob moved easily and silently in his hand. Martin took a deep breath and gently nudged the door forward.

It didn't resist him.

He waited again, but there was no noise, no shout.

Martin opened the door enough to poke his head in. The room was empty. Quickly and silently he slipped in and half-closed the door—just open enough for him to slip out if he needed to.

He listened again, and could hear muffled voices towards the front of the store. Ashley was pulling it off!

Filled with a new sense of confidence, Martin quickly surveyed things. It was a fair-sized room with shelves and work-tables covered in old antiques of varying level of repair. There were tools on some of the tables and more hanging from under wall cabinets. A few large bookcases went from floor to ceiling filled with cans of paint and varnish. There small boxes and large wardrobe-sized ones piled here and there. The place was quite cluttered except for a clear section near the front of the room where the largest work-table was. Above it was a light and what seemed to be a large magnifying device on a metal arm attached to the table. The door to the front part of the store lay just beyond that; thankfully it was shut.

Martin approached the table and his heart sunk. He saw almost immediately that the Cross wasn't there.

He quickly spun, glancing around the room for it. Nowhere!

What am I going to do now? Everything was riding on it being here in his workshop! He went from shelf to shelf and table-top to table-top, but could find nothing.

This was their only chance and it was wasted.

* * *

"Well what color *does* your grandmother prefer?" asked an irritated Sullivan O'Connell.

"I thinks she likes something with blue—royal blue," Ashley struggled to think of answers. He was doing what he could to keep the Old Wolf busy, but it wasn't easy. Ashley knew he wasn't that good at thinking on his feet, but he was trying his best. "She likes anything to do with royalty—loves Queen Elizabeth of England."

Mr. O'Connell sighed and rubbed his temples. "Are you sure it wouldn't be better if your parents picked something out for your grandmother's 80th birthday? The things in my shop are not what one would call *inexpensive*," the Old Wolf said and crossed his bone-thin arms across his chest. His thin frame took nothing from his *presence*, and Ashley had to admit the Old Wolf's name was appropriate. Here was an alpha male—confident and brutal, leader of his pack.

"If you don't even know what kind of item you're looking for, maybe it's better that you come back later." O'Connell stared at Ashley with penetrating green eyes.

"No," Ashley said, a little too quickly. "My parents, they said they want me to pick it—something from me, especially. Nanny loves when I picks her out presents." Ashley started to stroll as he spoke, staring around the store. "Besides," Ashley said,

Voyage to the Rock

turning back to the *Old Wolf*, "it's like my pops always says: 'It ain't the skill that catches the best fish, it's the time you puts in to find him', so I'm in no rush."

O'Connell sighed again. "Well what about one of these?" he said as he walked toward a wall full of commemorative plates. "This one commemorates the first official Royal Visit of Her Majesty Queen Elizabeth to Canada in1957 at which time this plate was issued."

Ashley looked at it as though seriously considering it. "Well..." he said, "I likes it, but do you have one where the trim is in blue instead of red?" Ashley looked from the plate to a visibly annoyed Mr. O'Connell.

"This is *one* of a kind," the old man said through gritted teeth. "It doesn't *exist* in any other color."

"Hhmm, too bad. I sort of liked it for her." Ashley pretended to be disappointed. "What else do you have?"

"Well..." Mr. O'Connell began again in irritated tones. "I have..."

Ashley wasn't listening. *Hurry Martin! I don't know how long I can keep him busy.*

* * *

Brigid could barely keep her eyes on the page for more than a few seconds before glancing up in either direction of the road, and then towards the antique store.

What was taking Martin so long?

He had said he'd be in and out, and it had already been five minutes for sure!

She hoped Ashley was doing alright. But how much longer could he possibly keep the act up? If Martin didn't appear soon, she'd blow the whistle—*even if* Ashley didn't come out first.

How could she have let Martin talk her into this?

She instinctively reached up for her blond braid and began twirling. He always seemed to push her into things she didn't want to do. Just because he didn't care about getting in trouble didn't mean she didn't!

Still, she had to admit that she liked *this* Martin a lot better than the sulky grump she'd lived with for the last six months.

She just wished he would get over himself and stop making things miserable for everyone else around him! She knew this was half the reason why she was so willing to go along with this whole quest.

Half the reason, anyway.

She was excited to solve the mystery, too. She might just be more careful about it, if Martin's mood hadn't lightened up so much since finding the Cross.

A hand touched her shoulder and Brigid jumped!

"Oh sorry, Brigid." It was the Russian grandmother from church. "I hope I didn't startle you much."

"Mrs. Petrovich, what are you doing here?" Brigid anxiously glanced past her down the street and then at the store's front door.

"Call me Babushka Ludmilla! Out for walk in afternoon sun. Is good for my health, no?" she said with a grandmotherly smile.

"I guess so." Brigid was unsure how to answer. *Not now! Of all times, I can't chat now.*

"And you? Reading on bench?"

"Well I sometimes like to get away and read in the sun," she said. "I like to... be alone and get away from the family."

Brigid forced herself to breathe. She even forced herself to drop her braid as she became acutely aware of the pain in her scalp.

"Yes, yes," the old woman said patting Brigid's arm, "is difficult to find time alone with family around."

Before Brigid could speak another word her heart suddenly froze.

Over the old grandmother's shoulder, she could see a van distantly approaching—Mr. Duffy's van. But he was *much* too early.

Voyage to the Rock

What was she going to do?

She couldn't very well blow the whistle in this grandmother's face and then have Martin tear out the back of the antique store. That would get back to their parents and they'd be discovered *for sure!*

She quickly rose and grabbed her whistle, holding it together with the book. "Are you going this way?" she asked the old lady. "Can I walk with you?"

"Oh yes, child, I would love that!"

Brigid took the old woman's arm. The best she could try to do was to stall the van to give Martin more time.

Was it ten minutes yet? It felt like hours. Was he already out?

Brigid didn't know, but she knew if she could give him five more minutes she was going to try.

The van was almost to the store.

Brigid and Babushka Ludmilla were now standing just before the driveway of the antique shop. Just as the van was approaching to turn in, Brigid released the old woman's arm and let the book and whistle fall forward from her hand as she pretended to trip.

The sudden sound of a horn and the squeal of breaks filled the air. A scream sounded behind Brigid as Ludmilla cried out in alarm.

Brigid's heart was pounding in her ears as she stood frozen in the driveway.

Mr. Duffy was leaning out his window with a fist raised. "Can't ye watch where yer goin'! I could'a hit ya!" he said in a thick Irish accent.

It really hadn't been very close; Brigid wasn't stupid after all. But she still felt shaky as she called back a weak apology before slowly grabbing her things and backing-up out of the way.

She prayed to God that Martin had heard the horn and gotten away.

"Well, anyway, no 'arm done. But be more car'ful next time!" the man said out his window, as he pulled the van down the driveway.

Please help him, St. Brendan! She said silently as the old grandmother began to fuss over her.

*   *   *

A horn sounded and breaks squealed.

Martin's head shot up! It couldn't be Duffy already?

He was at the far side of the room with a pile of different-sized boxes separating him from the open door.

He hesitated only a second before springing toward it.

Before he could make it, though, he saw Duffy's van pull up in front of the garage.

Martin had no chance of making it out the door without Duffy seeing him. He'd never be able to get away from the large Irishman!

Rather than panic—which was his first instinct—he quickly did the only other thing he could: with lightning speed he shut the door in silence and turned the lock on the handle.

Turned the lock! He almost groaned.

Not waiting a moment, he spun scanning the room for a hiding place. Where was he going to go?

A large wardrobe box stood at the far left side of the room. He ran to hide behind it.

At the door he heard the handle rattle and Duffy grumbling. There was the faint jingle of keys.

As he got around the box he almost stumbled down a small set of stairs that he hadn't seen. At the bottom of five stairs, Martin saw a door.

He hopped the stairs by two's and turned the old knob of the wooden door.

It opened.

Martin entered a dark room, and gently closed the door just as he heard the back door open and Duffy enter.

Voyage to the Rock

Martin jumped at a sudden rattle of keys as Duffy apparently tossed them onto one of the tables. He was muttering something about: "Foolish kid!"

Martin silently prayed Brigid and Ashley were both fine. He prayed for himself too! What had he gotten himself into?

Martin listened for a while at the door. He heard what sounded like Duffy carrying things in and then going back outside, only to return again.

There was nothing to do but wait and hope Duffy would go out front long enough for Martin to make his escape.

As Martin stepped back into the little window-less room, he noticed that it wasn't completely dark after all. There was a small light on a desk against a wall in the room. Martin couldn't make out much in the room except for what looked to be more cases of antiques, and clearly some of the most valuable.

He almost choked. The *Cross*!

On a stand to the left side of the desk in a small glass case stood the Cross. It was even more beautiful than before; it had been properly polished and cleaned of all the green tarnish covering it. The inter-twining weaves looked alive. The stone at the side of Christ—a red ruby—glinted faintly in the lamplight.

He had found St. Brendan's Cross!

As silently and carefully as he could, Martin lifted the top of the case. Reaching inside, he pulled the Cross out while letting the lid come to rest again. He pulled off his backpack and carefully placed the Cross in it. He then put the bag back on and headed for the door.

Silence.

Had he missed Duffy? Should he run now? He didn't know what to do.

In that brief moment he started to panic again.

What if he was caught? What would O'Connell do to him?

Martin shuddered as he imagined Sullivan O'Connell entering this little room—with no other way of escape—and coming upon Martin: the *Old Wolf* coming upon his little rabbit trapped in a hole!

I can't take it. It's now or never!

Just as Martin was about to burst from the room without a care to who found him—*anything* was better than the Old Wolf finding him there—he heard the scuffle of boots on the floor and a heaving grunt as Duffy laid something heavy on the floor.

Martin suddenly slumped against the wall, knees weak.

He had almost bounded out of the room and into the Irishman! He was an *idiot* for ever having come here. What had he been *thinking?*

Martin then heard the scuff of boots and a door open and shut. It wasn't the back door—it was much too light—but the door to the shop.

The room outside was silent.

Martin sprang from the room as silently as he could and carefully closed the door behind him. He flew up the stairs and headed around the boxes.

His heart was pounding in his ears so loudly that he couldn't have listened for someone coming even if he'd wanted to. This was it. He saw the back door—and still open!

But would he make it to the door? Or would either of the two men stumble into him as they came out from the front room?

He sprang.

And then... he was out the back door.

He was free!

He ran along the back of the house, not even pausing at the two windows he passed, and turned to follow the left side of the house.

When he made it to the edge, he quickly peeked out. There was no one to be seen—not even Ashley or Brigid. They'd be waiting up the street at their agreed meeting place.

Martin casually turned left, walking onto the sidewalk and heading up the road. At the first intersecting street, Martin turned left and then started trotting to the meeting place which was just down the next street at a park.

Voyage to the Rock

In moments, Martin burst through the bushes to see the red face of Brigid who let out a startled cry as he entered, and a worried Ashley.

"Where were you?" Brigid looked on the brink of fury and tears all at once.

"I'm sorry. I got stuck!" Martin said.

"You got *stuck*?" Brigid's lip started to tremble, and tears filled her eyes. "I thought... I thought you..." She raised a fist as if to hit him, but instead brushed tears from her eyes. "I thought they *caught* you, Martin!" This came out as a low wail.

"Don't worry, Brigid. I'm fine now," he said as he put a reassuring arm around her. She began to cry. "I'm sorry, Brigid. It was a stupid plan!"

She didn't look up.

"But look," he said as he pulled the bag off his back and unzipped it. "I got it!"

Brigid nodded weakly not even glancing at the bag, tears streaming down her cheeks. Martin looked to Ashley who didn't make eye contact with him and said nothing.

"We got it!" Martin repeated to them both.

"Yup," was all Ashley said as he looked with concern at Brigid who was still crying softly.

Darn it! Martin said to himself. *It wasn't supposed to be this way!*

Even Martin couldn't convince himself that he'd done the right thing today.

Chapter 18:
A Vacation Away

Martin was tired when they finally pulled into Terra Nova National Park for lunch. They had been on the road now for about five hours and he was glad for the chance to stretch his legs and get some fresh air. It was already mid-afternoon and they apparently still had another two hours or more until they would arrive at Jenny's house in St. John's.

Jenny was their father's cousin and she had made the trip up to Corner Brook earlier in the week. She had stayed at the house during the few days preceding their mission to get the Cross back, and Martin and Brigid had gotten to know her some. She was a nice older lady, never married, and a retired high school chemistry teacher. Jenny and his parents had spent late nights catching-up and chatting about family and old memories; Martin had awoken more than once to laughter.

The only difficult part about Jenny was that she liked to talk—*a lot*. She even talked to herself if there was no one else to talk to. Martin had faked sleep more than once in the last five hours just to avoid having to respond to her every: "Well what do you think about that tree?" "Who do you suppose lives in a house like that?" "Did you see those flowers, bushes, bunnies...[insert anything else you can think of]?" The three of them had heard Jenny's entire life story, knew about most of the students she had ever taught, and could imagine in *minute detail* the daily routine of her cat, Mr. Fuddle. Despite all that, Martin was surprised by how much he liked Jenny and how quickly all three of them felt comfortable with her.

Voyage to the Rock

It had been a long trip so far and everyone was tired—especially after yesterday. Brigid was still somewhat annoyed with Martin, but try as she might, she couldn't hide her genuine excitement at having gotten the Cross back. Ashley was back to his generally amicable self and had enjoyed immensely describing how infuriated he had made the *Old Wolf* by the end with all his moving from one gift idea to the next. Apparently, O'Connell had been so relieved to have an excuse to get rid of Ashley when the van honked and screeched that Ashley had gotten away without so much as a second glance from the *Old Wolf*.

Brigid also explained to them what had happened and why she was unable to warn them sooner. At that point, Ashley told her that she'd been "down-right heroic" and Brigid had blushed furiously. But Martin himself had agreed whole-heartedly and was looking at his sister with a new-found respect—even if she was overreacting about his own close call.

His story caused them to turn pale at moments and for Brigid to hit his arm at one point—and not lightly—telling him how stupid he'd been. But what really got Martin off the hook was seeing the immaculately polished Cross and its stunning blood red ruby; Brigid's eyes had nearly popped and Ashley let out a low whistle. And so in the end, they were all just glad to have the Cross back and the mystery before them—not to mention having two and a half weeks to puzzle everything out without any chance of the *Old Wolf* catching them.

Martin would have almost liked to have been there to see the *Old Wolf*'s face when he realized the Cross was gone—*almost*. As it was, they had enough of a challenge in front of them to think too much about Sullivan O'Connell. As stupid as it might have been—and Martin was pretty convinced it *had* been stupid—they had the Cross safely with them and another opportunity to solve the mystery of the poem.

They sat at a picnic table on a grassy slope with landscaped trees and bushes here and there. The place was actually quite active and there were lots of families. Nearby, they saw a beagle that danced around a family's toddler, who swayed this way and that as he tried to catch it. They were still laughing as they began unfolding sandwiches and taking out soda from the cooler. Martin, though, couldn't help turning his mind to more serious concerns: their mystery.

He had read and re-read the poem. On top of that, at the first chance they got last night they had put the Cross on the manuscript page. Nothing new jumped out at them, though, and in the end they had been too tired to try and concentrate on it more. Now all Martin could think about was the manuscript page and the Cross. He couldn't wait until later that night when all three of them would have a chance to try to tease out some answers.

Martin watched Ashley as he chewed a bite of his peanut butter and jam sandwich. The guy had actually turned out to be invaluable. He wasn't just some dumb kid; he saw things from a different perspective which at times really helped. Brigid had proved herself, too. Martin was proud of and irritated by her at the same time. He was glad to have the help, though.

Now if only he could live up to his part in all of this. He ran a hand through brown shaggy locks and dared to hope.

He spent the rest of the meal half-listening to the chatting of the others. He just ate and thought, occasionally laughing with them so that it would not be completely obvious that his mind was elsewhere.

After lunch, Martin dozed the last few hours until they were driving into St. John's. Maybe it was a city compared to Corner Brook, but it was still tiny compared to Boston; Martin couldn't help feeling a little disappointed. Like Corner Brook, it was built on a sloping hill that rose up from the bay and was dotted with trees and houses. The bay was to their right as they drove in and Jenny took them through the streets of the downtown which—except for a few large modern buildings—was a tapestry of brightly colored historic shops and houses: orange, green, yellow, blue, red, purple. The place was a bag of jelly beans that seemed to grow brighter the more the houses ascended the

Voyage to the Rock

slope. As they drove up from the water, the houses shifted from larger three-storey brick buildings to old Victorian style wooden homes. The place was nice enough—in a quaint sort of way—and it didn't really matter if it was a *big* city or not. He was there to work.

In no time they were pulling up to a large green Victorian house with white trim. The place must have been at least a hundred years old, but it looked great. They all got out and carried their bags up the wooden stairs to the long porch that ran the front of the house. Martin barely avoided knocking over one of the many potted plants that lined the stairs. They waited while Jenny fumbled for the key to the large red door.

She led them through a beautiful old home with hardwood floors and floral-patterned wallpaper. The house seemed very regal, even if it was a bit cluttered with plants and the occasional stack of books.

"Welcome to my home! I hope you'll enjoy your stay," said Jenny with a wave of her arm. "Right up here, now."

She led them upstairs. The boys she put in the room to the right. There were two single beds and a large window looking out on the backyard. Brigid was taken to one of the two rooms whose windows faced from the front of the house onto the harbor. It was a nice room with a canopied bed, but entirely *too pink*.

Afterwards, Jenny gave them a tour of the whole house. It was large—and *huge* for just one person. They'd have lots of space here, and that suited Martin best. The last thing he needed was Jenny stumbling onto their secret.

It wasn't until quite late before they all returned to their rooms for the night. Jenny made supper and dessert, followed by tea and cookies, followed by looking at album after album of pictures. To be honest, it was fun—for the first 15 minutes—but after two hours they were all exhausted. And so the Cross and manuscript would have to wait until the next morning.

After he was all washed up and both he and Ashley were in their beds, Martin took out the *Voyage* to read a bit before falling asleep. He was almost finished and now with the Cross back he was more eager than ever to keep reading. He opened the book...

*   *   *

A few days later a new island appeared with the memory of the last island still fresh in their minds. There stood a tall mountain as black as coal and shrouded in clouds with great smoke pouring from it. And with a rapid gust of forceful wind they suddenly flew towards it. Here the monk who remained of the three suddenly leaped from the boat as if carried. And with a wailing moan he cried aloud: "Woe is me, Father, for I am forcibly torn from you and cannot return!" And St. Brendan then saw that the wretched man was carried by a host of the demons and was already burning in an unholy flame. And from his own sorrow, St. Brendan then cried out: "O wretched man, how have you brought yourself to such an evil end?" But there was no answer and the monks then departed. Later that night, they saw bright flames shooting into the sky from the mountain's peak. But it went up and then landed upon the mountain again so that the whole place resembled a burning heap.

After this dreadful event, the holy fathers sailed for a further seven days, until they spotted something else sitting amidst the sea. It was the form of a man sitting soaked upon a sea-sprayed rock with some kind of cloth that whipped in the wind, hanging from two iron bars of metal. When the Fathers saw the sight, some thought it a bird, while others, a

Voyage to the Rock

boat. But St. Brendan silenced them all, waiting to know who this unfortunate creature was. And on they sailed toward him.

As they reached the man the waves were still except around the man and his rocky seat. But the waves crashed upon him, and then away, covering him at times, and at others revealing the small rock upon which he sat. The cloth that was before his face, which hung upon the metal prongs, was blown by the wind and the wild waves and whipped his eyes and forehead.

When the saint asked this man from where he came and who he was and for what crime he did suffer such punishment, the wretched man replied: "I am that most unhappy Judas, that most impure betrayer and greedy man, and it is not by my own doing, but by the unspeakable mercy of Jesus Christ, that I am allowed such comforts here away from the flames of Hell!" The monks all stared in stark amazement to hear words as "such comforts" there in that most awful place. "It is by the love and mercy of the Redeemer of the World, and in honor of His Resurrection on this Lord's Day that I am given to feel such cool relief! It is to me a paradise of delights, especially when I think to where I must return after this day of mercy shown—to the torments, my torments, which burn me up day and night. For me there is no place for repentance, but to you I shall share about the boundless mercy of God to me, that He gives to me at four seasons of the year, and on every Sunday—from Saturday vespers 'til Sunday of the same. I am here, in my place of cool respite, from Christmas Day until Theophany; from Pascha until Pentecost; and the last two times that I find such peace is on the feast of the Virgin's Purification, and the festival of when she fell asleep, her Dormition. The rest of the year I spend in my heritage of pain which I have purchased by an evil price, but pray the Lord for me that I may remain here until the morning's dawn and not be carried back at my accustomed time."

"The will of the Lord be done," replied the saint. "For God has granted that you be shown this further grace, and the demons will not come near you. Now explain to us the mystery of this cloth and why it whips you in the face."

"This cloth I once did give unto a leper, but since I stole it from the Lord's own purse, I find no comfort from it—despite the goodness of the deed. Instead by it I find only hurt, and thereby now I've learned, a good deed done in the wrong way, and not for God's own sake, is not counted as pleasing before the Lord. These iron poles upon which it hangs, I once gave to the priests for use in the temple. And finally, this rock you see, which is now my means of comfort, I once donated for a public road before I became the Lord's disciple."

And when the night had passed and the angry demons had come, St. Brendan with the might of the Lord kept the fearsome foes at bay and charged them in the name of the Lord to do no further harm to the wretched Judas. The monks then left to the horrible sound of the demons howls and Judas being taken away.

Voyage to the Rock

* * *

Martin shivered in his blankets despite the warmth of the evening. He looked over to Ashley for some comfort, but his soft, even, breathing was the only sound. The darkness of the room was oppressive. Was the rest of St. Brendan's *Voyage* going to be just like the last few times he'd read—all demons, betrayers, and fear?

Martin slowly reached up and made the sign of the Cross on himself. *Lord have mercy!* He couldn't help but feel even more guilty—and afraid—for the things he'd been doing lately. No one even knew what the monk did, but he was dragged off by *demons!* He thought of his own secrets—about Brendan Arthur's warnings, about Susan Arthur's death. Should he have been upfront with Brigid and Ashley about the danger? Had he gotten them mixed up in something he had no right to? He certainly had been manipulating them to get his way a lot lately, to do anything he could to keep his search alive—and to avoid *getting caught*. Was he like the monk with the secrets? Was he like Judas?

This thought terrified him. Hadn't Judas done good things for the wrong reasons and been tortured by them? *And what are you doing?* The thought formed in his mind. *Stealing, lying, manipulating, just to return the Cross?* The thoughts taunted him.

Was he acting like Judas? He shivered again. *Well I don't want to be like that.* He shouted back at the thoughts. *I do want to do this for St. Brendan! I'm not just being selfish.*

He stared at the ceiling trying to figure out what to do, and as his thoughts turned into dreams, his last words were: *Let me do things in the right way, O God.*

Chapter 19:
It's in the Little Things

Martin awoke to the noise of others in the hall. He looked over to Ashley's bed and saw that not only was the red-haired Newfoundlander not there, but his bed was neatly made and his stuff arranged on his bedside table. Martin hadn't heard a thing.

He scratched his head as he sat up on one arm. He couldn't help stifling a yawn. While he may have slept late, he hadn't slept well. His dreams had been filled with all sorts of dark images that lingered on the edge of his waking memory. All he could remember was the feeling of running, of being hunted by something.

But now, sitting in the sun that was streaming in through the open bedroom door, all his dreams seemed to melt into smoke. He sat there enjoying the simple warmth of his soft bed. Martin could feel his enthusiasm for the quest building as he relaxed. As long as they could escape Jenny for a while each day, he would be more than satisfied.

Brigid poked her head in the open doorway. "Finally you're up! You already missed breakfast, and Jenny sent me up to see how you were," she said. "Bacon and eggs are waiting for you downstairs—if you can ever get yourself out of bed. We're all waiting on you to go walking along the coast."

"A walk on the coast?" Martin said, feeling his mood sink.

"Don't worry, Martin. We'll have lots of time this afternoon to work on the poem; Jenny has a 'bridge party' with her friends. We'll be free to do whatever we like she said."

Voyage to the Rock

"Well, I guess I can wait. It's not like we have anything else to do for the next two and a half weeks. I'll be right down."

"Hurry then," Brigid said as she closed the door behind her.

* * *

"Yeah, yeah, the whales were cool," Martin said, waving Brigid's enthusiasm away and sitting on his bed in his and Ashley's room.

"Cool? They were awesome!" Brigid said. She was wearing pig-tails today and raised them into the air in her excitement. "I can't *wait* to take the boat ride to see them!" They had distantly seen the whales shooting water into the air on their walk around the harbor. "I'm expecting dolphins, too!"

"That's all great, Brigid," Martin said, "but we need to get down to work." He reached for his backpack concealed behind the headboard of his bed. "We'll only have a few solid hours." Martin checked again over his shoulder to make sure the door was closed; then he pulled the Cross out of his bag, got up, and laid it on the table next to the open book with the manuscript page.

"So where do we begin, B'ys?" Ashley asked smiling. He'd already taken a seat at the side of the desk.

"Well, I think we should look at the poem again and go over all the potential clues we have," Martin said, pulling up his own chair. "Then we'll be able to see what else we need to work through."

Brigid, standing over Martin's shoulder, said, "Why don't we make a list of the clues and answers so that we can see it all written out." She grabbed a pen and notebook and plunked down at the end of Martin's bed. Back against the wall, she started to write. "Okay. We have a guess for the first two lines: *There's more to verse than simply words, / The words reveal a shining gift.* One, there's a puzzle, and two there's a treasure or 'gift.'"

The other two nodded agreement, having turned their chairs to face Brigid.

Matthew Penney

"We also have an idea about—*A fruitful land unnamed by Birds*, and *A Three but One to where boats drift*," Brigid continued. "Line Three is talking about the Birds from St. Brendan's voyage, and Line Four is about the three fruitful islands that are really one: Newfoundland."

"Exactly," Martin said.

Brigid kept writing. "*A company of God—three lost/ Were first of Christ's own sons to land*. Line Five is about the three monks who don't return from the voyage, and Line Six is about St. Brendan's company being the first Christians to arrive in Newfoundland." Once she'd scribbled these down she looked up.

"Now, *But another comes to find the Cross* and *When unchanged faith arrives again*, are more tricky. It could be talking about Martin in Line Seven since he found the Cross." Brigid glanced at Martin clearly wondering if he would be annoyed by her "could" remark, but kept going, "and again about us in Line Eight with Dad's new church being built."

Martin knew they didn't necessarily believe the line was about him—but St. Brendan *did* know the future and *could* be speaking about him. Martin still had the feeling deep inside himself that the line was about him, so he responded aloud to their silent thoughts: "Even if it's not about us *prophetically*—which I still believe it is—it describes our situation pretty well, and it doesn't seem to affect the whole puzzle whatever we believe about it." The other two seemed to accept this. "Go on, Brigid," Martin said.

"Line Nine is a mystery: *A fiery portal shows the way*. But Dr. Arthur thinks Line 10, *To those before the Cross, they hail*, refers to making the sign of the Cross while standing 'before the Cross' laid on the manuscript. It's a pretty good guess," Brigid said. "At least, we don't have a better one."

"Agreed," Martin said. And Ashley shook his head in agreement.

"Line 11, *Not resting on or near the bay*, seems straightforward, but it's a bit confusing next to Line 12, *Between high water, rock,*

Voyage to the Rock

and whale. What is 'high water'? And how can something be between that and 'rock, and whale'?" Brigid looked up from her writing. "Any ideas?"

"Not me," Ashley said, tapping his chin.

"And not me, either, so let's keep going for now," Martin said.

"The next four lines seem to be connected. But we can at least make a guess about *To see the Cross as saving key*—Line 13, which seems to be about the Cross being some sort of 'key' just like Ashley and Dr. Arthur both thought. Line 14, *To guide one to the heavenly room,* seems to be a reference to the site or room that the Cross will be the 'key' for," Brigid said, readjusting the notepad resting on knees pulled almost to her chest. "But it's Line 15, *Recall: the first, the last shall be,* and Line 16, *And know the same when Crosses bloom,* that we don't even have a guess for. Any ideas for these?" She paused and looked from Ashley's silent shake of the head to Martin cracking his knuckles.

"Just go on, Brigid," Martin said. "We'll talk over the ones we don't know when we finish writing the list."

"Okay, okay," Brigid said, going back to her notepad. "Line 17, *To God's new children from afar,* again... maybe it refers to us, maybe it doesn't, but Line 18, *Ol' Brendan awaits his gifts to give,* certainly refers again to the treasure, whatever it might be. The last two lines also have us stumped: *With the blessing of the Stella Maris/ Faith to revive and to forgive.* There," Brigid said laying down her pencil.

They all looked at the list. It *was* impressive how many of the lines they had written answers for. But there were still a lot of question marks. They had no answer for at least eight lines of the twenty; and no guess at all for about five. Maybe they weren't so close to a solution as Martin had hoped. He didn't have time to think on it, though. There was someone coming up the stairs.

"Kids!" It was Jenny.

Martin quickly put the Cross back in his bag as Brigid hid the list and Ashley tucked the book into a drawer. They opened the door just as Jenny was reaching the top stair.

"Would you dears mind meeting some of my Bridge Club friends?" She was wearing a green and white striped shirt, and bright pink Capri pants with a daisy hair clip pinned in her hair. She couldn't have looked more "eccentric spinster" if she'd tried.

"Not at all, Jenny," Martin said. So much for *solid* work time.

* * *

Over the next few days, they found themselves scrambling to find time to work on their puzzle while being regularly interrupted when they did. It would have been more frustrating had they been making more progress, but as it was they were making little head-way. And so the interruptions for excursions and shopping and lunches out were not an entirely unwelcome break—just unwelcome *sometimes*.

Today, for example, they had all felt close to making a breakthrough. There was something that kept striking Ashley about the Cross and manuscript whenever they were placed together. Ashley would stare at the thing as though he expected the answers to just jump off the page. He just needed a little more time to figure out what it was he had said, and then... Jenny.

Today the plan was for them to come to where they now stood: Cape Spear. Jenny had been very excited to show them the easternmost point in North America. Martin couldn't bring himself to feel a similar excitement, but he could appreciate her enthusiasm a lot more than he would have before reading the *Voyage of St. Brendan*.

As he stood near the one hundred fifty year old lighthouse and looked out over the green grass and rocky coast toward the sprawling ocean, he couldn't help but imagine that this was something like what St. Brendan had done over 1,500 hundred

Voyage to the Rock

years ago. Maybe there *was* something exciting about that—or *inspiring*. A line of something seemed to float from his memory: "*Shall I turn my back on my native land and my face towards the sea?*" He tried to remember, to grasp at it, but as quickly as the thought had come it was gone again.

"So that's where this whole mystery began, eh?"

Martin turned to look at Ashley who had come up next to him.

"Across the ocean, I mean. It's hard to believe I've lived me whole life here and now with one old Cross, none of it's the same," Ashley said, staring out intently.

"What do you mean none of it's the same?" Martin said, turning to watch him.

"Well, I used to look out on the ocean and I just saw the ocean; but now it's the ocean St. Brendan sailed across. I used to see trees and rocks and they were just Newfoundland; but now I sees a land where ancient monks walked," Ashley said, his thoughts obviously stretching farther than his words.

Martin didn't know what to say.

"It's just weird, that's all, how someone knows something to be one way his whole life, and then suddenly... that thing he knows becomes something else—something *more*—right in front of his eyes." He paused and looked at Martin. "And the funny thing is, it was there the whole time and he just never knew what to look for."

Ashley shrugged and turned around to survey the large open green, interspersed with rocky patches. People walked here and there, sight-seeing and snapping photos. Ashley turned back to the sea.

The two of them continued to stare out at the ocean, neither of them speaking for a while. They just let the smell of the sea and the wind on their face hold them captive.

Brigid's voice broke the silence: "Hey Mart! Ashley! Come check out this Celtic cross."

Martin and Ashley turned to see her just down the bend from the grassy cliff on which they stood. They walked to meet her and the tall stone cross. It was a High Cross, Martin could tell that even at a distance. It had the characteristic circular halo—like the one on St. Brendan's.

When they got there all three of them stood looking at it. It overlooked the sea—as though this were the Cross from the poem, waiting to be found by travelers from across the ocean. But this cross was clearly something recently erected with its small brass plaque attached at the bottom.

"It's a memorial," Brigid said, her blond pony-tail blowing in the wind, "for all those lost at sea or on the rocky coasts of Newfoundland. It reminded me so much of St. Brendan and his monks that I had to call you guys over to see. It's even a Celtic—like the ones from the library book."

"Well if we don't solve that poem," Martin said, suddenly feeling oppressed by the vast uncertainty that still stood before them, "this might be the closest thing to finding anything related to Irish monks in Newfoundland." He turned and started back up the slope towards the lighthouse. Martin glanced over his shoulder and saw Ashley following, his own shoulders sagging a bit. Brigid lagged behind for a moment.

Martin glanced back again to catch sight of Brigid making the sign of the cross before the High Cross and leaning forward to kiss it quickly before running off towards them. But then... Brigid stopped dead, her mouth hanging open.

"What is it, Brigid?" Martin called back to her, stopping. "What's wrong?" Ashley also turned to look.

"Oh my gosh, guys! Oh my gosh!" she said clapping her hands and jumping up and down.

"What?" Martin said taking a step toward her.

"Not the east coast, Martin! The west! The west coast!" The words burst forth from Brigid's mouth.

"What are you talking about?" Martin said, his brow wrinkling.

"Dr. Arthur was wrong, Mart! The poem didn't mean the east coast! It meant the west! *A fiery portal shows the way / To those before the Cross, they hail;* He was making the sign of the cross

Voyage to the Rock

backwards! I just realized it after I made my own cross before *that* cross there," she said gesturing back at the stone high cross.

Martin's eyes became wide: "*Of course* he was! I can't believe it didn't occur to me before."

"Backwards? What are you B'ys talkin' about?" asked a puzzled Ashley.

"Orthodox Christians make the sign of the cross in the traditional way: from forehead to stomach, and then *right to left*, not left to right as Dr. Arthur would have thought. The Roman Catholics changed from the old way in the 11th century–long after St. Brendan and his monks, who would have done it the traditional way!" Martin said as he smiled, grabbing Ashley by the shoulders and shaking him. "That means it's on the western side of Newfoundland!"

Martin reached an arm around his sister as she bounced up to them and laughing said, "Great job, Brigid." She laughed with him, as Ashley echoed the praise.

"What's all the excitement about?" Jenny was coming down the slope. "Did I miss anything while I was searching for a washroom?"

They all froze a moment. Then Brigid said, "Oh, just a joke Martin told us, Jenny. Why don't you tell it to her, Martin?" she added with a mischievous smile.

Martin gave Brigid a wide-eyed look before he turned to face Jenny and tell her the *joke* that was so *funny*.

* * *

"Thanks for hanging me out to dry!" Martin said as soon as the door was closed. They were in Martin and Ashley's room. It was after dinner and they had graciously bowed out of watching 50's re-run movies with Jenny. Besides, Martin would have been too excited to watch a movie tonight even if it was the best one ever made. They had figured out another clue!

"I was sure you'd come up with something," Brigid said, holding her sides to keep from cracking up again. "The

'Hilarious Boar', though? Where did you ever come up with something like that? 'I park where I want?'... I didn't even get the joke!" Laughter was spilling out from both her and Ashley all over again.

"I would have liked to have seen either of you two do any better," Martin said, with mock indignation that he only *slightly* felt. He was in too good a mood right now for anything to spoil it. "Where's that map of Newfoundland?" he said looking through his bag.

"Right here," Ashley said pulling the map from under a book.

They laid it on the table. They also had out the manuscript page with the Cross on it, which they set next to the map. Martin touched the Cross from top to bottom and then right to left. There was no real reason for it, but he was just excited.

The Cross was impressive since being cleaned up. The bronze gleamed dully and caught the light of the lamp along its intricate weaving patterns. Martin could now make out every little detail of the sleeping Christ. He could even make out the imprint of little bumps for the nails in his hands and feet. But most impressive of all now was the shining red ruby that sat delicately on the little Christ's side—where the spear wound would be. The Cross was more beautiful than Martin could have ever have imagined. In some ways all the trouble with Sullivan O'Connell felt worth it just to be able to see the Cross like this.

"So," Martin said, moving to the map. He took his three fingers and tapped them on it as he had just done to the Cross: top—L'Anse aux Meadows; bottom—St. Lawrence; right—Fogo Island; left—Gros Morne. "Gros Morne National Park," Martin said leaning on the desk. "There's certainly more chance we'll be able to get there from Corner Brook to search. I had no idea how we were supposed to get to the eastern side of Newfoundland."

"Do you really think the treasure is in Gros Morne?" Brigid said starting to bounce again next to him.

Voyage to the Rock

"If Dr. Arthur was right about that part of the poem referring to the place of a campsite, then I'd say yeah," Martin said. Ashley had taken up his chair on Martin's left side again. "Still, I wish we had more to go on than just his guess. I wonder what the 'fiery portal' could be that's supposed to 'lead the way'. I don't see anything on the map that would give a clue. Ashley," Martin said laying a hand on his shoulder, "do you know of anything in Gros Morne that might be a 'fiery portal'—an area of red rock, or a patch of red maple trees, anything like that?"

Ashley stared at the map thoughtfully, but finally shook his head: "You gots me, B'y. 'I gots my line in the water, but not a single bite.'"

"Brigid, do you remember anything from when we drove through Gros Morne on the way to L'Anse aux Meadows?" He drummed his fingers on the desk.

She shook her head.

Martin sighed. "Maybe we should look at the poem again," he said as he reached for the book. Martin grabbed the Cross to slide it to one side.

"Wait!" Ashley said, grabbing his arm.

"What, Ashley?" Martin said, pausing.

Ashley released Martin's arm and Martin slowly lifted his hand from the Cross. Ashley then reached over and straightened the Cross back in its place on the manuscript page.

"Look!"

As he said this he reached up to the top part of the Cross to where one of the two "unconnected" knots—the "blemishes"—met the manuscript page. He slowly began to follow this single weaving thread with his finger up higher as it rose to a rounded peak and then dipped again and went across to meet the other "unconnected" weave on the top section of the Cross. Then he traced the weave down across the manuscript to the right where it met another "unconnected" knot on the Crosses right arm, and followed that across the arm, meeting the other spot where the thread met the manuscript.

In a matter of seconds, Ashley had traced his finger around the entire Cross and manuscript. He had passed eight of the "mistakes"—as Martin had originally thought of them when he had sketched the Cross—but now it was clear that they made up one continuous knot that moved along the Cross and the manuscript.

"It's in the shape of Newfoundland!" Brigid said, holding a hand to her mouth.

Brigid was right. It wasn't a perfect replica of a map by any means, but it was *clearly* a long weave in the shape of Newfoundland. The little image of Newfoundland was smaller than the Cross, and didn't fit top to bottom and side to side as Martin had originally tapped with his fingers on the map. Instead, the Cross was about an inch larger than the outline of Newfoundland on all sides.

Martin was dumbfounded. They had their proof now from this alone! St. Brendan and the monks *had* been to Newfoundland, and had made a Cross and a manuscript page to be a map.

"How did you ever see it, Ashley?" Martin said as he let himself sink into his chair.

"Just had a feeling I was missing something this last week—like I should see something that was right in front of me nose. Then all of a sudden—*Pop!*—it was like the thing just jumped off the page at me," Ashley said in a rush while waving expressive hands. "I guess having the map next to it just triggered it for me."

"Well, great work! Keep those eyes peeled for any other surprises," Martin said slapping him on the back.

"Mart, Ashley. Look!" Brigid tapped the manuscript page. "The ninth thread. Do you see? It connects too!" She put her finger on a section of the manuscript just where the arm of the Cross on the left side met the page. There was another thread that began there. She traced her finger along the paper to the side of the Cross where the ninth and final "unconnected" thread was, and continued to the end of the knot. "Here," she said, her finger resting next to the red ruby, "the Fiery Portal!" A smile split her face. It was mirrored on Martin and Ashley's. "It *is* in Gros Morne!"

Chapter 20:
Sharing Secrets

The bus ride back from St. John's had been a long ten and a half hours but hadn't been that bad. Jenny had lamented loudly that she could not reschedule her trip to New Hampshire and keep "her three Sweeties" longer. Honestly, Martin wondered if the bus had taken any longer whether she would have. Finally, though, they were driving away with Jenny waving from the sidewalk.

The two and a half weeks had passed surprisingly quickly, though they had gotten to see lots of St. John's and the surrounding area. Not for the first time, Martin thought about how beautiful a place Newfoundland really was—even if a bit rustic. And to be honest, even their time spent with Jenny had been enjoyable in the end.

The highlight for Brigid, of course, had been finally getting to take the whale-watching boat tour. And they *had* seen dolphins, too. But the most exciting thing by far was all the discoveries they'd pieced together. They were close now; Martin could feel it.

They had figured out on closer examination of the map compared to what they found on the Cross and manuscript that the 'fiery portal' was somewhere near the top half of Gros Morne National Park, and somewhere in from the coast. They had a general idea of where, but Martin knew it wasn't until they puzzled out the line *Between high water, rock, and whale* that they would know for certain. And so despite everything they'd learned, they spent much of the bus ride trying to solve that line—without much success.

Voyage to the Rock

They had a general guess that "whale" must mean some body of water—though not "on or near the bay"; so it must be a lake or river. This hadn't helped a lot, though, since there were at least three large lakes in Gros Morne even if the poem had discounted the two nearby bays. Plus, they still didn't understand how the "portal" could be *between* "high water, rock, and whale". Was it underwater: the whale being the deepest part, followed by rock, and then the "high water" which was nearer the surface of the lake or river? It didn't make sense. Plus none of them wanted to face the possibility that it would take a scuba-diver to find it.

Ashley had suggested that the "whale" could mean a lake, the "rock"—cliffs leading up from it, and the "high water" have something to do with rain. Therefore, he reasoned, the "fiery portal" must be somewhere under the open sky at the top of the cliffs. It was a better guess, but they all knew it was a stretch that just didn't seem to fit.

And so as Martin lay in bed that night, looking at the ceiling, he made a decision: he had to speak with Brendan Arthur again. He knew it was risky, and he *wouldn't* let anyone else learn of the existence of the Cross—not after what had happened with the *Old Wolf*. But he knew they had reached a dead-end, and if Dr. Arthur could help them get past that, Martin had to try. He would go on Saturday—the library would be an easy enough excuse and still leave him the whole day. They were close now to the end of their quest and he just needed a last bit of help to solve the mystery.

With that decided, Martin reached for the *Voyage* which lay on his bedside table. He had almost finished it—even if he hadn't managed to read much of it on their trip to St. John's. He had had too much to consider then. But now tucked quietly in his own bed, he pressed on to try to finish the *Voyage*.

* * *

Matthew Penney

It was after three days of sailing south that an island came into view. "Be of good cheer, my Brothers, for our seven year journey is nearly done, and here in this new place, we shall find a holy hermit. His name is Paul the Spiritual and for sixty years now passed, he hasn't eaten any physical food, and was brought food by an animal for thirty years before that!"

Soon they came upon his caves, in which this hermit dwelt, and coming out and greeting them, the hermit called them all by name. The monks marveled to see his prophetic gift and all gave glory to God and wondered at his appearance for he wore no clothes at all. Instead he had a long gray beard and long gray hair to match, and his figure was covered from neck to feet with his own gray body-hair.

And so after exchanging the kiss of peace, when St. Brendan was alone with Paul, he sighed and felt unworthy before this naked ascetic: "Woe is me, a poor sinner, wearing a monastic habit and ruling and leading over many monks while I see a man of angelic condition dwelling in the flesh!" But hearing his thoughts, Paul the Spiritual, replied: "God has also clothed and fed you these last seven years, and who could be more wretched than I who lack even covering."

Then Paul told his story of how St. Patrick had appeared to him and directed him to the island upon which he'd been for these past ninety years. "And God has now kept me alive for 140 years and for what may remain, I will await here in the flesh the day of my judgment before God. And so now travel again for your accustomed feasts of Holy

Voyage to the Rock

Thursday, Pascha, and Pentecost, and God, with the help of your friend on the Isle of Sheep, will lead you to the land you seek, the most holy of all lands—the *Land of the Promise of the Saints*."

*   *   *

Martin didn't remember falling asleep the previous night, but when he awoke in the morning his lamp was still on and the *Voyage of St. Brendan* was resting next to him on the bed. One thought stood out though in his mind as he awoke: *God, with the help of your friend...will lead you to the land you seek*. Martin shook his head; he was starting to see signs everywhere! But could this be the promise of success for his meeting with Dr. Arthur? Martin hoped it would, whatever the correlation between what he had read and Dr. Arthur.

And so it was with high hopes and great expectations that he found himself again at the top of the mountain in *Blow Me Down* National Park. This time he was accompanied by Ashley and Brigid, who had made it clear in no uncertain terms that they too were coming on this second trip. After all, this was *all* their mystery now, and not just Martin's. Reluctantly, Martin had agreed to their coming. But now as the three of them stood on the mountain with no sign of Dr. Arthur, Brigid gave him a rather dissatisfied look. *You wanted to come.* Martin thought, but didn't say anything.

After waiting for a half hour, Martin began to worry. Where would he find Dr. Arthur if not here? What if he was away? Then what would they do?

In the end, the three of them found themselves standing once again at the counter of *Lark's Song Café* asking about Dr. Arthur. The brown-haired Katie smiled to see them back. "Yes B'ys, I knows where you can find Ol' Brendan. His place ain't far from here, sure. Just go back down the road," she said, pointing back the way they'd come, "but turn right onto Little Port Road.

Then follow that for about five minutes and you'll see a dirt road that turns left. Follow that up the hill and on the other side of the bend you'll see Brendan's place. If you hit the water, you went too far, B'ys."

"Thanks, Katie," Brigid said as they turned to leave.

"You tells Ol' Brendan I says hello, would you, and that they'll catch the culprit!" Katie called out to them as they exited the café.

"What do you thinks she means by that, then?" Ashley said, shaking his head.

"I don't know, but it doesn't sound good," Martin said frowning.

Katie was right about her directions and they found the dirt road easily, even if it wasn't so easy to climb the hill on their bikes. With legs burning, they were soon looking down on a small house. It was more like a cottage than a regular house—it being only one storey and made of logs stained a deep brown. They approached the house which stood alone on the hillside of an otherwise grassy expanse interrupted by only a few sparse pine trees growing here and there.

They hesitated a moment. The house looked so rugged—not run-down exactly, but worn by age. "Well," Martin said, "there's no point in waiting here staring." They rode their bikes the rest of the way, then got off and went to the front door.

It was a sturdy wood door but where there had once been a window, there were now planks of wood sealing the opening. Martin looked for a bell. When he didn't find one, he gave a loud knock. They waited, listening. Inside Martin thought he could hear someone stirring and the faint sound of footsteps approaching the door.

"Yes?" he heard Dr. Arthur's voice answer from behind the closed door.

"Dr. Arthur? It's me, Martin," Martin said glancing at Ashley and Brigid, who shrugged their shoulders. "Remember, we met in *Blow Me Down* Park?"

Voyage to the Rock

There was a sound of a padlock being unlocked, and then the door opened to reveal Brendan Arthur. "Well," he said. "Back again, eh? And with some friends?"

"Yes sir. My sister Brigid and our friend Ashley."

"More questions?" he asked with a small huff and a knowing look.

Martin rubbed a hand through his hair and nodded.

"Come on then," Dr. Arthur said, gesturing them in. "Can I offer you something to drink?"

"Water would be fine," Martin said on behalf of them all.

"Water it is then," he said as he led them through a hallway cluttered with books, sheets of paper stacked on the floor, and other odds and ends. "You can take a seat in here," he said as they entered a bright living room which also seemed to function as a study by the looks of a desk to one side piled with more books and papers.

Martin sat down on a chair and Brigid and Ashley on the couch. He looked at the large bookcases with their many sized books. *The house of a scholar*, Martin thought. Yet, it was rugged as well, as if a fisherman also lived there. It had paintings of sailors and waterscapes, pieces of carved driftwood, and a mantle holding rocks, seashells, complete with a ship in a bottle.

"So what was so important," Dr. Arthur said as he entered the room carrying a tray with three glasses of water and a plate of cookies, "that you needed to come all the way back here from Corner Brook?" He laid the tray on the coffee table in front of the couch, and took his own mug and a cookie. He sat in a large armchair across from them. They took their water and a cookie each. As agreed, Martin would do the talking.

"Well...," he hesitated. "We didn't really know where else to turn. You see, we've being working on the mystery."

"St. Brendan's mystery?" Dr. Arthur said, his face darkening.

"Yes sir," Martin said, glancing at Dr. Arthur and then quickly looking down.

"I thought I told you to forget about all that, didn't I?" Dr. Arthur said.

"Well... yes, but..."

"But you couldn't just *forget* about it," Dr. Arthur finished the sentence for him, and his tone softened.

"Yeah," Martin said slowly unclenching fists that he hadn't realized he'd balled up.

"Well, I guess I can understand that," Dr. Arthur said with a sigh, "having a bit of experience with this business me self."

"It's just that we think we've figured out more of the poem," Martin said, gaining some courage. "And... something that you may have gotten wrong."

"I suspect there's lots I got wrong, me Son," Dr. Arthur said. "But you obviously have something particular in mind, so you might as well let me know."

"That part about 'hailing' before the Cross," Martin said. He shifted somewhat in the large chair. "We think you made a mistake because you made the sign of the cross backwards."

"What do you mean by that, then?" Dr. Arthur asked, his brow knotting.

"Remember how I told you my family is Orthodox?" The man nodded. "Well, we make the sign of the cross the way they did in the past: forehead, stomach, *right* then left. I've heard my dad answer why we Orthodox make our cross *backwards* about a hundred times. Western Christians changed some time after the 11th century," Martin said, with Brigid nodding slowly in confirmation.

As the words left Martin's mouth, the truth of what Martin was saying clearly dawned on Dr. Arthur: "Not in the east, in the west!" A pained expression came to his face: "We were wrong the whole time then," slowly running his fingers through his fuzzy beard. "No wonder we could never find anything..." He trailed off; his eyes were staring off, empty.

There was silence. None of them knew what to say. Only Martin understood what Dr. Arthur's pained look truly meant: his wife's death. He still hadn't been able to bring himself to tell the others—he just didn't know how.

Voyage to the Rock

Martin broke the silence. "We think it's somewhere in Gros Morne National Park."

"Yes," Dr. Arthur said, eyes still distant. "That would be about the right spot, I'd guess." But then he paused as if coming back to the present situation and seeing again the three of them sitting in his living room. "No! This is foolishness."

"What do you mean 'foolishness?'" Martin had to keep from raising his voice. "We just told you, we found out it's in Gros Morne."

"And how do you know you're right?" Dr. Arthur looked at him with an intensity that hadn't been there before. "How do you know you're not just chasing after fantasies and dreams, eh? And what are you willing to risk for something that may not even exist? Your life?" he asked, staring hard at Martin. "The life of your family and friends?" He pointed at Brigid and Ashley on the couch.

Martin shot a glance at a confused Brigid and Ashley.

"I told you it was *dangerous*. And you're just kids. You don't have any idea what you're getting yourselves into!" Dr. Arthur looked from the confused faces of Brigid and Ashley back to Martin. He shook his head and gave Martin a look like... well, a look like Martin's father had given him the day Martin learned they were moving to Newfoundland.

"You didn't tell them, did you?" Dr. Arthur's question was clearly a statement.

"Tell us what?" Brigid said, sitting up straighter. There was a tightness to the set of her jaw.

"You didn't even pass on the warning I gave to you, eh?" Dr. Arthur said as he shook his head and leaned back into his armchair.

"What *warning*, Martin? What didn't you tell us?" Brigid's face was flushed a hot pink. Ashley wouldn't make eye contact with Martin and wore a flat expression.

Martin felt himself wilting under the heat of Brigid's question; his mouth had gone dry.

"About that *Old Wolf*, Sullivan O'Connell," Dr. Arthur said as he crossed his arms on his chest. "About all the dangerous things that started to happen to me and...." He stopped himself sharply before going on. "All the sabotage and *accidents* that started happening when my wife and I were chasing this mystery fifteen years ago. I warned Martin, here, to stay as far away from O'Connell and this search as possible," Dr. Arthur said with a cool, level voice that was more intimidating than if he'd been shouting.

"You *knew* that Sullivan O'Connell was dangerous and you didn't tell us!" Brigid was leaning so far forward toward Martin it seemed as though she were going to leap for him. "You put us all in danger and didn't even *warn* us beforehand!"

"Look, Brigid, we already knew he was a thief and bad news. I didn't want to worry you guys." Martin was trying to calm his sister, but she didn't even hear his excuses.

"You let us go to his antique store and we were almost..." she abruptly cut-off, catching herself before finishing her sentence. She glanced at Dr. Arthur and then looked away.

"Ah," said Dr. Arthur raising his hands and then pointing at them. "So you're the reason I had my house broken into and my stuff taken."

"What?" Martin said almost jumping up. "No, we had nothing to do with anything like that. I swear we didn't!"

"He's telling the truth, he is, sir!" Ashley spoke for the first time, with Brigid still red in the face but nodding.

"Oh I knows you didn't do it, nor even know of it, but you three *caused* it," Dr. Arthur said. When they looked confused, he went on. "My house was broken into two days ago. Nothing valuable taken. Just some broken drawers," he said gesturing to a chest of drawers near Martin's chair that had clearly been forced open and the wood splintered near the locks, "and my notebook taken."

"A notebook and broken drawers? I don't understand," Martin said.

Voyage to the Rock

"That notebook contained all of my notes on my search for St. Brendan's campsite. It had all my maps, all my clues, and all my knowledge as to the whereabouts of the site. Now I thinks it would be a pretty big coincidence that you three fools," Dr. Arthur made a sweeping gesture over them, "were clearly poking your noses around O'Connell's store, and suddenly after fifteen years of peace, I gets a visit from someone who only cares about a worthless old notebook that just happens to do with St. Brendan and this mystery."

The three of them looked at one another and then looked back to Dr. Arthur who sat waiting with his coffee mug now in hand. What were they going to do? This had gone much further than Martin had intended. Would Dr. Arthur go to the police? Would the police start asking questions that led them to Martin and the Cross? If the police showed up at O'Connell's shop would he suddenly forget his aversion and give the description of Martin and the "stolen" artifact? What should he say now? Dr. Arthur spoke and solved his dilemma.

"And how do you know O'Connell is a *thief*?" There was a brief pause in which no one spoke. Dr. Arthur just stared—a wise old fisherman, waiting.

"Show him, Martin," Brigid finally said. Martin hesitated. "Show him now! He deserves to know—especially after having his house broken into."

"Show me what?" Dr. Arthur's eyes narrowed.

Martin looked helplessly at Ashley who only gave him a small, firm, nod. Martin sighed. That was that, then. He reached into his backpack which sat on the floor near his chair and pulled out the Cross. "This," he said, displaying it in his hand.

Dr. Arthur's face grew pale and his eyes wide as he laid his mug on the table. He reached forward for the Cross and Martin couldn't even hesitate before it was taken from him. Dr. Arthur held it as carefully as if he had received a baby from Martin's arms; his eyes were transfixed on it as it shone dully in the afternoon light.

What's that on the back of the Cross? Martin thought it looked scratched. Had O'Connell scratched it somehow? The thought of damage on the back of the Cross was scattered by Dr. Arthur's voice.

"Where did you find this? How...?" he trailed off.

"At L'Anse aux Meadows," Martin said simply. There was no use in holding back anymore. "At the bottom of a mostly-dry stream during low-tide, somewhere between the Viking settlement and the coast. Of course, it didn't look quite like this when I found it."

"It is *amazing*," Dr. Arthur said as he began to gently trace his finger over the interwoven knots that covered the Cross. "I just can't believe that you found it. It's...it's simply a miracle!"

"So you can tell it's genuine, too, huh?" Martin said.

"Tell? It's almost an exact copy of some of the most famous examples of Celtic religious art. The Christ himself looks almost to be an exact replica of the 'Christ Enthroned' from the *Book of Kells*," Dr. Arthur said, an awed smile spread across his face. "Though, I dare say, this would be the original and that a replica based on how much older this Cross must be. Exquisite! Well," said Dr. Arthur glancing up at them, "I guess I understand what made the *Old Wolf* desperate enough to try breaking into my little place seeking for answers. If he's seen this, he'll be more desperate than ever to find St. Brendan's 'heavenly room' and the 'shining gift' it contains. This Cross is the proof that his searching has not been in vain." He paused, staring at the Cross, "Nor mine."

"The *Old Wolf*, he stole it from Martin, Dr. Arthur," Ashley said perking up. "We didn't mean to cause no problems; we just wanted to get back what belonged to him."

"I'm not sure I'd be saying the Cross *belonged* to anyone, but if you found it after 1500 years, me Son," Dr. Arthur said, looking at Martin, "then I'd say St. Brendan must have wanted you to find it. *Christ's new children from afar*, eh? And so this explains why O'Connell took my book: to try to piece together my clues and whatever he may have learned from this here

Voyage to the Rock

Cross—*if* he learned anything other than that there is indeed a treasure to be found." Dr. Arthur had stood and carried the Cross over to the large window to hold it more directly into the light. "But that'll be enough to drive him on."

"There's more, Dr. Arthur. Look," Martin said, and pulled out the book with the manuscript page. He laid the book on the table. "Put the Cross over the poem." Dr. Arthur hesitated a moment and then did it. "Do you see it?" Martin traced his finger just as Ashley had done a few days previous to show the outline of Newfoundland that was formed.

Dr. Arthur's eyes widened.

"That's not all," Martin said as he traced his finger to lead to the red gem at Christ's side. "Here. *The Fiery Portal shows the way.*"

"By goodness, B'ys!" Dr. Arthur said, falling into his chair again and reaching for his pipe on the table next to him.

"We just need to know what *Between high water, rock, and whale* means so that we can figure out where precisely to look!" Martin said, looking intently at Dr. Arthur who was already stuffing the pipe with tobacco.

Dr. Arthur answered without a pause, still staring at the Cross: "On the cliff face."

"What?" Martin said from where he knelt next to the coffee table. "What do you mean?"

"The whale is a lake, the rock, a cave, where the site must be," Dr. Arthur said absently as he patted his breast pocket searching for his matches, "and the high water is one of the lakes that gather on the sprawling plateaus at the top of the cliffs. We were sure of it." He finally found the matches and struck one, puffing fiercely to get the tobacco lit.

"You were right, Ashley!" Brigid said beaming and pulling on his arm. Then she blushed at her own over-exuberance. Looking away she said more calmly, "Mostly right, anyway."

Ashley smiled at her.

"But which lake, Dr. Arthur?" Martin pressed.

Dr. Arthur still seemed somewhere else as plumes of smoke rose from his pipe and nostrils. "Western Brook Pond, it seems to me from that there ruby," he pointed with the end of his pipe at the Cross on the manuscript, but only glanced at it as if afraid to stare directly again after he'd finally broken his stare. "Makes the most sense, as well. Close to the coast but not on it, the largest lake, 2,000-foot-high cliffs, lakes that run off the plateau sending waterfalls sprawling down into the pond. That'd be my guess." Dr. Arthur took another long haul on his pipe stem; he was still a little pale.

Martin leaned forward more. He knew he had to press Dr. Arthur for more information: "But where? What cave?"

"The waterfall near Hopper's Pond maybe—one of the biggest lakes that feed a waterfall into Western Brook Pond." Dr. Arthur was staring off, as though his words weren't connected to his thoughts. "As to a cave, don't remember ever having seen one—not one visible from Western Brook Pond anyhow. I just don't know."

This was *perfect*! Martin had a location.

Then Dr. Arthur looked at the Cross and then at the three of them sitting in the room with him. "I'm at it *again*!" He brought a fist down hard onto the arm of his chair.

"At what again?" Brigid asked, a hand nervously gripping her braid.

"At this *fool-hardy* search!" the old man said. "Nothing good can come of all this. Not if Sullivan O'Connell has seen *this*!" he said raising the Cross. "He won't stop. He's a wolf on the hunt if ever I saw one!" Dr. Arthur closed his eyes and began to rub his temples, pipe still trailing sweet smoke. "But how to keep you safe now, that's the question, now that he knows you have it?"

"Is he *really* that dangerous?" Brigid asked, voice becoming urgent.

"Yes, he's *really* that dangerous, I'm afraid," Dr. Arthur said, opening his eyes and letting his hands drop. "And unlucky for you three, he seems to have a rather strong *aversion* to police. Most likely O'Connell doesn't want them snooping around and

Voyage to the Rock

finding out any of his past secrets," Dr. Arthur said, taking his pipe in one hand, "of which he has many, I might add, from the little I was able to discover. But I dare say Martin must have had some knowledge of this *aversion* or he likely wouldn't have gone after the Cross in the first place, eh?"

Martin's blush was answer enough for all of them.

Brigid scowled at Martin but then turned back to Dr. Arthur. "You said 'unlucky' a second ago? Don't you mean 'lucky?'"

"No, I means *unlucky*," he said emphatically. "If O'Connell had called the police, you'd have been in trouble, but you'd be *safe*. But now O'Connell wants this here Cross, and he wants it without any questions being asked about where he got it. So things are *real* dangerous for you three now."

Dr. Arthur paused as if considering and then continued, "But *lucky* for you, I've already thought of a way for you to save yourselves from this here mess."

"And what's that?" Brigid asked.

"You get rid of the Cross," Dr. Arthur replied.

"No," Martin said. "We can't just throw it away!"

"I didn't say *throw it away*, me Son." Dr. Arthur looked disgusted by the thought. "I said *get rid of* it. And the safest and quickest way is to tell your parents and have them tell the folks up at L'Anse aux Meadows what you've found. From there it'll be a *big* news story and you can confess how you found the Cross. They'll even likely overlook the fact that you didn't mention it to anyone seeing as you did find it at the bottom of a stream. But either way, Sullivan O'Connell certainly won't be able to go after you then, nor do I even thinks he'd risk trying to get back at you for what you did. It'll all be too public for his liking."

Dr. Arthur suddenly smiled broadly.

"What?" Brigid asked.

"Well, when you all tell everyone how *gracious* he was to examine and clean it for you before your big announcement, he'll be up to his ears in journalists." Dr. Arthur barked a laugh at the thought and slapped a thigh with his free hand. "Yes, that'll suit that *Old Wolf* just fine, and keep you all plenty safe!"

Martin's heart sunk. Even the news that he likely wouldn't get in trouble for having taken the Cross in the first place didn't cheer him up. This was *his* quest, *his* journey! How could he just abandon it right at the doorstep, when he was so close?

Dr. Arthur read his mind: "Tell your parents, me Son! There's no more time to be fooling around."

Brigid and Ashley both looked as dejected as he felt. Give it up when they now knew the likely location? "But if we just had a little while longer *before* we told everyone..." Martin said, shaggy hair hanging into his eyes.

"No. Now!" Dr. Arthur said with a touch of anger finally entering his voice. "Let me ask you a question: Have you been to St. John's recently?"

"How did you know that?" It was Brigid who spoke.

Dr. Arthur turned to her: "I thought so. You know what I did when I found out my place was robbed and my notebook gone? Hmmm? I went to pay a very discreet visit to Corner Brook to ask a few questions about Mr. O'Connell. Just as I'd suspected, Mr. O'Connell was 'away' for two weeks. And as I was able to discover, someone had overheard that brute of his, Duffy, mention something about St. John's for business."

All three of them turned pale. He was searching for them. But how did the *Old Wolf* know? Had he discovered who they were? Who would have told him about St. John's?

At least Jenny would be safe, Martin sighed inwardly, and noticed a similar sense of relief on the faces of Brigid and Ashley whose minds must have been running through the same thoughts as his. Thankfully Jenny had been booked to leave the same day they did on her trip to visit family in New Hampshire for three weeks.

I wish I never stepped into Sullivan O'Connell's shop! He wanted to say, that he'd never found the Cross, but couldn't bring himself to.

Voyage to the Rock

"So I can tell by your faces you're starting to catch on," Dr. Arthur said. His face had turned dark again. "Well, if you're not convinced yet, let me share with you one more piece of information that should convince you: that *evil* man had my wife killed... and tried to kill me."

Brigid gasped, and Ashley's mouth hung open. Martin just sat there feeling the weight of it all crushing down on him. When he had read it in an old newspaper he had been able to distance himself from it, to convince himself it didn't affect *his* search. But now, sitting in the same room as this man who had suffered so much, it was different.

Tears were in Brigid's eyes. "We're so sorry to hear that, Dr. Arthur," Brigid said barely above a whisper, "if we had known, we never would have bothered you with all this. Please forgive us!"

"I'm sure you wouldn't have, me Ducky," Dr. Arthur said with a real affection in his voice. "Just make up for it by keeping yourselves safe."

Martin felt a wave of anger flow through him. Why was everything so messed up? He just wanted to solve the mystery of a Cross he'd found forgotten and buried. And now look where they were: slammed up against a brick wall right when they were expecting to walk out of the maze. Ever since he'd gone to Sullivan O'Connell things had just gone from bad to worse. O'Connell really was a wolf—one who liked to prey on the innocent!

Well, Martin knew one thing for certain: he *wouldn't* let the *Old Wolf* find St. Brendan's treasure. He wouldn't.

Chapter 21:
Hard On the Trail

"Are you crazy, Martin!" Brigid said. Her face was bright red. "Didn't you hear a word Dr. Arthur said? They *killed* his wife. He *knows* about us. He's *looking* for us. We *have* to turn the Cross in. Tell him, Ashley!" she said turning to him while strangling her blond braid.

"I likes adventure and danger as much as the next B'y, Martin," Ashley said shaking his head. "But like my pops says: 'a small boat in a rough sea is more likely to end up sunk than back in the harbor.'" He shrugged broad shoulders. "I thinks Brigid's right."

"Oh you do, do you?" Martin said, fists clenching. "And you, Brigid," he stabbed a finger at her, "so now that *you* decide it's time to quit, we just quit?" Martin turned and began to stalk back to where they had left their bikes near the rest-stop sign. After two steps he spun around. "What about the poem, huh? What about the prophecies in it about us: *But another comes to find the Cross* and *To God's new children from afar / Ol' Brendan awaits his gifts to give?*" Even Dr. Arthur mentioned this last one being about us!" Martin threw up his hands. "Are we just going to forget about all of that, just hand this over to the Old Wolf?"

"No one's talking about giving the Cross to Sullivan O'Connell, Martin!" Brigid snapped. "We'll do what Dr. Arthur said and contact L'Anse aux Meadows. Then we can lead *them* to the treasure."

Martin chuckled. "And you really think that they're going to believe us about some treasure? A bunch of teenagers?"

"And Dr. Arthur!" Brigid said.

Voyage to the Rock

"Oh that's right, the sad, old man, off on a wild goose chase to find St. Brendan!" Martin said. He spat his words. "You know, no one believed him about O'Connell. They just said he *lost* it—had a nervous break-down—and saw things that weren't there! He even lost his job as a history professor from the university!" Martin was actually shouting, careless of who might hear. "They aren't going to believe him any more than us—maybe less!"

"You *knew?*" Brigid said, taking a half-step toward him. "You *knew* what happened to his wife and didn't *tell* us?" Her face would have sent pit bulls scampering away.

Martin didn't mean to let *that* slip; but maybe it was for the best anyway! "Yeah, I knew," Martin shouted. "But would telling have made a difference?"

"Yes!" Brigid's eyes were nearly popped from her head. "We wouldn't have gone along with your *ridiculous* plan!"

"*Exactly!* You wouldn't have done *anything!*" Martin said getting in Brigid's face. "And Sullivan O'Connell would have killed Susan Arthur, ruined Brendan, stolen the Cross, and then found St. Brendan's treasure, and likely *sold* it for millions! Would that have been a *better* plan?" Martin said, his heart beating a drum in his chest.

Brigid didn't shy away in the least, but did say, "Well, no! But you lied and manipulated us. You should have *trusted* us." She was again tugging on her braid. "But that's just like you, isn't it? Martin, the Center of the World; Martin, the only one whose opinion counts!" Brigid said beginning to yell herself. "You never think about anyone but yourself. You never care about how other people might feel, do you?"

Martin was caught off guard by this, but his eyes grew fiery.

"You just don't get it, Martin," Brigid said lowering her voice and shaking her head, her face twisted as if she'd eaten something sour. She stared him down. "You think you're so smart, think that you can always manipulate people to get what you want. Do you think we don't notice? Do you think we're stupid?" Brigid said taking a step forward. "That *I'm* stupid? I know that you've been trying to manipulate me, Martin." She gave him an ironic smile. "I did things I knew were stupid—were *wrong*, even—because I liked the Martin searching for the Cross more than Martin the selfish cry-baby!" Brigid turned to walk away and then turned back immediately.

"And you know what gets me the most, Martin? You think you know people so well and that you can manipulate them to get your own way, and you're totally clueless to what's really going on with them."

"What do you mean by that?" Martin was finally able to speak through his anger, though the blood was pounding in his ears.

"Dad, for instance," Brigid said.

"What about him?" Martin said, brow in a knot.

"See, you're not even aware," Brigid shook her head with a look halfway between pity and disgust. "Don't you see the way he tip-toes around you? The way he wants to do anything to make you like Newfoundland? To make it up to you?"

"You don't know what you're talking about," Martin said, folding his arms on his chest. But Martin had the sinking feeling she *did* know what she was talking about.

"Why do you think he's let you get away with being such a rude jerk so often? Why do you think he's always silently watching you out of the corner of his eye?" It was Brigid's turn to cross her arms on her chest. "He feels terrible, torn between following his *dream*—something so important to him and to others—and letting down his son! It's killing him, and you," she said jabbing a finger at him, "won't budge an inch for him."

Martin knew that if his face wasn't already red with anger at that moment, he would have turned red with shame. He glanced at Ashley, who just stood by scuffing his sneaker on the ground.

Was Brigid right? Was this what all his father's strange behavior had been about? About his feeling guilty for choosing his *dream* over Martin's comfort? Could that really be it? Martin knew it was.

Voyage to the Rock

"Well, congratulations, Martin. You got your way again. We listened to you; we helped you, and your plans worked without getting anyone killed," Brigid took a step back and glanced at Ashley. "Can we go?" Ashley began to follow her as she walked past Martin.

"Listen, Brigid. You're right," Martin said, turning to speak to her as she kept walking. "About everything! Please, Brigid. Wait." Brigid's shoulders slumped as she let out a deep breath while turning back. "The point is I knew O'Connell wasn't about to do anything to us. At most he would have caught me and handed me over to the police—caught in the act of stealing. No one was going to *die*! I wouldn't have put you guys in that kind of danger." Some of the fire returned to his words. "I do think these things over a little bit beforehand."

It was Ashley who spoke up. "Alright, B'y."

He came right over and pointed a finger at Martin, raising emphatic eyebrows. "But from now on, you 'think these things over' with all of us. Got that?" Ashley was actually somewhat imposing.

Brigid, still flushed, smiled. She raised eyebrows at Martin when he hesitated.

"Agreed." Martin sighed. "Now, about finding the site?"

"Martin, we haven't even *agreed* that we should keep the Cross!" Brigid said. "Besides, eventually, they'll have to believe us about a treasure, with all the proof we have."

"Alright Brigid, can we deal with this once and for all?" He waited. When they both nodded he said, "If we give them the Cross—a fifteen hundred year old relic from ancient Ireland, an artifact from St. Brendan himself, do you really think they'll let it out of their sight ever again? Do you really think they'll risk using it as a 'key' like the poem says? And," Martin brushed hair out of his face, "even if they were willing, how long do you think it will take for us to convince them, for them to research it all themselves and then for them to get the government approval and money to even *begin* the search?" He paused to let his words sink in. "When they finally arrive at the site there won't be anything *left* for them to find."

"And why's that?" Brigid said, tight-lipped.

"Because the Old Wolf will already have gotten there," Martin said. "He's seen the Cross, he has Brendan Arthur's notebook, he knows of the poem and manuscript, and we can't just count on him not having figured out the 'fiery portal' or the sign of the cross. If we could figure it out, so could he. Even if he doesn't know for *certain*, he'll have plenty of time to search Gros Morne—and there aren't that many lakes that fit all the clues. Sure he needs the Cross—it's the key—and maybe that's why he isn't already there searching Gros Morne. But that won't stop him once he knows the Cross is out of his reach *for good*."

Martin could see they understood now what he was saying. "It's either we find it or he does. Simple as that. And after everything he's done—forget whether St. Brendan was actually *prophesying* us doing this—after everything the Old Wolf's done, it would be just wrong to let him get his hands on it. Not to mention because of what he did to Susan Arthur."

Martin took a deep breath and wanted to knock his head on the biggest tree he could find for what he was about to say. Maybe Brigid's words had shaken him up more than he thought. He looked intently at them both. "I agreed that we'd decide together from now on, and I'll stick to that. You know everything that I do now: you know the danger; you know what's at stake. As I see it we have at least a week before O'Connell is back, based on what Dr. Arthur said. That's a week of safety. If we can't find it by the end of the week, then I'll willingly admit defeat and turn the Cross in. But it's up to you two. If you decide it stops here, it stops." He stuffed his hands into his jean pockets. "You know my vote, though."

He began to walk back toward the bikes as he heard Brigid and Ashley begin to talk quietly behind him. Martin looked across the road from the front of the rest-stop down to the flowing Humber River. Time seemed to stretch an eternity. And then a voice spoke from behind him.

Voyage to the Rock

"Okay. I'm in—for Brendan and Susan Arthur," Brigid said, peaking around one of Martin's shoulders.

"Me, too, B'y," Ashley said as he came up. "For St. Brendan."

Martin let out the breath he'd been holding and smiled.

"We have one week then," Martin said never taking his eyes from the blue water, "and I have a plan!"

*   *   *

"Anyone want to break for water and some trail-mix?" Fr. Gregory asked.

Martin, Brigid, and Ashley all nodded, red-faced and breathing heavily. They sat down on one of the large rock areas that covered the landscape before them. The four of them had just finished the hike out of the tree-filled gorge that led to the plateau that they had now entered. There weren't much for trees up here—only plenty of tuckamores and scrub bushes, as well as large sections of short green grass that grew among the rocks. There were lots of rocks.

"Here Martin," Fr. Gregory said as he handed Martin the bag of trail-mix.

"Thanks," Martin said, taking a handful before passing it to Ashley. Martin leaned back against his pack propped up behind him. His plan had worked perfectly. They had found out everything about this trail—The Hopper Trail—and had quickly worked to convince their father to take the three of them. It had helped that Martin had all the information ready about it, and that he knew his father *loved* any chance to go hiking.

He had had to work fast though, having only a week. He had persuaded his father to take time away from the Church in order to bring them this week since his mother had to be in Halifax for two days taking care of his grandmother after knee surgery anyway. The timing couldn't have been better. Maybe some things *could* actually work smoothly! So his father had agreed to let them try out this new hiking trail.

Martin still marveled and thanked St. Brendan that this trail even *existed*. He had initially discovered to his great horror that the only hiking trail that led anywhere near Western Brook Pond was the Long Range Trail—an expert hike through unmarked backcountry! He had thought everything was over. And then—like another miracle—he had discovered this new trail only opened *this* summer. Even Ashley had whistled when he heard of their *good luck*; Brigid had done a dance on the spot.

Now they had three days to make it to Hopper's Pond—the largest lake on the plateau above Western Brook Pond. Apparently, there was even a large waterfall that fell from it which could be seen from the Western Brook Pond tour-boat. It was that same boat that they needed to catch by 5pm on their final day so that they could leave from the trail-end. *But not before I search the cliffs near Hopper's Pond!*

They still didn't know what they would tell Martin's father when they got there. They just hoped they might figure out something by the time they arrived at the cave... or site... or whatever they might find. Since this was their one and only shot, they couldn't worry about that *minor* detail.

Besides, they still didn't know how the Cross was "the key" to the "heavenly room". Was there some sort of door-lock that he would just stick the Cross into and turn? It seemed foolish, but he couldn't imagine what else he might find; that was the problem really eating at him. Still, he was in Gros Morne, and *very* close now.

"I've got to tell you, you guys," Fr. Gregory said as he stood back up looking out over the gorge and the large lake, "this was a *great* idea. Look at how magnificent it is! I forgot just how wonderful it is up here." He turned to them, "You know I was about your age Martin when I first hiked up in this area with your grandfather? He was a real woodsman, though. No trail like this for him—just a map, a compass, and miles of backcountry." He took a deep breath of fresh air. "It's good to be back here."

Martin and the others reached for their packs and pulled them on, Ashley helping Brigid with hers. Martin was glad his

Voyage to the Rock

dad felt so good about the trip—it made his conscience feel a bit better about everything. He didn't *want* to keep his father in the dark; he just couldn't risk letting him in on it—not yet, at least, and not until he absolutely had to.

Martin led the way down the easily visible trail and could hear his father from behind him as they began to walk: "Have these two ever told you, Ashley, about the giant bull moose I saw while hiking here as a teenager?" Martin didn't hear Ashley's answer, but he did hear his father say: "They *didn't*! And I bet they never mentioned the herd of caribou I encountered either?" *Caribou?* Even Martin hadn't heard that one.

But Martin had no desire to hear about it right then; what he wanted was to get to Western Brook Pond, and to get there having solved the last two puzzles of his poem: the Cross as "key", and the most mysterious one yet, *Recall: the first, the last shall be/ And know the same when Crosses bloom.* What in the world did it mean? The first part was definitely a reference to Jesus' teaching in the Bible that the "last shall be first, and the first shall be last", but why did he need to "recall" that when *Crosses bloom*? And when *did* a cross *bloom*? What did it mean?

This puzzle, and all of the other clues combined, filled Martin's head as he hiked that day. But by the time he finally laid his head down on his makeshift pillow, exhausted, he didn't feel any closer to an answer. *But at least we're on the last leg of our journey*, he thought, and then snuggling up in his sleeping bag in their large tent, he fell asleep.

* * *

And so with many blessings they departed to the Isle of Sheep and found there as was usual their host with the readied feast. But this time when it was the hour to depart for the usual Pascha feast, their friend also came with them, to the back of Lasconius.

Now to add to the wonders of their final trip, when the Liturgy of Pascha was celebrated, Lasconius himself, with all of the Fathers upon him, swam to the Island of the Paradise of Birds and landed them all unharmed. After their time had passed from Pentecost and the eight days that followed that feast, their friend told them to ready the boat: "For I will be your companion and will lead you from here to the end of your journey that you've so long awaited—to the *Land of the Promise of the Saints*, which without me it would be impossible for you to find."

And so they set their course and headed their way until they were overshadowed by a misty darkness. "Do you know, Father-Abbot, what this darkness is? It's the mist that surrounds the island that you've sought for these last seven years. You will soon see it is the entrance to it."

Chapter 22:
Searching through Shadows

Martin awoke to the sound of the tent zipper. He opened his eyes to see his father dressed and slipping out with the small camp-stove in hand. Martin stretched and then sat up in his sleeping bag. His muscles were tight and his back ached slightly from a rock that had insisted on being a part of his bed last night. But otherwise he was refreshed and ready to go.

In a few minutes they were all up and getting ready. Martin and Ashley stepped out into the crisp morning air while Brigid quickly dressed. The day was clear and the sun reflected off the crystal clear pond that lay not ten feet away. From the cloudless blue sky above it was clear that it would be another perfect day for hiking. The rocky and grass-covered hills before them rose and dipped so that even the trail just a short distance away disappeared and re-appeared amidst them. At least the hills weren't too steep during the section they would be hiking this morning.

Martin looked over as Brigid emerged from the tent, rolled sleeping bag under her arm. After Ashley had dressed, Martin did the same. They each laid down their things before grabbing a bowl of oatmeal from Fr. Gregory. Thirty minutes later they had everything packed and were underway again.

The morning couldn't have gone more smoothly or more pleasantly. This section of the trail had provided some spectacular views of lakes and mountains, and they could even see all the way to the ocean in the distance. They were also not alone on the trail: they saw a little red fox, a few gray arctic hares, and even two caribou on a distant hill. Martin could see that they would soon be coming to one of the forested sections of stunted evergreen trees.

It was at this point that something happened which started a small nagging itch between Martin's shoulder blades. It had been just after they had passed over a rather steep rocky bald, making their descent towards the bit of forest in the distance. Martin still couldn't be sure it was anything more than a trick of the sun, but just as he had been about to descend the hill, his boot lace had caught on a scrub bush. He bent to unhook it from the gnarled plant and happened to glance back. In the far distance, near the top of a rocky hill, Martin could have sworn he caught sight of the silhouette of a man's head and shoulders. But by the time he had shielded his eyes from the sun, whatever may have been there was gone.

Another animal was his first thought. Were there *other* hikers out here? Martin didn't know what to think, and so he tried not to let it worry him.

For the next hour before they stopped for lunch, he hadn't been able to keep himself from periodically looking back over his shoulder. But he never saw anything else. Even so, Martin had to force away the uncomfortable feeling of being followed.

But then it happened again. It was after they had stopped for lunch and just before entering the small forested area. The others were already into the woods when Martin shot a parting glance back at the distant hills. He saw a form in the far distance which suddenly disappeared—as if ducking down. He *still* couldn't say for certain whether it was a man, but he now felt a sudden surge of urgency. He waited a few moments. Would it reappear? Stillness. He saw nothing. He had to catch the others who were now calling to him. He paused a final moment before dashing off to catch up.

"Anything wrong?" Fr. Gregory asked when he arrived. Martin saw a look of momentary anxiety on the faces of both Ashley and Brigid over his dad's shoulder.

Voyage to the Rock

"Nothing. I just thought I saw another caribou in the distance. Let's keep going!" Martin passed them as he said it, and started to set a good pace.

He tried to push them as quickly as he could without arousing suspicion. He was spurred on both by his anxiety for what might lay behind them and his excitement for what lay ahead. He led them through sections of trees, through large open areas, and then back through trees, occasionally glimpsing lakes along the way.

The further they walked, the more his anxiety moved to the back of his mind and the puzzle of the poem came to the fore. It filled his thoughts as Martin walked on silently, the voices of his father or Brigid occasionally breaking the stillness as they talked and laughed. Martin was just far enough ahead that he couldn't quite make out what they were saying.

To see the Cross as saving key / To guide one to the heavenly room. He thought he may have discovered something new about that line. He wasn't sure, but it had occurred to him that this "key" did not say that it *opened* the "heavenly room," but rather it said it would "guide" one there. He didn't know what that meant, but it made the problem of the Cross as some oversized key for a mysterious door vanish. That said, it didn't offer much of a clue for an alternative understanding. How would the Cross be a "key" to *lead* him to where he wanted to go? This didn't make any more sense to him. It held more closely to the literal sense of the words, but what did it mean?

Martin looked around suddenly. The path ended abruptly near a large evergreen tree. "What?" Martin looked side to side confused.

"Hey, Mart!" Fr. Gregory called from behind him. Martin turned around to see his father, Ashley, and Brigid. "You've turned down the wrong path. That's an animal trail!" Fr. Gregory said.

Martin looked down. The trail was thin and not nicely cleared like the Hopper trail. He had been so caught up in trying to figure out the poem that he hadn't noticed how the path veered sharply to the left. He would need to be *much* more observant if he was going to find St. Brendan's camp! *If only I could solve the poem, then I could put my full attention on getting to the campsite.*

"It's alright, Martin. You've been too long at the helm anyhow. It's time to reverse the order for a while," his father said chuckling. "Besides, don't forget that 'the last shall be first, and the first shall be last!'" With that he turned to the left, disappearing along the trail with the others.

Something clicked inside Martin. His father's words had struck like a hammer and he understood. If he hadn't just been puzzling over these lines he may not have seen it. But he *understood!* For the Cross to be seen as a "saving key" which would "guide" him to the "heavenly room" he needed to *recall: the first, the last shall be;* he needed to *reverse* it for it to become the "key" to "guide" him!

Martin didn't waste a minute but quickly reached into his pack and into another little black bag. He quickly unzipped the zipper and pulled the Cross out. Taking it he reversed it, so that instead of a Cross he had it upside down like holding a sword. He held it out trying to notice some new pattern in the weaves, some new answer. He didn't see anything new. Martin adjusted it in his hands, trying to examine the weaves from a different angle. Nothing.

He sighed. He was truly at a dead-end.

Martin picked up the little black bag to put the Cross back in. Just as he was putting it in something caught his eye. Scratches on the back of the Cross—the ones he'd glimpsed at Brendan Arthur's? He'd totally forgotten about them! He flipped the Cross over and to his amazement saw that the markings weren't *scratches* at all. They were faint and roughly carved—without any of the grace and beauty of the carvings on the front of the Cross, but they certainly weren't just some damage done through age or cleaning. This was a clue.

Martin stared at the carving on the back, and then held it farther away from himself. He let his eyes go out of focus a bit.

Voyage to the Rock

The "scratches" looked very similar to the sort of short twiggy bushes he'd been walking by all day. In fact, it was like the one he'd caught his boot lace on earlier, just before he'd seen the silhouette on the hill. But the carved one in his hands had a lone ridged-circle—a single flower on an otherwise empty bush: *when Crosses bloom*. This had to be the answer!

In the middle of the back of the Cross was a single line which started at the base of the Cross and led upward. From it he saw other lines branching off upwards and diagonally from the original line. Some of these were short, and some longer, but the main line continued to climb and curve a little as it did. Then this line stopped with one line leading right and branching off into many smaller ones, and another line to the left, which again branched into three. At the end of the rightmost of the three, there appeared to be some kind of ridged circle.

The Cross was a "key" because it was a *map*. It was a map to "guide" him to the "heavenly room." He had done it. He had figured it out!

Despite his exuberance at the discovery, he couldn't help feeling a little stupid as well. Why hadn't he remembered to check the "scratches" after their meeting with Dr. Arthur? How could he have missed something so obvious? *Like walking down an animal track when the real path is right in front of you?* He laughed at himself in his excitement.

He quickly tucked the Cross back in its bag and into his pack before running to catch up with the rest. They were waiting not too far down the trail. "I hope you buried it at least six inches, Martin. You know that's the rule, eh?" Fr. Gregory said.

"Yeah, Dad. I know," Martin said, glad that his time away had been interpreted so conveniently. "Sorry to hold us up."

Fr. Gregory took the lead again and they were off through the woods. Martin could barely keep his steps slow enough not to be stepping on Ashley's boots. He had discovered the most important mystery left! Likely it was a cave as Dr. Arthur had thought. Martin didn't think the caves could go too deep—at least he hoped not.

All that was left now was to get to Hopper's Pond and find an entrance near the cliff edge. Plus, he already had a plan for how to buy enough time to search and not have to let his father in on it until Martin himself could lead him to the treasure he'd find. Of course, Brigid wouldn't like that she and Ashley would also need to wait behind, but there was no other choice. From there it would be a short thirty minute hike down to the tour boat and on to fame.

The rest of the day passed with a lightness to their steps. They all talked and told jokes. Fr. Gregory asked all about Ashley's family and found out he was good friends as a teenager with a cousin of Ashley's father. Martin felt the pure joy of walking past the lakes and over the hillsides. He hadn't felt so care-free since... well, since he'd learned he was moving to Newfoundland. But things were good right now, and nothing could spoil that.

Gradually their trail began descending somewhat, while to their left the hills were starting to rise, turning into a small mountain-range. The trail clung to its side as it wound into another wooded area. It got much darker on entering between the cliff wall to their left and the trees to their right. Soon, the rocks climbed to a height of about 800 feet. The top was littered with tuckamores that turned into larger pine trees as they descended the side of the cliff to the trail.

The trail at this point had a campsite cleared to the right, ringed about by evergreen trees. The sound of a stream could be heard not far off.

"This looks like a nice place to camp, wouldn't you say?" Fr. Gregory said as they approached the spot. "It's about time to stop for the night anyway."

"Looks good to me," Ashley said.

"And a lot *softer* than last night's spot!" Brigid said rubbing a shoulder.

Voyage to the Rock

Martin remembered his own rock from the previous night, and agreed with the others.

"Good then," Fr. Gregory said. "I'll leave you guys to set up the tent, while I run down to that stream to get some water for cooking. I'll be back soon."

As soon as his father was gone, Martin pulled the other two close: "I've solved the last puzzle of the poem."

"What?" Brigid gasped. "How?"

Then Martin explained what he had been thinking and how Fr. Gregory had inadvertently answered the last clue for him. He then proceeded to tell them the rest of what he'd discovered.

"I wondered what was taking you so long. I thought maybe it was all the beans we've been having out here!" She winked at Ashley when she said that.

"B'ys, I just can't believe we had it in front of our own eyes, and hadn't seen it earlier," Ashley said. "We were two bites away from losing our worm, we were."

"Well, all we have to do is arrive at Hopper's Pond by lunch. Then we'll have the whole afternoon to 'relax' there until we need to catch the boat later that evening. We'll have hours to find the cave and make it to the treasure," Martin said. "After that, Dad should be so stunned and amazed that I doubt he'll have enough left over to be angry with us for keeping quiet about all this until now!" Martin prayed that it would go that way.

Ashley and Brigid both looked excited about the news. They'd all have trouble sleeping that night.

Chapter 23:
A Narrow Miss

Martin started awake in terror to a thunderous crackling that sounded something like crashing waves. A force slammed into the edge of the tent and Brigid screamed. The entire tent lurched backwards under the blow and Martin heard his father let out a sharp cry of pain. *My God, what's happening?*

In the next instant there was silence except for the fierce sobbing of his sister. "Brigid!" his father said in the darkness. "Are you hurt? Martin? Ashley? Is everyone okay?" There was a panic in his voice that Martin had never heard before.

"I'm fine, Dad!" Martin said quickly.

"Me, too, Fr. Gregory!" Ashley said.

Brigid was still sobbing, though not as loudly. "Are you hurt, Brigid?" Fr. Gregory asked again.

"I'm...not...hurt," Brigid said through her tears.

"God be praised!" Fr. Gregory murmured, but his voice sounded strained.

"Dad, are you okay? I heard you cry out!" Martin was straining to see his father in the darkness.

He heard, rather than saw, his father move and then came a sharp intake of breath. "My leg is injured," Fr. Gregory said, and Martin could tell his father was speaking through gritted teeth.

Brigid began to wail again.

"Calm down, Brigid!" her father said. "Calm down. I don't think it's serious. Martin, see if you can open the tent door."

Martin fumbled his way in the shifted tent, and found the zipper, opening it. Outside it was dark, but the faint light of morning was already beginning to lighten things. Martin saw what had happened. From the mountain side, across the trail, and into their campsite was the rubble of a large rockslide. Looking out and around the tent, Martin could see that if their tent had been five feet more to the left, the rockslide would have completely crushed them. He almost swayed from shock, but caught himself.

They had almost been killed!

As it was, the rockslide had only barely hit the left side of the tent and forced it somewhat askew. "It was a rockslide," Martin said. He then looked up to see where the rockslide had fallen from the cliff above.

Martin froze and for a second time had to keep himself from faltering. There had been someone at the top of the cliff—he had clearly seen the shadowy figure of a man! The rockslide *wasn't* an accident then. Sullivan O'Connell? How did he find them? It wasn't possible. He felt panic rise up in him. What would they do?

Forget St. Brendan's cave; that was for sure!

But how injured was his father? How would they get to the boat before another "accident" could happen? Martin's fears were cut short by his father's voice from within the tent.

"Martin," he said, his strain apparent, "can you find your flashlight?"

Martin ducked back into the tent, but Ashley had already found his and handed it to Fr. Gregory.

"Thanks, Ashley," Fr. Gregory said as he took it. "Now Brigid and Ashley, I want you two to go outside and get some cool air."

Ashley helped a stunned, but silent Brigid out of the tent. Martin was stunned himself. How hurt *was* his father's leg and how were they going to escape the *Old Wolf* now?

"Martin?"

"Yeah, Dad?" Martin said moving toward him.

"I need your help. There's a rock trapping my leg and I need you to take some of the weight off so that I can pull it out."

Martin hesitated then looked to where his father now shone the flashlight. There was a fairly large rock that had ripped through the side of the tent and was pressing against his father's sleeping bag. Martin carefully leaned forward, trying not to touch his father's legs and pushed against the rock. It was heavy but Martin lifted with all his strength, managing to keep it up long enough for his father to move his sleeping bag out. Martin let the rock drop with a thud.

"Martin," his father said, "move outside the tent. I'm going to get you to help me up when I get to the door."

Martin anxiously did as he was asked.

Once Fr. Gregory had shuffled over to the tent door, Martin grabbed one of his arms and put his other under his armpit. "1, 2, 3..." his father said, and struggled up with a grunt. Martin let Fr. Gregory put an arm around his shoulder and the two of them moved slowly to the large rock that they had used for a table the night before.

Brigid tried to muffle an anxious cry when she saw her father's leg. Martin saw that on his pant some blood had soaked through. Ashley had already gotten the first-aid kit and brought it over to where Fr. Gregory was sitting.

"Brigid I need you to heat me some of the water I collected last night on the stove." She nodded and ran off. "Ashley, could you open the package of bandages? I'm going to take a look at my leg," Fr. Gregory said. "Martin, give me a hand with my pant leg. Grab the scissors out of the first-aid kit; you're going to cut the pant."

Martin crouched in front of his father's injured leg, scissors in hand, and very gently began to cut from the bottom of the pant upward. *How much time do we have–an hour, two–before O'Connell finds us here?* His father winced as Martin tugged the material. "Sorry, Dad!" Martin said.

"You're doing great, Martin. Don't worry about me," Fr. Gregory's face was pale and there was sweat on his brow.

The next moment, Martin had cut the pant leg up to his father's knee, exposing a gash on the side of his lower leg. It was

Voyage to the Rock

bleeding and looked red and purplish in the area around it. His ankle was also swollen. Thankfully nothing was obviously broken.

"Good," Fr. Gregory said. "It's not that bad. Ashley hand that bandage to Martin. Martin, I'll get you to apply pressure to this cut for a few minutes. Also, help me lower myself to the ground." Both Martin and Ashley hurried to help. Once Fr. Gregory was down and leaning against the rock he said, "Now hand me my pack. We'll raise my leg."

Martin did as he was asked and then held some pressure on the bandage to help stop the bleeding. "Will you be able to walk, Dad?" Martin asked as they sat there.

Fr. Gregory sighed. "I doubt it. It may be broken or it may not be, but I'll never make it down that gorge to the boat on my own. You three will have to go for help."

Martin's heart sunk and he suddenly felt beads of sweat forming at his temples despite the chill morning. His father couldn't walk and they were the only chance for help with a crazed murderer following them! What would the *Old Wolf* do if he found them here? Nothing good, Martin knew. They *had* to go, and not just to bring help for his dad's leg.

"No, Dad!" Brigid cried. "I'll wait here with you. The boys can go!"

"Now none of that," Fr. Gregory said, obviously doing his best to sound reassuring. "I'll be just fine here by myself. I'd feel a lot better if you three were traveling together. It's safer that way. Besides Brigid, I need you to keep these two goofs in line. Otherwise, they'll go hunting moose or something and forget all about *me*!" He smiled at the three of them, who just returned weak smiles of their own. Fr. Gregory was trying to raise their spirits, but all Martin could think of was whether there were searching eyes above that still watched them. They *had* to get moving.

"Well, I'd say that's long enough with the pressure, Martin," Fr. Gregory said, gesturing him up. "Brigid, can you bring me some of that warm water and a towel?"

"Sure, Dad," Brigid said running over to the pot, while Ashley took it upon himself to grab a towel.

Thankfully, the gash had almost stopped bleeding, and in no time they had it cleaned and bandaged as best they could. It was a good thing his father knew what to do because Martin would have been helpless otherwise. As it was he *felt* plenty helpless.

"Brigid, Ashley, can you go to the stream and fill me a few more bottles of fresh water?" Fr. Gregory asked gesturing to the bottles on the make-shift table.

"Sure, Dad. We'll be right back!" Brigid said as she quickly grabbed the bottles and led Ashley away.

When they were gone, Fr. Gregory turned to Martin. "Martin," he said, "do you think you can manage this alright?" His eyes were intent, with just a hint of the worry-lines around them.

"I think so, Dad," Martin said suddenly feeling as though he were under water and couldn't breathe. There was a lump at the back of his throat. "I... I'm sorry, Dad," Martin finally got the words out.

"You don't have to be sorry, Martin," Fr. Gregory said shaking his head. "None of this is your fault."

If you only knew just how much it is my fault. But right now that wasn't what Martin was talking about.

"That's not what I mean," Martin said as he looked at the ground, his insides twisting in double-knots. "I've been a real jerk these last few months." He held up a hand as his dad was about to speak and went on. "Yes, I have been. Everyone knows it. I've been... angry, and I've been taking it out on everyone else." His dad watched him but did not interrupt.

Martin looked at his father. "I guess what I'm trying to say is that I think I can understand what it's like to have a dream, and to want to chase it. And not just to chase it for yourself..."— Martin's voice grew quieter—"but for a greater purpose, because sometimes what you're after is so valuable it needs to be shared."

The two of them were silent for a moment. Then Fr. Gregory reached over to pull Martin in with an arm around the

Voyage to the Rock

shoulders. "Thanks," he said into Martin's hair and gave him a squeeze.

There wasn't time to say more as Brigid and Ashley appeared on the path with water bottles in hand. Martin stood and moved to grab his backpack emptied of all but the Cross and the basics. They went to Fr. Gregory with the water.

"Well, it's time you guys were off," Fr. Gregory said as Martin came over. "If you hurry, you can catch the earlier boat." Fr. Gregory shifted against the large rock. They had placed a sleeping bag under and behind him and had covered him with another.

"But we need to make you a warm breakfast, and we should maybe wait with you to make sure you're feeling better." Brigid was clearly still reluctant to go.

"Dad's right, Brigid," Martin said, as he played nervously with the strap of his backpack. "We should head out. It's getting late." He prayed not *too* late.

Brigid shot Martin an accusatory look. Unfortunately, Martin knew he deserved just such a look, even if not for what he had just said. He had almost gotten them *killed* with this stupid idea of his. And now they needed to get help—and *quickly!*

"Martin's right, Brigid," her father said. "We have plenty of food and water left. It's better that you get moving."

"Oh, alright," Brigid said, only pouting slightly. "But we'll be back soon!"

In another ten minutes they were ready. They wore their jackets to help stay warm as a foggy mist began to form among the trees. They had pulled the tent over to their father in case it started to rain, and had patched the hole as best they could with duct tape.

As they started down the path, Fr. Gregory called to them, a confident smile visible on his face: "Don't worry, guys. I have the Mother of God and my Guardian Angel to keep me company!" They waved one last time, and Martin could hear his father singing the familiar Supplication service. "*With many temptations surrounding me, searching for salvation, I have hastened unto thee...*" His voice floated through the chill morning air and filled Martin with at least a bit of courage. *Most Holy Mother of God, save us*, he thought, *and keep the Old Wolf far away!*

They hadn't been walking for more than a quarter of an hour when Martin stopped them. "What is it, Martin?" Brigid asked. "What's wrong?"

"That rockslide was no accident."

"What?" Brigid eyes filled with sudden terror. "What are you talking about, Martin?"

"I saw someone on the ridge—when I first looked outside the tent," Martin said, brushing damp hair from his forehead.

"The *Old Wolf*?" Ashley asked, as he looked from side to side.

"I couldn't say for sure—but a man."

"And you let us *leave* Dad? What were you *thinking*, Martin?" Brigid nearly screamed. "He's helpless back there!"

"Calm down, Brigid. Don't you think I know that!" Martin snapped back at her. "That's why we *had* to go. Do you want O'Connell to come looking for us and find us there with Dad? What do you think he would do? He wouldn't just let us walk away! His word against a bunch of teenagers is one thing. His word against a priest and his children is something else. And I don't want to put the *Old Wolf* in the dilemma of having to find a solution. It won't work in our favour, I know that much!" Martin glanced around. They couldn't waste too much time with this.

"Still, you should have at least *warned* Dad!" she said, one hand squeezing her blond pony-tail.

"Oh, yeah? And do you really think he would have let us go, knowing there was a murderer on the loose?" Martin said, his own frayed nerves showing. "We're the only chance of bringing help before O'Connell finds him—and us. If we don't bring the police, the *Old Wolf* is free to do with us whatever he wants."

"And St. Brendan's treasure?" she said. The words stabbed their accusation. "It has nothing to do with that?"

Voyage to the Rock

"That's enough, Brigid!" Ashley said, putting a hand on her shoulder. "We all know Martin's been foolish at times, he's admitted that himself, but it ain't right to say that to him."

Brigid reddened, but didn't completely back down.

"St. Brendan's treasure?" Her words had cut Martin and he could feel his own face flush with anger and shame. "Forget it. I'll throw the Cross off a cliff and to the bottom of Western Brook Pond if that's what it takes to get help!"

Brigid's face softened and her eyes began to fill with tears. "I know you would, Martin. I'm sorry. I'm just afraid, that's all."

"It's okay," Martin said. "We all are, I think. But we'll get help. I figure we have about an hour on him at least. He has to climb all the way down the mountain-side before he can make it to the trail, and just look how high it still is." Martin pointed to the cliffs above. "We should get moving, though."

Brigid nodded and wiped her eyes before the tears could spill out. With that the three of them were off again.

They continued to weave their way along the trail which alternated between being closer and farther from the mountainside. The trail stayed among the evergreens but they were much smaller in size than they had been. They could see the cloudy gray sky above the treetops and a light fog clung to the trail.

It began to feel so desolate and lonely that they started walking side-by-side, each of them occasionally glancing around. Martin slid his prayer rope off his wrist and started to quietly say the Jesus Prayer as they walked: *Lord Jesus Christ, have mercy on us!*

Soon Brigid had begun praying as well, and they were alternating aloud between him saying one Jesus Prayer, and her saying one *Most Holy Mother of God, save us!* They continued like this for some time and Martin could feel himself relaxing somewhat and the heaviness of the woods around them seemed to lighten.

Ashley then asked in a half-whisper: "Is there something for me to say?"

Martin turned to look at him, not immediately sure what to answer. "Well... I guess you could say: *St. Brendan, pray for us,* if you want. We could certainly stand to have him listening to us right now."

And so the three of them spent the next while alternating prayer after prayer as they walked and tried not to think of what still lay before them. The trail was now staying close to the mountain which was looking much more like a hill than it had before. The trees were also getting thinner.

"Martin, look!" Brigid hissed as she pointed a finger towards the descending cliff.

Martin suddenly felt nauseous. It was the *Old Wolf* and Duffy—both of them! They were clearly visible through the thinning tree-tops on the ridge. They were descending from the mountain-side quickly. Martin looked ahead to the trail and silently thanked God that it veered sharply to the right away from the base of the mountain and moved deeper into the forest of short—but sheltering—trees.

Had the men seen them? Martin couldn't say for sure. But altogether the three of them tore off at a run. They had to get far enough down the trail that they could stay ahead of their pursuers. Martin knew it would still take the men some time to clear the end of the rocky slope and backtrack to find the trail, but they had been too close. They needed speed now in order to keep their lead.

And if you don't keep your lead? The thought loomed in his mind like a taunt. What would Martin do? Could the three of them really keep up this pace all the way down to the boat at the edge of Western Brook Pond? He knew the answer even as the question formed in his mind: it was impossible.

Martin tried to think as he ran but between his heart pounding and his rapid breathing, he couldn't come up with anything. All he could do was to will Brigid and Ashley to run faster in front of him, to push themselves harder. They kept this up for a while but Martin knew by their panting that they were quickly reaching their limit.

"Guys...stop!" Martin said through gasping breaths. Ashley and Brigid hesitated, then both slowed and stopped.

Voyage to the Rock

There was a hunted look on Brigid's weary face: "Why are we stopping? We have to keep moving. They'll be here soon!"

"We can't keep moving at this pace," Martin said putting his hands on his head to catch his breath. "We'll be exhausted in no time."

"He's right, Brigid," Ashley said, following Martin's example and breathing deeply. "We got to pace ourselves. We got a good lead on them anyhow."

Brigid looked from the one to the other as her chest heaved with the effort of catching her breath. Then with a tired nod, she agreed.

They started down the trail at a slow trot while continuing to watch the trail behind them. To the right of them the forest thinned and became a very steep hillside; to their left was the forest. All was quiet except for the crunching of ground under their feet. The air was damp with the fog that still lingered under the gray sky. Martin could feel sweat turning chill on his back. The mood was oppressive.

He was such a *fool*. Whatever the others might say, Martin knew that this was his fault. He had been so *driven*. He had known all the dangers and had ignored each one. And now where were they? They were hunted, had almost been killed, and had left their father bleeding and trapped in the forest. *It wasn't supposed to be like this St. Brendan! I never meant to do things like this.*

As if to further accuse him, he remembered what the tortured Judas had said in St. Brendan's *Voyage*: A good deed done in the wrong way, and not for God's own sake, is not counted as pleasing before the Lord. Had he become like Judas? This wasn't the first time he'd asked himself the question. Had he betrayed those around him, those closest to him? He had stolen, lied, manipulated... and had he now handed his family and friend over to those who would hurt them—maybe *kill* them? Martin shuddered.

It hadn't begun like this, had it? There was a sickening feeling in the pit of his stomach now. He knew the answer—and had known from the beginning. The voice inside him, which he had struggled so hard to silence these past few weeks, was now accusing him: *The moment you picked that Cross out of the stream, you knew what you needed to do. It all began there, and everything else has just been a justification of what you did that day.* The voice was right.

I swear, St. Brendan, Martin cried out within himself, *if you get us out of this safely, I will confess everything. I will accept everything. I will do whatever it takes to make things right again—whatever the cost! Please... forgive me!* There was no answer, but he remembered something that gave him courage to hope: *Ol' Brendan awaits his gifts to give...Faith to revive and to forgive.*

Martin looked back as the other two continued in front of him. There was no one behind him for as far as he could see. He inwardly sighed and glanced at an opening to the left—an animal trail similar to the one he had mistakenly gone down the previous day. He glanced down it as he passed. It was empty, thank God. The last thing they needed was to stumble upon a black bear or bull moose!

They continued to move down the trail which curved around a bend just ahead. A loud crack behind them sent Martin and the others jumping!

"Stop. Now!" a voice cried from behind them.

The three of them turned in horror to see Duffy with a gun still pointed to the sky, and next to him was Sullivan O'Connell. They were standing in front of the animal trail, not more than twenty feet away.

"But how did you...?" Martin started to sputter.

"How did we catch you so easily?" O'Connell said, his lip curled in a sneering smile. "Do you think me so *dull*, as to chase after you like a dog chasing a rock? Mr. Duffy here's a good man, and good at finding his way through the woods."

They both wore dark hiking clothes and brown hiking boots that seemed out of place for the rugged Duffy as much for the stately O'Connell. "The real question is how you little fools have evaded me for as long as you have." The sneer became almost a snarl.

Voyage to the Rock

"You tried to kill us last night!" Martin felt sudden anger boil within him despite his nearly petrifying fright. "You caused a rockslide above our campsite!"

"Tried to *kill* you?" the Old Wolf asked with feigned innocence. "By a rockslide? I don't think so."

"We saw you two up there!" Brigid stamped her foot in anger.

"You did, did you?" O'Connell's voice was becoming dangerously quiet. "And how will you prove it? *Accidental* rockslides happen all the time."

"What do you want, O'Connell?" Martin said, his fists clenched.

O'Connell looked annoyed at being interrupted, but started to speak in a mocking voice: "What do I want? What do I want?" His face grew dark. "What do you think I want, you filthy little thief? I want my *Cross* back!"

"It's not *your* Cross. It's St. Brendan's!" Brigid shouted.

"You had better shut that girl up, *boy*," O'Connell said to Martin, "before I have Mr. Duffy shut her up." Duffy took a half-step forward; he was grinning.

"He'd better not try!" Ashley said, stepping in front of Brigid.

"I'm tired of this," The old man waved a dismissive hand. "Give me the Cross!" His voice came out somewhere between a shriek and a snarl. There was none of the "gentlemanly" O'Connell of the antique store here. He was literally transformed into a beast of a man.

"And if we don't?" Martin said, backing closer to Ashley and Brigid.

"If you *don't?*" the Old Wolf asked wide-eyed, looking at Duffy. "If you don't, I'll have Mr. Duffy here *shoot* you all." His green eyes seemed to shine as they looked back at the three of them.

"That won't look like an accident!" Martin had to play this right. "Not like it did with our campsite... or like with Susan Arthur."

"Ah," the *Old Wolf* chuckled, "so you know about poor old Susan, do you? Maybe you're not quite as stupid as I thought you were. Yes, the two Dr. Arthurs were less than... cooperative. You'd do well to learn from their mistakes."

"You're a monster!" Brigid shouted.

"A monster?" Mr. O'Connell looked as if he were considering the word. "No, not a monster. Just someone who has spent a life-time in *exile* waiting to find what that Cross will lead me to. Besides," he said waving a dismissive hand, "I didn't cause the rockslide that killed her—my assistant Mr. Duffy did. Now give me the Cross before I have to let Mr. Duffy deal with *you* three as well."

Martin didn't know what to do. He was pretty sure that O'Connell wasn't likely to shoot them, not with how many questions that would raise. But he also knew that they could just as easily be killed by *sliding down* a rock as by a *rockslide*. And there were plenty of steep cliffs around where an "accident" was all too possible. His only guarantee that they stayed alive was still having the Cross. After O'Connell had that, there were no guarantees left.

"Duffy, go get the Cross from him!" the *Old Wolf* ordered. His face had become pale and he actually shook as he pointed at them.

In panic Martin instinctively cried out within himself: *Lord Jesus Christ, have mercy on us!*

Martin started. What was that noise? He saw that Duffy, too, hesitated from where he stood before the animal trail. Just then he and O'Connell jumped back as a large animal burst from out of the animal trail! A massive bull moose now stood swinging its antlered head back and forth on the trail directly between them and the men. Martin could hear its low grunts as it stomped its front hooves on the ground.

Martin hesitated a moment. The moose clearly wasn't sure in which direction it would charge: toward them or toward the two men. God help them if it decided to charge in their direction! With no choices left, Martin did the only thing he could: he shouted "*Run!*"

Brigid and Ashley responded instantly and leapt to make it around the bend of the trail. Martin, too, sprang as fast as he could. Behind him he again heard the crack of Duffy's gun, and something whizzed by his head and struck a tree in the woods ahead of him.

He just made it around the bend when he heard the gun fire again and a man scream from behind them. He could hear thrashing and grunts from the moose, but didn't go back to look. As they ran, the screaming continued behind them. The three of them moved as fast and for as long as their bodies would allow. They couldn't stop; they had to keep going.

They had been caught in the deadly grasp of the *Old Wolf* and had survived again. But they weren't at the boat yet.

Chapter 24:
The Rabbit and the Wolf

"No, Martin," Brigid said, grabbing the front of his jacket, "we're not leaving you!"

The three of them stood at a fork in the trail. The one arm led down through the trees to the large mirror-like lake below, while the other continued to climb toward the plateau above the rock walls and Western Brook Pond below. The sun shone out of the now clear blue sky and calmly illuminated the majestic scene before them in sharp contrast to their own grim situation.

"I've made up my mind, Brigid." He gently pulled her hand away as he spoke. "This is the only way to guarantee that you guys make it safely to the boat for help, and Dad needs help soon." Martin said this more confidently than he felt. "Besides, I'm the reason why everyone is in this mess in the first place."

"We all decided..." Brigid began, but Martin raised a hand to silence her.

"Yes, we decided together, but I'm the one responsible for having gotten us here. If I hadn't been so *selfish* from the beginning, we wouldn't be running for our lives now. You know it's true—both of you," Martin said looking from Brigid to Ashley, "even if you won't admit it to me. If I hadn't been so sour about moving to Corner Brook, if I hadn't been so set on *not* liking it here, on *not* fitting in, maybe I wouldn't have done all the stupid and dishonest things I've done so far."

"Martin, we forgive you for all of that. You know we do. But you can't just run off on your own because of it!" Brigid said, gesturing to the rising trail.

Voyage to the Rock

"It is exactly because of that that I *have* to: because I could never forgive myself if I didn't and something happened to you guys like what almost just happened," Martin said looking away. "Besides, we need to waste some time. There's still an hour before the boat will arrive, and it's only thirty minutes from this spot down into the gorge and to the edge of Western Brook Pond. We can't risk going down there and having one or both of O'Connell and Duffy finding us—thirty minutes before any help will arrive."

"But how do you *know* he'll follow you and not us?" Brigid asked.

"He wants the Cross, Brigid. If he sees me," Martin said, "he'll know it's his last *possible* chance to get it before we reveal it to the world. Then, he'll never get his precious treasure! He'll come—just as long as he sees me." At this tears started to form in Brigid's eyes.

"He's right, Brigid," Ashley said softly, and put a hand on her shoulder, "and we needs the extra time."

"I know he's right," she said wiping her eyes with her sleeve. "Just... be careful," she said as she threw her arms around Martin's neck and hugged him tightly. "We'll be back with help soon!"

"Don't worry," Martin said. "I'll find the cave of St. Brendan and hide there until you guys come with help. Let's see the *Old Wolf* find what no one's found in fifteen hundred years—and without the Cross for a map! I'll be fine. Now go on." With a final wave, Brigid and Ashley started their descent into the gorge while Martin headed in the direction of Hopper's Pond.

The trail climbed as he moved up the rocky hillside. Martin had already worked out his plan. He would head up the trail to the farthest point where he could still see the junction between the Hopper's Pond Trail and the path to Western Brook Pond. When, or *if*, someone came up the trail, Martin would be clearly visible; they had all agreed that after the screaming they'd heard it wasn't likely that more than one man would be coming for them. Once he had drawn any pursuit, he would head for Hopper's Pond.

The only problem that remained was finding St. Brendan's campsite. He *had* to find it. There would be nowhere else to hide.

Martin waited, eyes fixed on the trail below. How much time had passed? Were Ashley and Brigid far enough away? *Thirty minutes must have passed—enough time so that they can't get caught before the boat arrives.* He breathed a sigh of relief. If no one had appeared by now, chances were *both* O'Connell and Duffy were injured in the meeting with the bull moose. That meant he would be safe, too...

A tall, thin man came lopping down the trail into view: Sullivan O'Connell. Martin felt a stab of fear as he clearly made out Duffy's gun clutched in his hand.

Martin didn't leave his spot, waiting for the *Old Wolf* to see him. It was the hardest thing he'd ever done in his life. O'Connell's gaze slowly fell upon him and the old man raised his free hand to wave—as though to an old friend. Martin felt as though he could see the old man's intense green eyes enveloping him as they had on their first meeting.

He turned and ran.

He continued to ascend and could see nothing but sky above as he scrambled, trying not to fall. In a moment he had crested the hill and was staring at a large lake. The water looked clear and cold and he could see the cliff edge to the right which led down 2,000 feet to Western Brook Pond. He sprinted in the direction of the cliff.

"Is this the spot?" He said aloud as he reached a grassy area between Hopper's Pond and the cliff edge. There was a stream that flowed from the lake and turned into a waterfall at the cliff's edge. Beyond it was another hillside—green and rocky, but not very tall. He scanned it for any openings in the rock... *nothing.* How long did he have before the *Old Wolf* crested the ridge behind him? He had to move quickly!

Voyage to the Rock

He raced to the edge and began to peer down. All he saw was waterfall, rock, and the water far, *far* below. Where was it? He ran back and forth along the edge and saw nothing. He scanned the hillsides again. Nothing!

Save me, Jesus!

Martin was almost beside himself with a gripping panic that threatened to overcome him and send him running as fast as he could over the hillside and into the wild back-country. He had been wrong. There was nothing here—just water and cliffs and the *Old Wolf* with his gun approaching. No campsite of St. Brendan, no treasure, no nothing. He had been a fool, and now he would be a *dead* fool!

Martin was moving back and forth, searching near the cliff edge. He tripped and lurched forward. He hit the ground hard and all the breath was knocked from his lungs. He lay at the very *edge* of the cliff—not two feet away. He gasped for air as he scrambled back on hands and knees staring in shock down to the water below. He had almost fallen off!

Then he saw something. Was that a small ledge leading down? He moved over to the right to look. It *was* a ledge.

As he carefully scrambled down he understood why he hadn't seen it before. The ledge passed under a portion of overhanging cliff which actually extended about five or six feet out from the rest of the cliff wall. Unless someone hung themselves over the edge, it would be nearly *impossible* to see the ledge from above. If Martin hadn't nearly tumbled over himself, he may never have seen the beginning of it.

Once he was down on it and moving along the ledge, Martin could see what he had dreamed of seeing for the last week: a cave entrance, not ten feet away.

Thank you, St. Brendan! Dear God, thank you!

He had found it, and not one second too soon. If he was lucky, the *Old Wolf* would never see the ledge, and would think that Martin had fled into the back-country.

Martin hugged the cliff wall as he shuffled along the rock ledge which was even smaller than the rocky outcrop just above him. As Martin neared the cave, his breath caught in his throat. Half the rock ledge had fallen away from the section just before the cave, leaving a walkway of about two feet only. How was he going to make it across that?

Suddenly a flurry of rocks and dirt tumbled in a cloud and spray from the edge of the cliff right above him. He froze, laying his back as flat against the cliff as he could. There was someone on the ridge just a few feet above his head.

He could faintly make out muttering above and there came another spray of rocks and dirt. Martin closed his eyes and mouth against the dirt cloud that blew against him. It was the *Old Wolf*.

There was nothing left for Martin to do. If the *Old Wolf* caught him now, he was done for. He started shuffling again toward the cave. He steeled himself as he came to the broken section and flattened himself as much as he could to the cliff wall, arms extended left and right in an attempt to keep himself to the wall. He slowly and carefully shuffled his way across. Below all he could see were rock and water.

There was a flurry of stones that suddenly fell, kicked off by Martin's feet as he shuffled. He paused, terrified. Had O'Connell heard it? Was he watching on the ridge, just above Martin's head? Would he spring down and fling Martin from the cliff wall?

There was silence above.

Martin only waited a moment more before quickly shuffling the rest of the way past the broken section. With two large steps more he was in the cave entrance. He covered his mouth as he let out a silent breath and wiped the sweat and dirt from his forehead with the back of his sleeve. He was giddy from relief. *Can't stay here, though. It's still too dangerous.*

Grabbing his flashlight, he flicked it on and shone it into the darkness while taking the Cross in his other hand. The cave was surprisingly wide and was tall enough that he couldn't touch the ceiling with his hands. The ground was solid but filled with dirt and in places rock debris. Martin could see that the tunnel clearly descended.

He quickly turned the Cross over to the map-side. He examined it briefly, noting the four passages that he would pass before he came to the one where he needed to turn. He'd start with that. He began to descend at a light trot, still trying to be as silent as possible.

He discovered something very quickly: the cave was not as shallow as he had initially hoped it would be. He knew this would be to his advantage if the *Old Wolf did* get in, but he had to choke down his own growing sense of claustrophobia. What was once a bright opening behind him was now a faint light in the distance, but he continued to move.

Martin passed the tunnel on his right, then the second on his left farther on. Now as he continued forward the passage began to veer slightly to the right. According to the map on the Cross, he should be going straight, but there hadn't been a fork, so Martin just trusted what was on the Cross; the last thing he needed was to get lost in here. He looked back with one wistful glance at the light behind him and then continued to veer to the right as it winked out. It was just him, the Cross, and his flashlight now. Martin had to restrain a groan.

Martin noticed that the walls of the cave were shining. He reached his hand over and felt cold water trickling down the sides. *Must be from the lake above,* he thought.

As he continued down the passageway, the sounds of water filled his ears as the cave walls were now running steadily with it. His feet began to slosh in the mud of the now wet cave floor beneath, and more than once he had to skirt large puddles. A few times he couldn't skirt or jump them and had no choice but to walk through; his feet were soaked by this point. Martin was getting nervous; would he find the whole place filled with water? He went on; there was nothing else to do.

The air had become stale and Martin found it harder to breathe than before. He was also getting cold from the chill and the water that was now splashing and spraying off the walls at points.

Then he saw a fork in the path in the looming distance. He looked down at the Cross which showed that he needed to take the left tunnel, and avoid the middle and right ones.

Martin hesitated a moment when he saw that the left tunnel clearly continued to descend while the other two seemed to ascend. He swallowed and made the sign of the Cross. He prayed he was following the map correctly!

In this passage the water gushed down the walls, soaking the ground to mud and leaving a stream in the middle of the path descending into the darkness. Martin shook slightly—and not just from the cold.

He could see that this tunnel wound more like a snake than the relatively straight line on the map. The turning and the darkness began to feel oppressive. Martin was starting to feel panicked. What was he doing here?

And then Martin heard a sound that froze him to the bone. He paused—had it been real, or was he just freaking himself out?

He listened.

There! Martin distinctly heard the grunts or shouts of a man. It was distant, but Martin also heard splashing—as though someone were heading his way and not caring to slow down at the puddles. The *Old Wolf* had found the ledge and the cave. He was coming!

What am I going to do? He looked back and in horror realized something. The water! It had made so much mud that Martin had left muddy tracks right to himself. He needed to move. He started running, not caring about the water and any noise he made. He had to get away.

He felt trapped; *hunted*.

The image of a giant gray wolf formed in his mind. He could almost hear it howling; feel its hot breath on his neck.

Martin slipped and caught himself in a spray of water, but he barely slowed. The cave shook and gleamed sickeningly with the bouncing light of his flashlight. He had to keep moving, had

Voyage to the Rock

to lose his pursuer amid the water and gathering pools that he sloshed through along the passageway.

He saw a fork looming before him again. He hurriedly checked the Cross. He needed to go into the center tunnel this time. Martin rushed for it, water splashing everywhere as he ran. He could see that the tunnel floor was covered with a thin layer of shallow water.

Maybe I should go down one of the other tunnels? Set a false trail? He flashed the light to the right and the left.

Above the noise of rushing water, he thought he made out the sounds of an irregular sloshing still coming from the passageway behind him. The wolf was gaining on him. *There's no time! What if you get lost? Or worse–double back and stumble into O'Connell?* He had to press onwards and try to lose him at the points where the water was deepest. That was all he could do. *It's up to you, St. Brendan. God help me!*

Martin was starting to shiver continually now. The water was freezing, and despite his layers of clothes he was wet and cold. How long could he manage this? How long could he camp out in here before he froze to death? He couldn't think of that now. He had to keep moving.

He came to another junction in the tunnel. He took the right as his map indicated. He paused to listen for sounds. No grunts, no irregular sloshing. Had he lost the *Old Wolf*? Had his wild running through water obscured his path? He sighed with relief. *He can't be as close at least.*

Martin started moving more slowly now, trying to keep from leaving any trail. Was this path starting to ascend? He couldn't tell but there seemed hardly any water in this tunnel. The ground was drier–even if still muddy.

He walked on for a while; he wasn't sure for how long. Time had lost all meaning. Had the boat arrived yet? Were Brigid and Ashley bringing help?

Suddenly the path dipped considerably in front of him. Below he saw a large pool of water before the trail ascended again sharply on the other side. The pool was at least ten feet wide, and there was no chance Martin could jump it; besides, he needed to stay quiet anyway. But as he waded into it, Martin quickly realized that this pool was *deep*. He was already up to his knees and it was getting deeper.

Hesitating he looked down at the Cross again. This was definitely the way it pointed. He had to keep going. Gripping the Cross tightly in one hand and shining the flashlight ahead with the other, he continued wading. His breath caught in his throat as he waded in past his waist. He lifted up his hands to keep the Cross and flashlight dry as the water rose to his chest. The water was so cold that Martin could barely get his body to respond.

Come on, Martin!

He urged himself onward. Step by step he managed to make his legs move and as the trail ascended, the water-level lowered. Martin was up to his waist again and nearly across.

A sudden explosion to Martin's left slammed him into the cave wall in a rush of icy water. With a jolt of intense pain in his right shoulder, Martin was forced under the freezing pool by the spray. Sputtering and gasping for air, he drove himself up out of the water. He could feel a torrent of cold water pelting him from the left.

The light had vanished. Martin groped in the darkness. It was pitch black!

The flashlight and the Cross were *gone*.

Chapter 25:
A Light in the Darkness

Martin dove despite his cold and fear—a new terror driving him to dive and dive. He *had* to find his flashlight. This went on and on until finally, exhausted and numb, Martin pulled himself up out of the water and onto the ascending tunnel floor.

Martin lay in a blackness he had never known.

He was trembling with shivers that wracked his whole body as he curled in a ball for warmth. There was a fogginess to his thoughts that only seemed to fade slightly after getting out of the water.

He was in darkness. He was in the depths of a cave in impenetrable darkness!

Martin felt a terror in that moment that nearly drove him out of his mind. Only one thought kept him from starting to scream over and over: it was the image of a large gray wolf with intense green eyes. With the little clarity of mind that Martin still possessed, he knew that if he began to scream he would not stop until the wolf had its jaws around his throat.

Had the *Old Wolf* already heard his shouts during the burst of water? Was he coming toward him now in this deep darkness?

Martin suddenly had the irrational feeling of tearing back down the cave through the darkness shouting for Sullivan O'Connell. Anything to end the oppressive blackness! In his absolute terror, Martin squeezed his eyes shut and hugged his body for warmth.

He silently screamed from his very depths: *Lord Jesus, save me, save me! St. Brendan!*

Martin lay huddled in cold and terror; but he began to feel something. Was there a warmth returning to his body? Yes, there was. It began to fill Martin's limbs and his chest until it seemed as though he was on fire—but not a fire that burned, one that warmed and calmed him.

Am I dying? Strangely, he felt no anxiety. *Is dying really so peaceful—and* warm?

The warmth he felt alone was enough to make him forget everything else. How could this warmth feel so *good?* Did he smell something now? What was that fragrance? Like a thousand fresh roses gathered beside him, the fragrance overwhelmed him and he almost forgot the soothing warmth.

Martin opened his eyes then, and to his amazement he could see. Yet, for some reason he didn't feel surprised, as though this were the most natural thing to have happened. He just felt peaceful and warm. His shoulder had also stopped throbbing and he felt as though he could suddenly run a hundred miles. What was happening to him?

He looked back at the rushing torrent that flowed from the cave wall; he saw the deep cold pool of water, and yet he didn't feel afraid. He turned to look up the passageway and now saw the source of both the light and the fragrance. There appeared to be a luminous cloud of smoke, like sunbeams catching on the incense at church that he had seen so often. The luminous cloud was coming from up the tunnel. Martin arose and with a calm and protected feeling, he followed it.

As he walked toward the cloud, he never seemed to pass any farther than the very edge of it—its fragrance strengthening and pulling at him. But whenever he looked behind him it was gone; he wasn't walking through it, he was walking *with* it.

It continued to lead him upwards along the curving passage. He barely noticed passageways to his right or left as he passed; he was transfixed on the luminous cloud. All of his anxiety had melted away to be replaced with a deep sense of peace.

Voyage to the Rock

He was now standing in a large cavern. Martin vaguely noticed shapes at the edges of the darkness where the shadows were still deep. Were they pots? And tools? He noticed something that looked like a long table, and a stone fire pit? There were still logs beside it. Martin saw all of this as in a dream, though. It was the luminous cloud that still drew him on.

He followed it toward a wide opening at the highest point of the cavern. As he moved toward the entrance his vision could no longer penetrate the brightness of the cloud which had begun to shine brighter and brighter as he approached.

Strangely, he suddenly pictured his father stepping out of the darkness at Pascha holding a brightly lit candle and chanting, "*Come receive the Light.*" The light filled the large opening, but was so bright now that it almost hurt Martin's eyes. He squinted as it increased, and Martin stopped a few feet away from the entrance.

Then the bright light was gone.

It wasn't dark, but the cloud had resumed its soft glow as before. From where he stood he could see that the room was a chapel. It looked like pictures he'd seen of a Roman catacomb church.

Directly ahead against the far wall he could see a small holy table carved into the rock-face. He made out what looked to be a Celtic icon of a young Christ on his Mother's lap carved into an alcove just above the small flat surface of the holy table.

In awe, Martin followed the luminous cloud into the chapel; the fragrance was even *stronger*–as impossible as it seemed. As he entered he gasped and stood dumbstruck! He saw the source of the luminous cloud and the fragrance.

To the right of the room on a long slab of carved stone lay the incorrupt relics of a monk. The cloud was densest and brightest around him, and the fragrance filled Martin with a sense of awe and joy.

But this was not only a monk, but a priest-monk judging from the Gospel book that he held on his chest. He wore a long, but simple grayish-white robe that covered him from head to toe, and he had a hood that was pulled up. His eyes were closed and he had a long reddish-gray beard that ran to his chest. The skin of his face was a golden brown color as were the hands that grasped the sides of the Gospel book. A simple rope of knotted beads hung from one wrist.

Martin knew that what he was seeing should be impossible under normal circumstances, but he didn't feel any fear in the presence of a fifteen hundred year old dead body. He just couldn't! The light and the fragrance, the warmth inside him and the *peace* were so overwhelmingly strong that he felt the opposite of fear; he felt love, and a desire to thank the priest-monk.

Martin was an Orthodox Christian. He had heard of such miraculous things before in his life and always thought he believed them. But now he believed in a way he *never* had before.

"Thank you, holy Father," Martin spoke in a whisper. "Thank you for bringing me here to you!"

Martin then studied the book the monk held as if now seeing it for the first time. It was breath-taking! There was a large cross in the middle of carved gold as well as the familiar Celtic knots twining in patterns around the edges of the cover. There were gems-stones of every color—blue, red, green, yellow—that glittered in the luminous cloud. The metal work was fine and beautiful—like the pictures Martin had seen in the books from the library.

As Martin stood before the Irish monk with the Gospel in his hands, he had the overwhelming desire to kiss the book. Making the sign of the cross over himself, he leaned forward to kiss the Gospel as he would on any Sunday when his father held it up. But before his face was yet six inches away, the book raised to meet his lips. He kissed it, and again—strangely—felt no fear. Then with great awe he kissed the priest-monk's fragrant hand.

Martin stood up to see that the priest-monk held the book up and away from his chest. Martin waited, his breath caught in his chest. The priest-monk looked as though he wasn't just

Voyage to the Rock

holding the Gospel for Martin to kiss, but... *offering* it for him to take!

Martin didn't know what to do. Could *this* be the treasure, the answer to the line of the poem: *To God's new children from afar, Ol' Brendan awaits his gifts to give?* Martin hardly hoped to imagine that it was. This was a treasure beyond his wildest dreams.

But how did he know if it was God's will for him to take it?

He hesitated. All he could think to do was to pray and see. Could he sense an answer? He concentrated with all his attention on saying the Jesus Prayer and listening for an answer. He didn't know but decided that if the holy monk really did want him to have the book that he would have to let it go when Martin placed his own hands on it.

Martin took a deep breath and reached his hands carefully to grasp the sides of the Gospel book just below the golden-brown fingers of the monk, who, to his amazement, simultaneously lifted them. They moved just a few inches, but they *did* move—enough for Martin to take the holy Gospel. Martin did so, almost beside himself with amazement.

Immediately, as though being absorbed into the luminous cloud itself, the relics of the priest-monk seemed to shimmer and become transparent, and then they were just... gone—and with them the radiant cloud.

Martin clutched the Gospel to his chest now and his nostrils were still filled with the scent of the priest-monk's ineffable fragrance. He was alone in the chapel but he was surprised to notice that despite the fact that the cloud had left, there was now a warm glow emanating from the Gospel book *itself*. He seemed to feel the glow right into his heart as he clutched it to his chest.

The soft glow tugged at him.

Martin slowly lifted the gold and jeweled cover and what greeted his eyes was magnificent: page after page of a sea of color and design. Martin stared in amazement as he flipped through. The book was in the *exact* style of the *Book of Kells*! The figures, the knots, the weaves, the colors, were just like those he had seen in his library book.

But then it occurred to Martin: this book wasn't a copy of the style of the *Kells* book, the *Kells* book was the copy! Martin felt suddenly overwhelmed by what he held in his hands. He carefully closed the book again and held it pressed to his chest once more.

Martin then noticed something that wasn't mystical or miraculous—but it was beautiful. It was air: fresh, crisp, beautiful, Newfoundland air.

A way out!

He had been so caught up that he had forgotten the situation he was actually in. He looked for the source of the air, and saw to the right of the altar table, a tunnel. It was smaller than the others he'd passed through, but it was a tunnel. At the end of it he even made out light. This was his freedom!

As he was about to head into the tunnel, Martin turned to cast one final glance back. It was just then that Sullivan O'Connell entered the chapel. He barely looked like a man anymore with wild green eyes and a gaunt face black from the filth and water. His eyes found Martin's and the Gospel book held in both Martin's hands.

O'Connell suddenly came alive with a terrifying speed. He seemed every bit to transform into the hungry wolf and Martin, the helpless rabbit.

Martin turned and ran.

Behind him he heard a vicious snarl. He clung to the book as he scrambled for the blessed light ahead. He moved as fast as he could.

It was with a shock that Martin felt his foot knocked from under him as he slammed to the tunnel floor. He tried desperately to return the air that had burst from his lungs, but just lay there gasping momentarily. Then a strong hand grabbed at his backpack and yanked him around.

The distorted visage of the *Old Wolf* loomed over him as the shadows played on his face. "You filth! You little filth!" He

Voyage to the Rock

shook Martin and spittle was running down his terrifying face. "You try to steal *my* book—MY BOOK!" he screamed the words. "Do you know how many years I've sought for this? How many others I've had to get *rid* of who were getting too close? And you—a *boy!*—are going to take it from me? Going to steal my reward and my *freedom*? No!" he shrieked, and simultaneously there was a crash and an explosion of rock and rushing water in the chapel below. Martin could see the entire room filling with a massive torrent of water that poured in. The lake above must have been crashing in to fill the caves!

"You filthy thief!" the *Old Wolf* raved with a mad look in his eyes. "You want to follow the path of Brendan and his monks? Then you can follow it to the bottom of this lake—into a dark and watery cavern grave!"

As he said this O'Connell began to drag Martin down toward the chapel that was roaring with the water and rock that were close to completely filling it now.

"No!" Martin screamed. "Please, no!"

The *Old Wolf* pulled Martin to take the Gospel and then cast him into the depths of icy black water. Martin with his last breath yelled: "St. Brendan, save me!"

As if in response, the rock wall exploded right in front of Martin, slamming a mighty torrent of water and debris into O'Connell. Martin sprang back from him just in time.

With a horrified scream, the water swept Sullivan O'Connell down into the chaos of the collapsing chapel. His scream echoed in Martin's ears as he scrambled up the tunnel—still clutching the Gospel in one arm to his chest.

Martin slammed with all his might through the large loose stones sheltering most of the tunnel mouth onto the plateau above. He climbed out of a sheltered hollow on the opposite side of a small hill from the lake.

Martin scrambled away just in time to see the mouth of the tunnel he'd just escaped fill with water. It left a pool as though there had never been a tunnel at all.

He suddenly felt the weight of exhaustion and cold crush down on him. With his remaining strength he climbed up the hillside, and placed the Gospel on a dry flat rock. Laying down numb and exhausted, the last thing he could remember saying before he lost all consciousness was: *Thank you, Lord Jesus. Thank you, St. Brendan.*

Martin awoke briefly to the faces of three men staring down upon him. He vaguely heard one of them say, "It's alright. We've got you," before he slipped again into a deep, dreamless sleep.

Chapter 26:
Land of the Promise of the Saints

And so they set their course and headed their way, until they were overshadowed by a misty darkness. "Do you know, Father-Abbot, what this darkness is? It's the mist that surrounds the island that you've sought for these last seven years. You will soon see that it is the entrance to it."

After an hour had passed a great light shone around them, and the boat suddenly stood by a shore. And when they had disembarked they saw now before them the *Land of the Promise of the Saints*. It was all filled with forest and trees thickly covered in all sorts of lovely rich fruits. And all the time that they explored the land it never became night, but always was shining like the light of the noon-day sun. For forty days did they travel and found marvelous refreshment and still could find no end to the place. But on the fortieth day they discovered a river flowing toward the middle of the place.

Then St. Brendan said: "Dear Fathers from here we cannot pass-over and must therefore be happy to remain ignorant about the rest of this place."

And suddenly there appeared a youth radiant in splendor with features so striking and handsomely set. He embraced all the Fathers and addressed them as brothers and said: "Peace be with you, and with all who practice the peace of Christ. Blessed are they who dwell in Thy house, O Lord; they shall praise Thee unto the ages of ages."

And turning to address St. Brendan, he said: "This land you have sought, but you could not discover because Christ wished to first show you his many mysteries. These mysteries of the ocean you've now seen and can tell, and it is time to return to the land of your birth. But take much of the fruits and precious stones all around, for the days of your earthly pilgrimage must draw to a close. And after many years this land will be made manifest to those who come after you, when days of tribulation come to the people of Christ."

But when St. Brendan inquired as to when this would happen, the shining youth said: "When the Most High Creator has brought all nations under His subjection, then will this land be shown to all His elect."

And so preparing his boat for the return trip, St. Brendan and the monks took leave of their guide and host, who had helped them so much for seven long years. And setting sail directly, and under God's guidance, the saint and his monks arrived at their own monastery, where all the monks gave glory to God for their safe return and learned of the marvelous wonders of God which were seen on the voyage of St. Brendan their abbot.

Voyage to the Rock

* * *

The doctor had put Martin on strict bed rest for the three days since his narrow escape from Sullivan O'Connell. He had been found suffering from mild hypothermia and exhaustion, along with a multitude of cuts, scrapes, and bruises. The whole rescue was quite fuzzy in Martin's memory. He had slept most of the way, though he vaguely remembered the noise of the helicopter as it had come for him.

He still lay in his bed when the door to his room opened a crack, and then wider; it was Brigid. Martin sat up in his bed as she came in and shut the door.

This was the first time they had been allowed to speak together since he'd gotten back. He figured that would be the lightest part of his punishment.

To say his parents had not been happy with him would have been the gentlest way to have put it. But there was something about parents seeing their only son almost die that had a softening effect—*somewhat*.

He had been true to his word, though, and had confessed everything that had taken place since the trip to L'Anse aux Meadows to both his parents and the police. It hadn't been easy or pleasant, but he had survived it.

Heck, what were two furious parents next to the *Old Wolf*. He felt a chill when he thought of *him*, though he was glad that the truth would now be known about Susan Arthur's death.

And so now he'd be working long days at the church for the rest of the summer and not going *anywhere* without an adult for quite a while.

No jail time, though—not even a criminal record, though it seemed for a while his parents might have pushed for one had the police not been so willing to overlook his stunt at O'Connell's shop. All things considered, Martin thought he had gotten off pretty easy.

"How are you feeling, Mart?" Brigid asked quietly, her long blond hair hanging uncharacteristically loose.

"I'm doing better," he said, stretching. "Just a bit tired and sore still. So you two obviously made it to the boat?"

"Yeah," she said while staring at the floor.

"And no sign of Duffy?" Brigid shook her head. "What happened to him in the end?"

"No one knows." Her voice grew quieter. "They found a lot of blood on the trail, though. Just no sign of him. The police are now convinced he was the one Sullivan O'Connell had gotten to cause the first rockslide—with Susan Arthur. There's a warrant out for Duffy's arrest."

"So did you hear what happened from Mom and Dad about the cave and Sullivan O'Connell and everything?" Martin asked.

"Well, not from Mom and Dad," Brigid said, peeking up at him and then away with a guilty grin. "But I did listen at the door when the police were here as you told them everything."

When Martin's eyes grew wide, she said, "I know. I'm sorry. I couldn't help myself!"

Martin smiled and shook his head. "Now don't start developing my bad habits. I'm in enough trouble as it is without getting into more for having taught them to you!" He winked at her.

"Thanks, Brigid," he said becoming serious. "You saved my life—you and Ashley."

Brigid blushed.

"Well," she said, "it was really more Ashley than me. If he hadn't been there I don't know how I would have managed. You know we watched those cliffs from the moment we got to Western Brook Pond."

Brigid was sitting on the end of Martin's bed with her knees pulled to her chest. "I was terrified for you, to be honest. But Ashley said you'd managed so far, and you'd continue to manage. Then the boat arrived with Mom and a Park Warden. Did you know Dr. Arthur had actually called her and told her everything he knew?"

Martin looked surprised.

Voyage to the Rock

"Yeah, he had been trying for the two days before she got back from Halifax. He knew something was up when he didn't hear about the Cross in the news, and then tracked Mom down. So when the tour boat arrived, Mom and a warden were on it."

Martin felt grateful that Dr. Arthur had cared that much to protect them.

"You know, Martin," Brigid said, looking away. "When we were watching for you, Ashley and I saw a waterfall suddenly shoot out of the rock face above... all the people did. Then it stopped, leaving the sound of crumbling rocks. It became so quiet suddenly, I couldn't help..."

She stopped, choked up.

"Well, I started to cry a little. But St. Brendan gave me strength," she said looking at Martin. "I knew he wouldn't let anything happen to you!"

She hopped up and knocked him back by throwing a hug around his neck. "I'm glad you made it!" she said softly.

"Me, too, Brigid," Martin said putting his arms around her. "Me, too."

* * *

Martin was surprised by how many people had showed up on the front lawn of their new church. There must have been hundreds. They all stood in a semi-circle around the bishop and the many clergymen who stood before two elaborately decorated stands. His own father was standing next to the bishop, wearing his brilliant golden vestments gleaming in the sun.

Martin, along with his friend Nick from Boston, stood near them holding large processional candles. They were both shining in their own golden server's vestments.

The rest of the summer had flown by. Despite his punishment, he had been able to escape occasionally with Brigid and Ashley, and so the rest of the summer had still been enjoyable.

To his amazement the church was actually ready. It wasn't finished inside of course, and the walls were still bare and waiting for their finishing coats of paint, but the altar area and a simple iconostasis had been prepared with the icons that his mother and Brigid had been working on all summer.

They had even placed a wall-fresco in the large alcove above the altar area: of the Mother of God with a baby Jesus upon her lap, his hand raised in a blessing. It brought back memories of a similar one he had seen—the one from St. Brendan's chapel, and he couldn't help smiling when he thought of it.

Today they would celebrate two events. The first was the consecration of their new Church so that they could begin holding services in it. The second had to do with what lay in front of them on the decorated stands; this was the real reason so many had shown up.

Before him the two objects gleamed in their glass cases: the Celtic Gospel book, and St. Brendan's Cross. He still marveled at this last miracle of St. Brendan.

After he had explained everything to his parents and the police, and had told them how he had lost his flashlight and the Cross, they completely surprised him by reaching over and showing him the Cross. They said it had been in his bag slung across his back when they had found him. Martin could do nothing but smile. And so now, two of the most precious objects in the world now stood before him and all these people.

The greater surprise still was that they would be allowed to keep the objects at *their* church. They had had to agree to have a security system and cameras installed, and to undergo yearly inspections to assure that everything was being cared for properly, but the precious objects were theirs to take care of.

The last line of the poem had taken on a new significance for Martin. All of this hadn't just been for him. It had been for all of the people here today, and all of the people who would come in the years to follow. It was for anyone who—*With the blessing of the Stella Maris*', came with faith and love to visit God's precious gifts: *Faith to revive and to forgive.*

Voyage to the Rock

Martin smiled at Brigid and Ashley, who stood nearby with his mother and Brendan Arthur. They returned his smile with their own, just as the bishop, the clergy, and the choir began to chant the hymn to St. Brendan, the new patron of their church. Their song rose like billows of incense-smoke from a censer: to God and to His servant, St. Brendan.

But the words that now filled Martin's mind were not those of the hymn, but of a prayer he had struggled to memorize over the past weeks: *Shall I abandon, O King of Mysteries, the soft comforts of home? Shall I turn my back on my native land and my face towards the sea? Shall I put myself wholly at the mercy of God? Shall I throw myself wholly on the King of kings, without food and drink, without a bed to lie on? Shall I say farewell to my beautiful land, placing myself under Christ's yoke? Shall I leave the prints of my knees on the sandy beach, a record of my final prayer in my native land? Shall I then suffer every kind of wound that the sea can inflict? Shall I take my tiny boat across the wind and sparkling ocean? O King of the glorious heaven, shall I go of my own choice upon the sea? O Christ, will you help me on the wild waves?*

St. Brendan had helped him to leave behind the past, and to embrace what lay ahead in the uncertainty of the future. The little church overlooking the blue waters of the Humber River was not his cathedral in Boston; his life here wasn't his life there.

But as Martin stood amid the people gathered together in that place, he prayed that St. Brendan would guide this new "ship" of his—not one filled with monks, but one filled with people who also desired to set foot upon the shores of the *Land of the Promise of the Saints*.

To God be the Glory, through the Prayers of His True Servant, St. Brendan the Navigator

Lumination Press

Infusing Light into the fiction genre

Lumination Press publishes works of fiction which reflect the mystery and miracle of a world filled with the Light of Orthodoxy: a world in which passions rage, miracles abound, blood is shed and kingdoms are won. Such a world comes alive in *Lumination Press* stories, not to distract us from the reality of this world, but rather to reveal the spiritual reality all around us - if only we have the eyes to see it.

Acknowledging the notable scarcity of fiction from an Orthodox perspective, *Lumination Press* hopes to fill that need with quality works. With a focus on youth and the youthful at heart, *Lumination Press* will offer a variety of stories of spiritual struggle and victory for the whole family.

For more titles check us out at:

luminationpress.webs.com

Also, don't forget to go to

voyagetotherock.webs.com

to separate *the fact from the fiction*, and to discover other interesting information.

About the Author

Fr. Matthew Penney's dreams of being a writer began with a question to his father at age 12: "Can I be a priest *and* a writer?" And thus his journey began. Half Newfoundlander himself, it was his personal experiences of *The Rock* that inspired the story. He is an Orthodox priest in the Canadian diocese of ROCOR, and along with his Matushka Catherine, resides in New Brunswick, Canada. In the fall of 2014, he will begin a PhD in Education.

Made in the USA
Charleston, SC
30 September 2016